CW01663140

the girl with the baby

BOOKS BY SAM VICKERY

One Last Second

My Only Child

Save My Daughter

Her Silent Husband

The Guilty Mother

The Child at My Door

The Perfect Baby

One Big Happy Family

The Promise

One More Tomorrow

Keep It Secret

The Things You Cannot See

Where There's Smoke

NOVELLAS

What You Never Knew

the girl with the baby

SAM VICKERY

bookouture

Published by Bookouture in 2026

An imprint of Storyfire Ltd.
Carmelite House
50 Victoria Embankment
London EC4Y 0DZ

www.bookouture.com

The authorised representative in the EEA is Hachette Ireland
8 Castlecourt Centre
Dublin 15 D15 XTP3
Ireland
(email: info@hbgi.ie)

Copyright © Sam Vickery, 2026

Sam Vickery has asserted her right to be identified as the author of this work.

All rights reserved. No part of this publication may be reproduced, stored in any retrieval system, or transmitted, in any form or by any means, electronic, mechanical, photocopying, recording or otherwise, without the prior written permission of the publishers.

ISBN: 978-1-83525-862-0
eBook ISBN: 978-1-83525-861-3

This book is a work of fiction. Names, characters, businesses, organizations, places and events other than those clearly in the public domain, are either the product of the author's imagination or are used fictitiously. Any resemblance to actual persons, living or dead, events or locales is entirely coincidental.

For my brother, Daniel, who always puts family first.

PROLOGUE

I had thought I had more time. That when it came to my escape, I'd be ready, prepared. Not like this. Waterloo station was packed as usual, tourists gathered in crowds, blocking my path, making me want to scream at them to move out of my way, to ask if they were blind to my urgency as I tried to battle my way past, my free arm forming a protective cage around the tiny baby sleeping soundly against my chest.

I looked down at my newborn daughter, blind panic fizzing through my veins at the thought of what would happen to her if I didn't make it on time. The liquid evaporated from my mouth, my milk-swollen breasts tingling as her tiny lips sucked at air from the depths of her slumber.

There was a shout from behind me, male, angry, and I felt my body tense as I dipped deeper into the crowd, unable to stop myself from peering back over my shoulder. An argument had broken out between two strangers, seemingly over a dropped takeaway coffee. I cringed away as the security guard went to intervene, my heart racing as I stopped briefly to look up at the huge screens, scanning the reams of information to see which platform my train was waiting at. There were just three minutes left until it would leave. And I could not miss it. Everything would be over if I did.

My heart thumped hard against my ribs, my eyesight blurring, unable to focus through the fear threatening to overwhelm me. It was never supposed to be like this. I'd had a plan. I'd thought it would be so much smoother, safer. I couldn't believe I had been so stupid. Left myself open, vulnerable...

Ahead of me, I heard the hiss of a train pulling in, the doors bursting open, the hordes of passengers disembarking onto the platform.

Was he amongst them? Would he see me, find me here?

I blinked, dragging my gaze back to the board, finally seeing the words clearly. Platform 10. I needed platform 10. I turned, tripping over the foot of the man next to me, grabbing his lapel to right myself.

'My apologies,' he said through a thick Italian accent. I only shook my head, already breaking into a jog, my palm cradling my daughter's tiny skull to keep her from bouncing into my chest.

The train was there, the guard striding alongside it, passengers sprinting for the doors. On the platform opposite, another train pulled in, and I didn't dare turn to it.

I pulled the hood on my raincoat up over my ears, sweat prickling down my spine, and launched myself through the nearest door, into the blissful quiet of the carriage. My hands were shaking hard, my head spinning, and I felt a trickle of warm liquid seep down my leg. For a moment, as I gripped the back of a seat, I just swayed, black spots exploding in my vision.

'Here, sweetheart. Sit down.'

I opened my eyes to find a middle-aged woman gesturing to the seat she'd vacated, and gave a grateful nod, lowering myself into it with a breathless thanks and stripping off my coat, my skin steaming beneath the plasticky fabric. I stared at the window, watching every person who passed, waiting for the inevitable moment he would appear at the glass and find me. Catch me. I willed the train to move, and when at last it did, I sent out a silent thanks, slumping back against the headrest.

I had bought myself some time, but it wasn't over. He would come for me. And when he found me, he would be more furious than I'd ever seen him. Of that I was certain.

ONE

ANNIE

I held my secateurs against my chest, letting the hot sun warm my upturned face as I waited for the fat, fuzzy bee to finish pillaging the lavender I was attempting to cut. The smell of the purple flowers brought back a thousand happy memories of my childhood in this very garden, made me picture my mother out here, her small bare feet on the hot stone path as she tied ribbons around bundles of fragrant bouquets, leaving them in my clothes drawers to ward off the moths. The yellow stone of the manor house behind me shone like buttercups in the late-afternoon sun, and I smiled to myself. Was it any wonder I felt so safe here? It was my own little slice of heaven. The prettiest house in the village, at least to my mind.

The bee buzzed over towards the honeysuckle bush, and I took my opportunity, humming to myself as I cut through the long stems, placing the bundles into the woven willow basket slung over my arm.

'Beautiful day for gardening!'

I turned, a smile already on my lips as I saw Aaron at the gate. His words never seemed to carry any hint of sarcasm, though living right next door to me, he knew more than anyone that I would be out here whatever the weather. I liked routine. *Needed* it. It made me feel safe.

Like clockwork, from 2 p.m. every day, come rain, snow or baking sun, I was out here. In the winter months, I might only last an hour or so, but in the summer, on a balmy June day like this, I could stay out until the sun went down. This garden, tending to the plants, watching them grow, gave me a sense of peace I had lost for too long. I never took it for granted.

'Hello,' I said as he opened the gate, heading up the path towards me.

'I was watching you from the window. You look very relaxed.'

I screwed up my face, trying to work out how his confession about watching me made me feel. If it had been anyone else, I would have been uneasy, but Aaron had become a friend to me over the past three years.

'You of all people should know that stalking is a crime,' I said, though I couldn't help but grin.

He held up his hands, his brown eyes sparkling, the tanned skin around them crinkling. 'You got me. I'm a disgrace to the police force. Do you want to handcuff me now?' he teased, flashing a playful wink.

I felt my cheeks turn hot, the blush creeping up my neck, and turned my attention back to the flower beds, moving over to the rose bushes, snipping at a few of the blooms and adding them to my basket. I was grateful that he stayed put on the path, not following me, always so careful not to invade my space. He seemed better at reading my cues than any other man I'd met. Perhaps that was why I'd accepted his presence in my life. That and the fact that life without his help would be pretty damn hard, considering the restrictions I'd put on myself.

'Anyway,' he said, moving past the joke, sensing my change in mood, 'I'm popping down to the village to get some bits for my dinner. Do you need me to pick anything up for you while I'm there?'

'Thanks, but I'm okay today.'

He gave a nod, already turning for the gate. 'I'll check again tomorrow. Oh, and I've got an abundance of strawberries out the back. I'll drop some round for you sometime.'

'That would be lovely. Thanks, Aaron.'

'Don't mention it. See you later, Annie.' He flashed me another cheeky smile, and I tried not to look like a smitten schoolgirl as he waved, taking long strides down the lane towards the village centre.

He stopped suddenly, turning as if he'd forgotten something, and I glanced away, guilty at having been caught staring. 'Oh,' he said, walking back and stopping by the gate, 'I meant to tell you...' He reached into his pocket and produced a folded piece of paper. 'It's about the birdhouses... Ron gave me this when I dropped off the last collection yesterday.' He cleared his throat. 'It's a contract.'

'For what?'

'Online sales.'

I frowned, stunned. I'd been making the birdhouses for as long as I could remember. Back at school, I'd fallen in love with woodworking, and from the moment I held that first smooth, warm block of wood in my hands, I'd felt a sense of peace that had stayed with me. As the years had passed, and I found myself with nothing else to fill my time, the quiet time spent sanding, chiselling, carving had become an escape I couldn't live without. It had been a hobby, done for my own mental health, but since moving back here, I had begun to sell them as a means to pay for my simple lifestyle. Aaron had contacted a shopkeeper in a tourist town five miles away and made all the arrangements for me, but in the past year, the shopkeeper had grown increasingly insistent that we were missing out on profits by not advertising online. Aaron had hand-delivered a letter from him pushing me to allow him to expand, and reading his words – *growth, opportunity, international potential* – had made me want to refuse to send any more of my birdhouses his way. The thing that made them sell so well was that they were distinctive, different from anything else on the market. Made from a single block of wood and hours of patient, intricate work, with tiny flowers adorning the edges, squirrels and blue tits carved into the borders. If they were plastered online, they would be recognised... and it would only be a matter of time before the wrong person saw them, tracked me down. The thought made my mouth dry, a shudder working through me, my fingers curling into a tight ball.

I shook my head. 'Aaron—'

'He's offering you fifty-fifty,' he said, interrupting me. 'He'll pay for the social media ads and manage the website. He asked if you might be willing to make some videos showing how you work, but I told him that would be out of the question. They sell so well in the shop, he just wants you to make more money.'

'No, *he* wants to make more money. This isn't about what I need. The answer is no. I've told you before. Local sales only. I won't risk my privacy. You of all people should understand my reasons for that!'

He met my eyes. 'Annie... he already did it. He wanted me to tell you that he's sold more online in a week than in a month in the shop. He's asked me to let you know he can take as many as you can make.'

I shook my head, horrified at the revelation. 'He did it already? Despite my saying I wouldn't allow it? You told him that, right? That I didn't consent?' I hated that I had to rely on Aaron as a go-between, but the idea of speaking to the man myself was out of the question.

'Of course. Maybe I didn't make it clear enough, though. I didn't want him asking too many questions.'

'Tell him to take it down. Today. I mean it.' I glanced at the contract still clutched in his hand. 'You can bin that. And remind Ron that if he tries anything like this again, we'll find another shop willing to sell my stuff. I've a good mind to do it now anyway. The trust is broken.'

He met my eyes. 'I'll sort it. I promise. But you have nothing to worry about, Annie. I'm right next door. You're safe here.'

I shook my head, feeling anything but.

I watched him leave, then sighed, pressing my lips together before turning back to the garden. The clang of the bells striking 5.30 p.m. from the church two lanes away filled the air, their distinctive tune so familiar it was almost a part of who I was now. The village was famous for those bells. It was one of the oldest churches in the whole of England, and the tradition had been going for almost five centuries.

I couldn't understand why anyone would object to the sound, but Aaron had mentioned that a new couple who had moved to a house at the far end of the village last month were furious that they kept getting woken up by the bells. They'd turned up at a meeting at the community hall to demand something be done, and according to Aaron's retelling, it had cemented them immediately as difficult outsiders.

They would tune them out soon enough. It was easy to let them fade into the background.

The ringing stopped, and I heard the bang of the gate behind me. I turned, wondering if Aaron had forgotten to latch it, to find a woman standing on the path.

'Oh, hi,' I said, instantly tensing at the unexpected arrival. 'Can I help you with something?'

She rushed forward, the sudden burst of movement startling me, and it was only then that I saw the cotton baby hat, the bundle strapped close to her body. 'You have to help me!' she whispered, grabbing my arm tightly, looking over her shoulder as if she felt sure someone was chasing after her. 'I need help.'

I shook my head, yanking back my arm as if the touch of her

fingers had burned, and stepping away, wanting to turn from her, to run inside and bolt my door. I didn't let people into my home. Not ever. Not even Aaron. But this woman looked like she was running for her life. Like she had no other option.

I opened my mouth to say something, to tell her I wasn't any use to her, but she stepped closer, gripped my arm again, tighter this time, as if she could sense the refusal on my tongue. There was something about her expression that gave me pause, and I stared at her, wondering if we'd met before.

'*Please*,' she begged. 'Please help us!'

I bit my lower lip, fighting against every instinct in my body, then gave a slow, reluctant nod. 'Okay,' I conceded. 'You had better come inside.'

TWO

I placed a mug of tea on the low walnut coffee table, hoping the woman didn't expect sugar as I had none to offer her. She looked at it without picking it up. 'I... I'll just go and get the biscuit tin,' I muttered, turning from her and rushing back to the kitchen. There were a pair of comfortable armchairs beside the enormous stone hearth, the grate of the open fire lying empty, having been swept for the summer months. In the winter, I loved nothing more than curling up in one of those chairs, the smell of a roast drifting from the Aga behind me, chopping boards full of fragrant vegetable peelings on the huge table in the centre of the room, a dog-eared paperback the only company I needed.

The flagstones were worn and smooth, a divot worked into the floor beside the sink where I still washed every pot and pan and plate by hand, refusing to let anyone inside to fit a dish-washer. It was an unnecessary luxury, and so far since being back here, I'd managed to avoid any need for workmen, trying to ignore the mounting list of little jobs that were crying out to be done around the two-hundred-year-old building.

I pressed my palms into the scratched wooden countertop,

leaning heavily against it as I tried to gather my thoughts, adjust to this intruder in my private space. It felt so wrong to have her here, sitting in *my* chair, in *my* living room. The instant I'd invited her inside, I'd regretted it. I wasn't the person to help her. I couldn't, even if I wanted to.

I took a deep breath and grabbed the tin filled with biscuits Aaron had picked up for me. Heading back into the living room, I plonked it down on the table with more force than was necessary. 'I'm afraid you can't stay long. I'll have to ask you to go as soon as you finish your tea.' Even as I said the words, I felt terrible. The look of panic that flashed across her features confirmed just how rude I had sounded, but I didn't apologise. She had no idea what she was getting into coming here.

'Are you from the village?' I asked, wondering if she might be one of the new residents, the ones who'd complained about the church bells.

She shook her head, her face red and flushed. It was cooler here in the sitting room than it had been in the garden, but the lowering sun was glaring through the bay window, and I walked over to open it, letting a soft breeze flow in as she stripped off the raincoat that was entirely inappropriate for a balmy day like today. As she let it fall to the cushion behind her, her thin cotton cardigan slipped off her shoulders, and I caught sight of the bruise on her upper arm, purple and fresh and the size of a fist. My stomach lurched and dizziness swept over me. 'What happened?' I asked, my words thick, slow as I nodded towards her arm.

She glanced down at it, then looked back to me, her eyes wide and frightened. 'I...' She took a breath, then looked away, pulling her cardigan up, her hands wrapping around herself, obscuring the bruise from view. 'I'm not sure... I don't remember.'

I stared at her, watching as she moved to unstrap the baby from the carrier. 'How old is your baby?'

'She's five weeks,' she replied softly, pulling off the baby's hat to reveal a head of tight black curls. 'Her name is Amala. And I'm Jade.'

'You shouldn't be rushing around yet. You should be resting.'

She gave a wry smile. 'I know.' She turned the baby to nestle in the crook of her arm, and I saw her tiny face for the first time. Smooth dark brown skin, with sparkling eyes a few shades darker. Nothing like the freckled pale skin of her mother, with her fine waist-length light brown hair.

'Where's her father?' I asked softly.

Jade only shook her head, laying the baby on the seat beside her as she reached for her tea.

'Why are you here?' I asked, the words a low hiss, panic making me lose my manners.

'I told you, Annie. I need your help.'

I froze, my eyes widening. 'I didn't tell you my name,' I said softly. I looked again to the baby, her black eyes staring up at the ceiling. The anxiety I'd been feeling suddenly morphed into something more urgent, fuelled by a sense of suspicion that seemed to seep down my spine like tar, acrid and burning. 'Who sent you here?' I whispered. 'Why have you come?'

Jade shook her head as if I was crazy. As if I'd made a mistake. 'I read it on your post while you were making the tea. Look,' she said, pointing to the catalogue on the table. 'Annie Balfour. I'm sorry, I didn't mean to unsettle you. I'm not thinking straight. It's been a long and exhausting day. I haven't been sleeping. I'm so sorry, I know it must be strange to have me turn up like this, but I saw you there in the garden and I just knew you'd help me. You look kind, and I heard the way you laughed with your neighbour. And to find a woman around the same age as me... I knew you'd be understanding. We have to stick together, don't we? Us women.'

I frowned. She had no idea what kind of person I was. The

secrets I kept. The things I'd done to secure this life, this safe haven for myself. *None*. And despite her innocent explanation, I didn't believe her.

I swallowed, a question playing on my lips, though I didn't want to ask it. Aaron had unsettled me in the garden, and now this. I was letting my imagination, my *fears* run wild. But still... she was here, and there was no doubt she was running from something bad.

'Is it because of him?' I whispered. 'Are you... in danger?' The words stuck in my throat, and I suddenly didn't want her to answer – didn't want the responsibility that would fall at my feet if she confirmed my very worst fears. I'd been waiting for this day, I realised. Expecting it... expecting *her*. Ever since I received that letter from my Aunt Betty last summer. I got a lot of letters from her and my Great-Aunt Susan. They were my only real link to the outside world – aside from Aaron – and they both loved to send me gossip and news from old friends and estranged family members. I didn't think Aunt Betty had any idea of the impact *that* particular letter would have on me. The news that the man I'd walked away from after a decade-long relationship had found a new girl and got married just two years after I'd left him.

Ryan had been dismissive of my family throughout our relationship, never bothering to get to know them, but his grandmother had kept in touch with Betty – a fact I was certain Ryan was unaware of – and had shared the news with her over coffee. She'd said the new wife was some twenty-seven-year-old girl, five years younger than me. And staring at this woman now, I recalled the photograph my aunt had enclosed of the woman in the simple white satin wedding dress. The pale, freckled skin. Long, fine brown hair. Wide, innocent hazel eyes. I'd held that photograph in my hands and worried that I should warn her. That I should break my pact to never leave this place, to go and tell her about the danger she was getting into. But I hadn't. I'd shoved the photograph back in the envelope and pretended it didn't exist. That I didn't know the truth.

And now, looking at this woman, I couldn't help but think that the father of her baby, the reason she was here, was the man I'd gone to the ends of the earth – the ends of my moral compass – to escape. Could this really be Ryan's new wife here in my house?

THREE

I didn't wait for her to confirm my fears as I leaped to my feet, panic chasing through my veins like wildfire, my heart threatening to burst free of my chest. If he'd tracked me down having seen the birdhouses online, this could all be some sick game on his part. I could just imagine the thought process he would have gone through. He'd force his young, vulnerable bride to come here and gain my trust, using the baby as collateral, and then he would find a way to get into my home... ruin everything I'd strived to create for myself in the embers I'd been left with. The grudge I knew he had over my leaving would never fade. The hatred he carried, the need to punish me for the humiliation, the pain I'd caused him... he would stop at nothing to make me pay.

'You have to leave,' I demanded, clasping my fingers tightly in front of me, digging my fingernails into my flesh as a reminder to myself not to physically grab this woman and throw her out of my house. Beside her, the baby began to whimper, and Jade lifted her up to her chest, her eyes beseeching as they met mine. 'She needs feeding. I don't know what I'm doing... how to raise this baby. I don't have a clue about any of it.'

'You must have family, friends you can ask to help?' I snapped, though I recalled how isolated I'd become over the years I'd spent under Ryan's roof. By the end, he'd made sure I'd had nobody to turn to. Nobody who cared about me.

'I don't,' she replied simply. 'I know it's a lot to ask... that you don't know me. I realise how much of an imposition—' She broke off, sucking in a deep breath as if she were trying not to cry. 'I just need somewhere safe to stay for a day or two, just while I can get some things organised.' She pressed her lips together. 'And yes,' she said softly. 'In answer to your question... yes, I'm running from someone... someone dangerous.' Her fingers touched the spot on her cardigan below which I'd seen that fresh bruise. 'I can't go home right now. Please, I really have no one.'

I gave a short nod, hating myself for what I was about to say. My voice sounded too high, like it didn't belong to me. 'There's a women's refuge in town. It's about twenty minutes' drive from here. I can ask my neighbour to take you. He's a policeman.'

'No!' She gripped the baby closer, Amala's cries growing louder now. 'I can't go to a refuge. And I don't want anyone else involved. Especially not the police!'

I knew exactly why she was afraid. Why she felt that was an impossible choice. 'Jade... I can't have you here. Look, there's a bed and breakfast down in the village. It's nice, and it's not the summer holidays yet, so I'm sure they'll have a vacancy. I can give you some cash if you need it...'

She frowned. 'I don't want money. I just wanted your help.'

I shook my head, feeling sick with guilt. 'Is it *him*? Is it Ryan you're running from? Please, I have to know!'

She dipped her head in silent confirmation, and I felt the ground sway beneath my feet. This couldn't be happening. It just couldn't!

'I'm sorry.' I remained standing, my eyes flicking pointedly towards the door. I couldn't meet her gaze, couldn't stand myself for being so weak, so pathetic. 'I can't do this... I can't help you.'

'Please! I wouldn't ask if I weren't desperate... *Please*, Annie!'

'I'm sorry. I can't.'

There was a long, uncomfortable pause. Finally, she gave a resigned nod, then slowly rose to her feet, the baby clutched in her arms. Her hands were shaking, and I looked away, pretending not to see.

'I'm so sorry,' I repeated. 'I'm not good with people... strangers. I'm a private person. I don't have guests. I don't know how to help you,' I admitted, disgusted with myself for having to say those words. I didn't add that I'd barely known how to help *myself* when I'd been in her position. That it had taken embracing a side of me I hadn't known existed in order to gain my freedom, and it wasn't a path I was willing to take again. What I had done – the terrible things that had followed – had nearly killed me, but she couldn't possibly understand that what she wanted from me was out of the question. She was just a scared girl.

She bowed her head, picking up the changing bag she'd arrived with and heading for the door. 'Thank you for inviting me in. And for the tea.'

I didn't answer. Guilt and self-hatred swirled in my belly as I followed her silently to the door, showing her out. I closed it behind her, sliding the bolt across, then rushed back to the sitting room to watch her through the net curtains. I hated myself for being such a coward. For pushing a young, vulnerable mother and her baby onto the street. Not just any woman, I reminded myself. She was in this position, running with her newborn daughter, because of me. But what choice did I have? She was a threat to everything I'd tried to create, to protect this past three years. I had to find that photo, the letter Aunt Betty had sent after Ryan had got married. I had to know for sure that she was his wife. That this was my fault.

Amala's cries were growing more frantic as Jade opened the front gate, stepping out onto the quiet lane. I watched as she glanced one way and then the other, lost, frightened, alone. She jiggled the baby, trying to calm her, then perched on the low stone wall of my front garden, trying to position her so she could feed her. I should have at least waited until she'd taken care of that before tossing her out onto the street. I felt my cheeks heat at the thought of how little I had offered her. At the knowledge that if it hadn't been for this house, this safe, secret bolthole that had provided an escape in my darkest hour, I might have been in the very same shoes as this poor girl was now.

The baby screamed louder, struggling to get into the right position, and the sound of her cries sent goosebumps rushing down my arms. I was a coward not to help. I'd jumped straight to the worst possible conclusion. What if this *wasn't* a sick game Ryan was playing with me? She could have tracked me down herself, come to me because she knew that I, above anyone else, would believe her story. That I would know what it meant to belong to Ryan Avory. How could I turn her away knowing what would happen to her, to that innocent little baby, if she went home to him? The thought made me sick to my stomach. I was a terrible, terrible person. I was weak – just like he'd always said.

I gripped the net curtains tight in my palm, my mouth dry, my heart pounding, then, with a sudden rush of brave determination, I took a deep breath and turned from the window, striding back to the front door and sliding the bolt back. Before I could talk myself out of my decision, I stepped outside and walked purposefully up the path. 'A week. No more than that. It's all I can offer, but it should give you time to figure out your next steps.'

Jade turned her face to me, her cheeks streaked with tears,

mascara smudged beneath bloodshot eyes as the baby suckled ferociously at her breast. 'Really?' she asked, as if she didn't dare to believe what she was hearing.

I gave a short nod. 'I don't know anything about babies. I won't be much help in that regard, I'm afraid, but I'm sure we can manage.'

'Thank you,' she said softly, wiping at her cheek.

I peered over the gate, down the lane, conscious that Aaron would be making his way back from the village any minute. I didn't want him to see her here, to have him asking questions. 'Come on then – let's get you inside and I'll show you where you can freshen up, and where you can sleep. Will the baby be okay in the bed with you?'

She stood, the baby still latched onto her nipple, and nodded. 'Yes... we'll be fine. Thank you, Annie. Thanks so much.'

Once we were back inside, I closed the door, locking it again, then pointed to the staircase. 'It's creaky, but it's well built. Go on up.'

I followed her slow, careful footsteps, and when we got to the landing, I showed her along the long, bright corridor to one of the guest rooms. There was a four-poster double bed in the centre, a bright patterned rug beneath it and a soft green velvet headboard against the wall behind it. The bare duvet was folded, the pillows stacked in a pile on top of it. 'I'll get some sheets. I never bother making this one up. There's an en suite just through that door to the left. The water takes an age to come out hot, but it will in the end if you're patient. Please don't go in my bedroom or my bathroom. I like my privacy,' I added.

She nodded. 'Of course.'

I gripped my fingers together again, circling my thumbs over and over, anxiety pulsing through my veins. It was taking all my concentration not to toss her back out again. Not to take back my invitation.

There was a bang at the sash window across the room, and Jade jumped, her whole body stiffening, her arms wrapping tighter around her daughter as if she were readying herself for someone to snatch her from her arms. Her nerves were so obvious, and it only made me feel all the more on edge, as if someone was about to come for us. As if he might already be out there, waiting for his chance. I closed my eyes briefly. 'The catch on that one is noisy. It rattles if there's a big gust of wind. Sorry.'

'No, it's fine... I'm just tired. Silly of me to be so jumpy.'

I met her eyes, wanting to ask more, to hear the whole story, but I could see how blanched and exhausted she was. 'I'll get you those sheets. I was just going to heat up some soup for my dinner. Can I get some for you?'

'That would be great.'

'Why don't you settle in. I'll bring everything up.'

I left without waiting for her to answer, pulling the door closed behind me. Then I stood in the corridor and pressed my hands to my face, hoping that I hadn't just made a terrible mistake.

FOUR

The light summer breeze ruffled my hair, and I tucked it behind my ear, unable to stop myself from anxiously fiddling with it, along with the bracelet on my wrist, which I couldn't seem to stop from looping and unlooping around my fingertip. Every few seconds, I found my gaze flicking back towards the house, homing in on the window of the spare room. Jade had drawn the curtains against the setting sun, perhaps exhausted from the high emotion of the day, or maybe in an attempt to settle Amala, who'd been fractious and grizzly when I'd taken a tray of supper in.

The thought of her sleeping in the room that had always been reserved for my grandmother – the woman I'd begged to stay just one more night each time she left, who had read me stories at bedtime, something I'd never experienced with my mother, and baked the most delicious cakes on the planet – was beyond uncomfortable to imagine. There was a part of me that wanted to keep it as a shrine to her, that imagined the vanilla smell of her hand cream wafting from the drawer in the bedside cabinet each time it was opened. But none of the other bedrooms were in any fit state to house guests right now, and I didn't have time to prepare them. It would only be for a few days anyway... Jade would be gone before I knew it.

I hadn't been able to stop myself from coming out here to check the lane, though my instincts had screamed at me to stay inside and bolt the doors, protect myself no matter what. But the unknown was worse. I couldn't stop picturing Ryan out here, leaning casually back in the driver's seat of his parked car, just waiting to catch my eye and wink, a sign that the game was only just beginning. I was grateful – not for the first time – that the house was on its own up here at the end of the dead-end road, with the exception of Aaron, of course. There was no way for someone to casually drive by, watching me as they passed. Just a narrow country lane, low nettle bushes opposite the two houses, and farmer's fields beyond, all filled with ripe strawberries offering no place to hide.

I was safe here, I reminded myself. Well, I had been.

'Hello, beautiful!'

I snapped my head up, my heart racing at the sound of the male voice, though I recognised it at once, and came face to face with Aaron as he pushed open his gate, his warm eyes searching mine as if he'd asked a question I'd neglected to answer. He'd long since given up inviting me to come on an evening stroll with him, though he often commented on how lovely the village looked at dusk.

'Oh, hi.' My voice sounded shaky, and I cleared my throat. I forced a smile to my lips. 'Just the person! I meant to tell you earlier, I finished that birdhouse – the one with the badger carvings.'

'Great. You figured out how to balance it, then?'

I nodded, gesturing for him to follow me, and he pushed the gate open, walking a few steps behind me. I forced myself to keep my pace steady, not slowing to make him pass, ignoring the fact that I felt as though I was being stalked in my own garden. I kept my eyes straight ahead, refusing to glance again at Jade's window. I knew I should tell him. Any sensible person would. What was the point in having a policeman living next door if I didn't call on him for favours from time to time? And he would want to know. I swallowed. If I shared with him that I was harbouring a victim of abuse, a vulnerable young mother – and that in her need to protect her daughter, she might have led danger on a whole greater level to my doorstep – he would help. He would know what to do. But I knew beyond doubt that I couldn't say a word. I couldn't risk the consequences that might follow.

'Yes,' I said, my voice scratchy. I cleared my throat again. Usually, I made weighty, removable stands – huge twisted pillars of polished oak that screwed into the base of the birdhouses. But lately the hanging birdhouses I made, suspended by a thick chain from the bough of a tree or a pergola, had grown in popularity. And if I didn't get the design of the house perfectly balanced, it would lean too heavily to one side. 'I added a couple of hares to the opposite edge,' I said. 'That did the trick.'

'I knew you'd work it out.'

I walked down the path past the house, through the arched gateway and on towards the workshop, opening the latch and stepping into the gloom. Behind me, I heard Aaron take a deep breath, knowing exactly what he was smelling. The scent of sawdust and varnish was both familiar and comforting to me. It was the smell I associated with safety... escape. It had taken the best part of a year before I'd let Aaron come in here, after he'd made the arrangement with Ron to stock the birdhouses in his shop. Before that, I'd met him at the front gate every time, having heaved my completed pieces through the garden to hand over to him. I hadn't been able to stand the idea of anyone in my personal space, and to his credit, he hadn't pushed.

'Did you speak to Ron when you got back from the shops?' I asked. 'Did you make him take down the stuff he put online?'

He gave a rueful nod, and I could see he thought I was

being overly cautious. 'He was a bit put out – he hired someone to photograph the birdhouses and set up a website, and was making mutterings about recouping his costs, but I pointed out that you hadn't signed any agreement and were likely to take your work elsewhere if he didn't respect your wishes.'

'And he agreed? It's off the internet now?'

He nodded again, but the comfort I should have felt was glaringly absent. It was too late. Somehow, Jade had found me. I chewed my lower lip, reaching for the badger birdhouse on the shelf and placing it down on the workbench in front of Aaron.

He broke into a grin. 'You're so talented, Annie. You really can't blame Ron for wanting to show the world that.'

I raised an eyebrow. 'You and I both know he's not trying to make me into a world-famous artist. He's only interested in making as much profit as possible from our arrangement. Not that I'm not grateful to him, but still...' I sighed, running my finger over the little cub between the two adult badgers.

'The detail on that is phenomenal.' Aaron's finger touched the badger's pointed snout, the edge of his hand grazing mine. I felt my heart rate quicken but kept my eyes trained on the wooden carvings, feigning indifference, as if it was of no significance to me that the heat from his skin burned into mine. Energy crackled through my veins, neither one of us pulling away. It would be so natural to give in to whatever this thing was that had developed over the past year. This unspoken *wanting* I felt between us. I wasn't naïve enough not to realise he felt it too. We both knew something had changed... grown.

When at last I looked up, his brown eyes met mine, and I held his gaze, frozen to the spot, not wanting to end the moment. He wouldn't make the move. Wouldn't lower his head those last few inches to bridge the gap. He'd wait for me to show him I was ready...

The memory of another first kiss struck me. The way I'd felt like I was safe, those huge arms wrapping around me as if I were his to protect. Every muscle in my body tensed as I remembered how quickly that had changed. How those arms had become a vice, a prison... I'd been stupid to let myself trust him. It had nearly cost me my life, and in the end, I'd paid a far greater price than that. I'd lost my values, my sense of right and wrong. Become someone I couldn't stand to face in the mirror. I wouldn't make that mistake again.

I snatched my hand away, sliding the birdhouse across the bench towards Aaron. 'Tell Ron *local* sales only or I won't do business with him again. I mean it, Aaron. Make sure he's under no illusions when it comes to that.'

He gave a stiff nod, then heaved the cube of wood into his tanned arms. I watched him go without following, angry at myself for succumbing to a fantasy that could never materialise. Being alone was the only choice. The only way to ensure no one got hurt.

FIVE

JADE

My stomach gave a painful rumble, and I pressed my free hand to my still soft belly as I stood at the bottom of the stairs listening for movement. Sleep hadn't come. The bed in Annie's spare room was ancient and sagging, and despite my exhaustion, I couldn't relax, too afraid of Amala rolling into the centre, of waking up to find her face pressed into the mattress, a lifeless shell of a doll. I didn't know if it was my hormones – the potent cocktail of new motherhood – but I didn't feel like myself. I kept having flashes of horrific images, premonitions I hoped wouldn't come true.

Coming here hadn't made it any easier. I would have loved to be able to stay in the home I'd created, in my own bed, recuperating from the birth of my first child. But I had made my choice. And despite the difficulties I was facing now, I knew this was my only option.

So I'd stayed awake. Kept vigil, though my head had drooped again and again. I'd got up, pacing the room, peering out through the little sash window at the still, moonlit summer night, and longing for the moment I could go downstairs.

Annie had kindly brought me up a tray with some soup and

a couple of slices of buttered bread last night, but I got the impression she had no idea of the appetite of a breastfeeding mother. She was a tiny bird of a woman, her skin deeply tanned and starting to show the signs of sun damage, her golden-brown hair scooped into a messy bun on top of her pretty face.

She'd been wearing a knee-length blue-and-white floral summer dress, buttons running the full length of it, and she flitted around as if she had too much energy to contain in such a small body. I got the horrible impression she wasn't much of a foodie. And people like that always assumed that because *they* were full, everybody else must be too.

It had been a long night, feeding Amala every other hour with nothing more than half a tin of soup to keep me going, accompanied by endless glasses of tap water from the en suite, and now I was ravenous, desperate for her to come down and offer some form of breakfast. At nearly midday, my hopes were dwindling.

I could hear her up there. She'd been awake for hours. There was movement coming from behind the closed bedroom door, creaks in the floorboards overhead. What was she doing up there? Did she even remember I was here?

I hitched Amala upright on my chest, her tiny head wobbling as she tried to peer over my shoulder.

How long would I have to be here for? Would a week be enough? Annie had made it quite clear that I was an unwelcome imposition on her life, her home. So it would have to be enough. It wasn't like I had another option – time wasn't on my side.

A shiver ran through my body as I thought of the man I'd evaded at the train station. The consequences of this week not going to plan. It wasn't a choice. If I'd had more time, like I'd anticipated, things might have been simpler. But now the decision had been taken out of my hands.

I looked at my daughter and felt more determined than

ever. I was doing this for her. For us. For our future, our freedom. I wouldn't let her down.

I shoved the last bite of the flapjack I'd found stashed at the bottom of Amala's changing bag into my mouth, chewing it rapidly as I left her sound asleep on the makeshift bed I'd made out of the sofa throw on the sitting room carpet, hurrying into the hallway and pausing by the stairs. I waited a moment to see if Annie was going to respond to the quiet tap at the front door, but she didn't appear. I hesitated, not keen to open the thick wooden door myself and find out who was behind it. I didn't think it was him. If it *had* been, the door would be swinging on its ancient hinges by now, but still, I couldn't help the nerves that swirled inside my belly.

The knock came again, and I approached slowly and slid back the heavy bolt.

The man on the front step did a double-take when he saw me, his brow creasing in confusion. 'Who are you?' he asked, his brown eyes narrowing as they met mine.

'Uh, you knocked on *my* door. I don't give out my personal information to strangers.'

He blinked, then shook his head, letting out a slow breath. 'I'm Aaron Williams. I live next door. I help Annie with things... things she needs. So...?'

He waited pointedly, folding his arms.

'I'm Jade. Jade Ashton.'

'And what are you doing in Annie's house?'

I shrugged, finding his attitude strange and overbearing. 'Why do you care? I'm staying for a few days. I'm a guest. Is that okay with you, Aaron?' I knew I was being abrasive, but I was tired and hungry and his whole demeanour put me on edge, the way he stood blocking the front door with his tall, muscular frame, as if he thought he'd trapped me so I'd have to submit to his interrogation. I instantly disliked him. The way he assumed he was entitled to know everything about me.

He looked over my shoulder, as if he was checking to see if Annie was coming, and when he saw no sign of her, he stepped closer to me, his feet breaching the threshold. I sucked in my cheeks, biting the soft skin inside them as I forced myself to hold my stance, refusing to back away, though every instinct in my body told me to move.

'Annie doesn't have guests,' he said softly. 'Not ever. And *you* shouldn't be here.'

The words sent a shower of goosebumps racing up my arms, and I suppressed a shudder. He stepped back and bent down, picking up a blue ceramic bowl full to the brim with fat red strawberries. He handed them to me, and my stomach growled. 'Give these to her, will you? And tell her I'll be back later... to see if there's anything she needs.'

I nodded wordlessly, my jaw stiff, my mouth unsmiling, and as he turned towards the path, I remembered that Annie had told me that her neighbour was in the police force. Was *this* the man she'd expected me to turn to for help? As I closed the door, holding the bowl against my chest, I wondered why his words had sounded so much like a warning.

SIX

ANNIE

I pulled the last box from the very back of the wardrobe, dropping it onto my unmade bed and flipping off the thick cardboard lid to peer at the contents inside. The room was a mess, papers and envelopes and photo albums and letters spread across every surface, the floorboards carpeted in old bills and statements I'd opened and discarded. It was going to take forever to clean it all up, and still I was no closer to finding what I was looking for.

I caught a glimpse of myself in the mirror, noting the dark circles beneath my eyes. There'd been a time I could go all night without even closing my eyes, and still look fresh and full of life the following morning. That was long before I met Ryan. Back when I'd lived a whole different life. Had friends. Travelled. Socialised, almost to excess, though to look at me now, it was difficult to believe. Those old friends wouldn't even recognise me now. It felt like that Annie had died long ago.

I rubbed at my face, trying to wake up my circulation and bring some colour to my tired complexion. I knew Jade and the baby must have been up for hours, but I didn't want to have to go downstairs and face her – not until I'd found that letter from my aunt, that photograph. I had to see it again, to prove to myself that this girl, this intruder into my sanctuary, was indeed Ryan's new wife.

I'd spent the whole night lying in the dark, fully dressed, unable to even think of falling asleep with the presence of a stranger under my roof. Every creak manifested into a footstep outside my bedroom door. Every muffled sound a whispered conversation between the man I had done terrible things to escape and his new bride. It took all my willpower not to jump out of bed and toss Jade and her baby out into the night. It was only that expression of desperate fear, the way she had held her daughter as if she was fighting off invisible demons, that had stopped me from doing just that. I knew I was doing the right thing helping her, even if it put me at risk of being found too.

I hated that my safe place no longer felt hidden and secure. And on top of that, there was something else that plagued me. That tiny baby. What if something happened to her under my roof? Would the finger be pointed at me? Would Ryan spin his story so it looked like *I* was at fault? If he brought up the past, the secrets I'd kept hidden from the world, hidden from *him* even, there was a chance he'd be believed. What would happen to me then?

There was a quiet knock at the bedroom door, and before I could ask for a moment to gather myself, it swung open.

'Sorry,' Jade said, stepping inside without waiting for an invitation. Not that I had any intention of offering any such thing. The baby was cradled in the crook of her arm, and I saw her curiosity as she took in the pandemonium surrounding me. 'I just wanted to let you know, your next-door neighbour popped round earlier. He gave me some strawberries. I hope you don't mind, but I ate a few.'

Shit. Now Aaron would be bursting with questions. Concern.

'You didn't let him in?' I asked, my tone bordering on rude. I didn't like the idea of this stranger answering my door, inserting herself into my business.

'No.' She shook her head.

'Good... that's good.'

'So... the strawberries?'

'What? Oh, yes, help yourself,' I said, glancing at the box in front of me.

'Are you... do you need some help in here?' she asked, gesturing to the mess.

'Oh, this... no, I was just looking for something. A document I need,' I said, grasping for an explanation.

'I can help if you'd like?' she said, offering a tentative smile. 'I had a really messy roommate at uni. She was always getting me to find her latest piece of coursework – I have a knack for it,' she added, using the hand that wasn't cradling Amala to delve into the closest box, plucking out a typed letter and scanning it.

I shook my head, striding over the heap of papers and holding out my hand pointedly. 'That won't be necessary, thank you.'

'Are you sure?' Her tone was filled with doubt and her expression was concerned as she glanced around the room once more.

'Yes. I'm sure. Go on down. I'll come and make some sandwiches in a minute. You must be getting hungry.'

She gave a slow nod, then opened her mouth as if to say something else before changing her mind. 'Okay,' she said softly, casting a final glance at the mess.

Once she had left, pulling the door closed behind her, I rushed back to the bed, tipping the box out and meticulously going through every single sheet of paper. It wasn't there. I knew I'd kept it. Tucked the letter and the photograph back into the envelope it had been sent in. I *always* kept letters. I liked to read them back years later, to remind myself of the past, living through the stories on the page. It was a way for me to remember, to feel less lonely – my only connection to my remaining family and the outside world.

The only photos I'd ever burned were the ones I'd found of Ryan. But *he* hadn't been in the picture. It had only been her. The bride, that long brown hair and simple satin dress. I couldn't have thrown it away. But where was it? I *had* to find it.

I heard the stairs creaking as Jade descended and felt panic course through me. One thing was for certain, I wasn't safe any more.

SEVEN

I pulled the block of cheese from the fridge, cutting thick, uneven slices and slapping them onto the roughly sliced bread, trying not to make eye contact with Jade, who stood beside the hearth watching my every move.

'I hope you don't feel like I'm expecting you to wait on me,' she said softly. 'I just didn't want to rifle through your cupboards. I wasn't sure you'd be okay with that. I can give you some money towards the shopping,' she offered, her voice quiet, uncertain, as if she wasn't sure how I might take the suggestion. 'I have a little bit of cash on me.'

I looked up, seeing her pale face crease with awkward embarrassment as her stomach gave a loud rumble. 'That won't be necessary.' I hadn't given it much thought – feeding her, telling her to help herself to food. I couldn't be sure if my poor hosting skills were down to a lack of practice on my part or a pointed way to let her know she was unwelcome here. Sighing, I had to admit to myself that the latter was probably more true than I'd like to admit. The realisation made me feel ashamed. If she was on the run from abuse, the last thing she needed to encounter was a host who barely fed her.

I finished making the sandwiches, then, on second thoughts, flipped open the fridge door again, pulling out a yoghurt. I added some crackers and hummus to her plate before carrying it over to the table. 'I'll make a pot of tea,' I said, gesturing for her to sit down. She hesitated only a moment, then, her eyes lingering on the food, walked over, pulled out a chair and slumped into it, holding the baby with one arm as she ate.

I watched, pursing my lips as I assessed the situation. There was nothing here to make life with a newborn easier. No bouncy chair, no bassinet, and the kitchen floor was hard and cold, too dangerous for the baby to be set down on.

Jade glanced up to find me looking at her, and raised an eyebrow. 'Aren't you having something?' she asked through a mouthful of crackers.

I nodded towards my plate, where my solitary sandwich sat untouched. I was too nauseated to face it, my belly churning with anxiety. 'Do... do you want me to hold her? So that you can eat with both hands?' I didn't know why I made the offer. It was the wrong thing to do. I knew it. But despite that knowledge, a part of me wanted to feel the weight of the baby in my arms. To hold her against my chest and breathe in that newborn smell.

'You don't mind?' Jade asked, her eyes widening in hope.

I pressed my lips together, not offering a reply, instead walking over and taking Amala from her before I could change my mind; before I could make the sensible choice and walk away. Amala's head wobbled, and I held my breath, hyper aware of the solid flagstones beneath me, flashes of horrific images, terrifying premonitions of the consequences of me losing my grasp on her, burning through my mind's eye. My hands trembled as I adjusted her, each move slow and careful.

Jade turned back to her plate, seemingly unbothered about handing her baby over to a stranger. It was crazy to me that she might not sense the danger in that. How easily she had given her up, how willing to believe she could trust me to care for the most important person in her world. How very stupid.

I walked slowly over to one of the armchairs by the unlit fireplace, lowering myself into it and taking in the baby's tiny features. The tight black ringlets. The long curling eyelashes. The round chubby cheeks. The tiny pink lips, pursed in a little triangle shape. I stared at her and felt sick. It had been a mistake to take her, hold her, but despite knowing that, I couldn't seem to bring myself to stand up and give her back to her mother. I placed a hand over her back, letting it rise and fall with her every breath, looking around my kitchen, at the mess on the counter, the sun shining through the latticed window, anywhere but down at the baby I held on to, the only sound coming from Jade as she methodically worked her way through her lunch. She must have been starving. Guilt and shame flooded me again. I wasn't the person to help her. I had barely managed to save myself.

'The man who came round with the strawberries,' I said suddenly, angling myself to look at her. 'He's a policeman. And he's a friend of mine. He can help you if you're in trouble.'

Jade paused, her mouth full of food, her eyes widening. She swallowed thickly. 'He gave off a vibe,' she said softly. 'I didn't trust him.'

I nodded. I could understand that. I'd been wary of men too, when I'd first come here. But Aaron wasn't Ryan. 'If it wasn't for him, there'd be no food in this house. He does all my shopping. And he does it without my ever having asked him. He's a good person.'

'Why don't you just order what you need online?'

I flushed, aware that I was going to look even stranger than I probably already did. 'I don't have the internet here.' I glanced at the mobile phone she'd placed beside her plate on the table. 'I don't even have one of those. Just a basic landline for emergencies. Actually—' I broke off, not wanting to ask.

'What?'

I sighed. 'Could you do something for me? I just want to see something.'

'Online, you mean?'

I nodded. 'I... I sell these birdhouses at a local shop – hand-made ones.' I pointed out the window to the huge one that stood in the centre of the lawn.

'Wow... Did you make that?' she asked, her eyes wide as she took it in.

'I did.' I watched her for a sign that she already knew. That she'd found me because she'd seen Ron's ad online. The timing was too close to be coincidental, and yet Jade remained unruffled as she studied the birdhouse.

'It's so detailed. The little wooden animal carvings look so realistic. You're very talented; it must have taken for ever.'

I shrugged. 'Not too long. But I think someone might be selling them online and I just wanted to check. I can't, you see.'

She glanced down at her phone, and again I watched her face carefully. There had been so many of the birdhouses at the flat when I'd finally left, and somehow I couldn't imagine Ryan destroying them. She *must* have seen them there. And if she had, she'd have recognised them instantly if she'd seen an ad online. That was if Ryan hadn't seen them first. He was addicted to his phone, always online. Either way, it would have been so easy to find me once they'd tracked Ron down. Ron knew I was Aaron's neighbour, and it wasn't like there were any other houses nearby. It was just the two of us here.

She typed something I couldn't see, shaking her head as she clicked her tongue, and I felt relieved that she was coming up empty-handed. Aaron had done as he'd promised and got the ad taken down. But then she held up the phone, showing me an image that made my heart turn to stone in my chest. 'This one looks similar. Is it one of yours?'

I stared, balling my hands into fists to stop them from trembling. She clicked the picture and nodded to herself. 'It takes me to a website: Annie's Hand-Made Birdhouses. It's a pretty basic site, not very professional-looking... oh, and there's a Facebook page attached. Hold on. The signal is awful here; it's taking a minute to load.'

I stood behind her, watching the screen. It finally loaded, and I saw the profile picture was one of my most recent pieces. Jade clicked on the 'about' page, and there was a description. *English woodworker Annie Balfour, who lives in a charming Cotswold village...* The words blurred in front of me, and I felt myself sway. I gripped the back of her chair. 'Are there ads?' I whispered. 'That people will see on there?'

'I can check.' She clicked a few buttons and then nodded. 'Yes. There are four running at the moment. Three in the UK and one for North America.'

'Oh my God...'

'You're very talented, Annie,' she repeated, smiling up at me. 'It's a good idea to sell them online.'

I shook my head at the horrible realisation that not only were the photographs being pushed to the world, but my name was tied in with them. It would leave no doubt in his mind. I glanced down at the phone in her hand and something caught my eye. 'What does that mean?' I frowned, pointing at the screen where a little button said *Following*.

'Oh... I must have just clicked it while I was searching,' she said, her cheeks turning pink. 'I'll leave it, though; I want to see what you make next.'

'You won't see anything. I'm going to get it taken down.'

She dipped her head as if she might argue with me but said nothing.

'And I'd appreciate it if you'd turn off any location sharing or tracking apps on that thing while you're here,' I said, my tone curt.

'On the phone?' She frowned. 'I don't have any tracking.'

'Is there anyone who might want to find you? Follow you here?' I retorted pointedly.

She placed her sandwich down slowly. 'Nobody knows where I am, Annie. Only you.'

'You just had a baby. Surely someone is going to notice your absence?'

She bowed her head but didn't answer.

'Look, if you won't talk to Aaron about whatever it is you're running from, why not try that women's refuge I told you about?'

'You don't want me here.' The words were an accusation.

'I don't know how to help you.'

'You're helping already. Just offering a safe space, a roof over our heads. You're helping more than you possibly know. Look, I know we're invading your privacy. Making you uncomfortable. But if you can just give me a little time to gather my thoughts and figure out what I'm going to do next...' She took a deep breath. 'That's all I'm asking for. I don't want to take my daughter to a refuge. Those places aren't safe for a baby. I'd be constantly afraid that someone's angry ex would turn up and be violent – that we wouldn't be safe.'

'What about *your* ex?'

Amala shuffled in my arms, and I felt a sudden explosion in her nappy, her eyes shooting open as the warm, sweet-smelling liquid seeped from the sides.

'Oh!' I cried.

Jade was up and over in a second, scooping the baby from my arms. 'Sorry, it's the breast milk. Oh, the nappy's leaking! I'll go and change her.'

She darted from the room, leaving me with empty arms and a feeling that she was keeping secrets she would do anything not to share.

. . .

The bedroom was back in order again after a lot of hard work on my part. I felt pent up and jittery, my long summer afternoon in the garden over far too soon today. I'd barely managed twenty minutes out there, unable to relax for fear of who might creep up behind me, jumping at every sound, every passing voice, knowing that a stranger was at that very moment moving around inside my house, taking up space I didn't want to give. After some half-hearted pruning, I'd rushed back inside, taping a note on the front door asking Aaron to pick up eggs and yoghurt and an extra packet of pasta on his evening stroll to the village shop, and to leave them on the step. I knew he'd do it, though the questions when I next saw him would be unbearable. It wouldn't be the first time I'd gone into my shell and retreated from the world.

Now, with the June heat making me feel restless and irritable, I didn't want to get into bed despite the lack of sleep last night. I yanked my silk dressing gown off my shoulders, letting it drop to the floor, sticking my head out the window and breathing in the warm, sweet night air. The moon was high and bright, and I longed to head out into the garden to sink my bare toes into the cool grass, feel the breeze on my skin. I felt like a prisoner – trapped – and that brought back memories I'd long since suppressed, boxed up, unwilling to ever delve inside them. I hated that even now, all these years later, *he* was still able to have such an effect on me. And with thoughts of him came the memories of what I'd done... the person I had become when backed into a corner, the depths I'd sunk to. I didn't want to think of that. To be reminded of any of it. The baby being here was bringing it all back, as if it was fresh, raw, and it made me want to run, to shed my body and find a new skin to inhabit, pretend that the person I had once been, that woman who had done those unforgivable things, was a stranger to me. Not real. Not someone whose guilt I had to carry.

I'd spent the past three years crafting a new reality for

myself, becoming someone I could live with. Someone I liked, much to my surprise. I'd protected my space, my solidarity, knowing that any chink in my armour could cause it all to spill free, unleash the person hiding beneath the surface. I'd done well to adapt, change. But now I felt as if I was teetering on the brink of a breakdown. Jade and Amala were rocking the foundations I'd thought were so strong, and I couldn't cope with the uncertainty of what was coming next. What I might do if I was right.

I glanced at the clock, shocked to realise how late it was. Almost 3 a.m. I *had* to try and sleep. I checked the lock on my bedroom door for the tenth time since coming in here, then climbed into bed, pulling a thin sheet around my body. I lay back, trying to breathe through the panic attack that was fighting to be released, closing my eyes, listening to the frantic sound of my heart racing in my chest.

My eyes snapped open at the sound above me. A footstep. Was it coming from the loft? I couldn't be sure. My mouth went dry as I listened, frozen to the bed. There it was again. Another creak of the floorboard. A scrape of something being moved aside. It was an old house. It was prone to unexplained noises. But this was different.

My heart pounded, my hands fisting the sheets, sweat coating my palms as I lay utterly still, useless, unable to produce an ounce of fight. Instantly reverting to the weak, pitiful, pathetic girl I'd let myself become over those long, torturous years with him. I hated myself for my fear, for my Pavlovian reaction, the instinct to make myself small and quiet rather than roar, defend this space, this sanctuary I held so dear. I was better than this. I had changed, hadn't I?

With a burst of determined fire, I leaped from the bed, dashing over to where I'd dropped my dressing gown on the floor and yanking it on, ignoring the way my hands trembled, the convulsions spilling through my body. I pulled back the bolt noisily, throwing open the door and heading along the narrow hallway to the little alcove below the loft hatch. I wrapped my arms around myself, looking up at it. It was closed, just as I'd left it. No ladder in sight. No sign that anyone had been here. Accessed the space. But I'd heard movement. I'd definitely heard someone up there. I was sure I had.

I balled my hands into fists, staring at the hatch, wondering what to do, then turned and walked to the opposite end of the corridor, to Jade's door, listening, unsure what I was hoping to hear. There was no sound, and despite my desire to open the door and check she was in there, I managed to resist. Instead, I went to the stairs. My bare feet were silent on the thick carpet, and I walked slowly, my eyes darting left and right, trying to pick up on some change, some clue as to what I'd heard. When I reached the bottom, I froze, hearing a voice coming from the sitting room. *Jade*.

Ice encased my belly, trickled down my spine, as I realised she was talking to someone in there. Every instinct in my body screamed at me to run back up to my room and bolt the door again. To hide beneath the covers until morning broke. But I was in *my* house. This was my safe space. And I wouldn't be cowed. Not now.

Two heavy silver candlesticks stood on a small table just inside the front door, and I took one in my hand, the weight of it reassuring, comforting as I walked as quietly as I could manage towards the sitting room. Taking a deep breath, I flung open the door and stepped inside.

'Oh, hi, Annie,' Jade whispered.

I took in the scene. She was standing in the middle of the room, rocking the baby vigorously back and forth.

'Did we wake you?' she asked, her voice apologetic.

'What are you doing?' I looked past her to the window, open far enough to fit a man through.

She paused, noticing the candlestick in my fist. Her eyes

widened for a moment, then she looked back to my face, resuming her rhythmic movement. 'Amala has trapped wind. She was getting upset, and I didn't want her crying to wake you, so I came down here to settle her. The rocking helps.'

'I didn't hear her cry.'

'She didn't make much noise. But she was getting fidgety. I'm sorry for disturbing you. It's late... You should go back up. She's much more settled now; I think she'll go back to sleep in a minute.'

I stared at the window. Had *that* been what I'd heard? Her opening the creaky old window for a bit of air? Or walking past my door to come down here? It was the simplest explanation, and yet it didn't feel like the right one. Jade's eyes were trained on the baby, avoiding mine, and I had the sudden urge to scream at her that she was lying. That she'd brought danger into my home. I wanted to pick up the landline and call a taxi, make her leave right this second so that I could go back to the life I wanted, *needed*. I couldn't live like this. Not again.

I bit my lip, forced myself to speak calmly, despite the terror bubbling inside my chest. 'You shouldn't open the window that wide. We get foxes in the garden... one might get in and hurt the baby.'

'Right,' she said quietly, clearly trying not to disturb Amala. 'Sorry, I didn't think.'

I gave a short nod, walking over to the window and closing it, double-checking it was tightly shut. Then I turned and walked from the room, leaving her standing there swaying from side to side.

As I headed slowly back up the stairs, I felt as if the stress of her being here might actually drive me mad. I took a deep breath and told myself I was doing the right thing. Jade needed my help. She just needed a place to rest while she figured out her next move, and suspecting otherwise wouldn't help either of us.

EIGHT

My eyes itched with exhaustion, and for the tenth time in as many minutes, I raised the back of my gloved hand to rub at them, the dry, sawdust-filled air making me cough. I gripped the sandpaper in my pinched fingers, pausing again to listen.

The door to the workshop was open to the dawn, birdsong filling the garden beyond, the soft orange-streaked sunrise promising another clear summer's day. It should have made me smile, but I was too tired, too damn tense, to take any pleasure in it. For three years I'd created a routine, coming out here to work after a long, leisurely breakfast. I'd spend two or three hours absorbed in creating my latest piece, then go in for lunch. The afternoons were for the garden. It was a routine that had brought both comfort and pleasure after so many years of not knowing what to expect, what horrors might be waiting for me on any given day, but having barely slept last night, I'd given up trying and had been out here since the first signs of light, not bothering to eat before creeping out the back door.

It was probably for the best I got it done early. Down here, at the end of the garden, with the tools banging and whirring, I couldn't hear a thing from the house. I could at least *try* to relax.

I sighed, resuming my sanding, my small fingers working into the soft wood. Despite how this hobby came about, woodworking was still my happy place. It had been a surprise to me that Ryan had supplied the wood, the kit, long after he'd made me give up anything else that had brought me pleasure. But it hadn't taken me long to work out why. He thrived on praise, and my unusual skill set, showing off what I was capable of to his friends, his colleagues, had brought him a sense of smug satisfaction. *His* girlfriend was thinner, better dressed, more talented than theirs – at least in his warped view.

He would take the houses as I finished them and present them as gifts to his circle – a subtle reminder that while they had wives and girlfriends who answered back and forced them to do their share of the housework, he had me waiting at home to cook his dinner and wash his pants. And make little gifts for his friends. He saw it as a mark of pride that I didn't need to work, though the truth was we couldn't really afford it, and a second income would have meant a lot less sacrifice. But I had never objected to his thinly veiled bragging, the illusion that he was so good to me, so nurturing of my *talents*, because it meant I could continue to do the thing I most enjoyed. An escape from the hell that was my reality. It was interesting to me that given all the other things he'd done to hurt me, he had never once destroyed a single one of the birdhouses.

It was only now, feeling vulnerable and exposed in a way I hadn't for a very long time, that I wished I'd thought to create something different after moving here. Something less distinctive.

I sighed, pausing to listen again, wondering if Jade and the baby would be waking soon. I didn't want her wandering around in there freely. I wanted to be back before she had the chance to snoop. The memory of that Facebook site, the 'about' page complete with my full name, sent a shiver down my spine. If Ron had led Jade to me... if he'd inadvertently led Ryan here, things were about to get very nasty, and I didn't know what I might have to do in order to clean up his mess.

'You want me to *what*?' I asked, hot water sloshing out of the overfilled kettle onto the counter as I spun to face Jade. Her long brown hair was tied back in a low ponytail, making her look even younger than usual – like a girl of eighteen rather than the twenty-eight she'd claimed to be. There was no sign of Amala, and it made me anxious to think of her alone upstairs, the horrible things that could happen to a tiny baby in a split second with nobody watching.

'I... I need nappies,' she said, clasping her hands together. 'I only came with Amala's changing bag, and I'm down to my last few. I could do with wipes too. And probably some more sleepsuits.'

I knew my expression was betraying my exact feelings – absolute shock and anger at what she was asking me. I could feel the deep furrow in my brow, my red, bleary eyes sore and dry from the lack of sleep over the past couple of nights – caused by *her*, as it happened. I had emerged from the workshop just now feeling stiff and angry, and before I'd even had a chance to drink a cup of coffee, she was trying to get me to run her errands as if I was her fucking employee. I couldn't believe the cheek of her.

'*So*?' I asked pointedly, still gripping the kettle. 'Go down to the village. It's only ten minutes' walk from here.'

She nodded slowly, as if I was somehow missing the point. 'I saw the shop the other day. It's only a little Co-op. They won't have baby clothes there. I thought maybe you could drive into the town and get what I need.'

I blinked.

'I... I saw the garage round the side of the house,' she continued. 'That red Mini. It's yours, right? And I don't have a car... I don't drive, and I don't have a seat for the baby.'

I pressed my lips together, reminding myself that I had agreed to help her. I didn't know when she'd been close enough to the garage to see the rusting old Mini through the window. Had she been snooping? The idea sent a chill down my spine.

'It was my mother's car. It hasn't left the garage in years,' I said, turning at last to pour water over the generous spoonful of instant coffee waiting in my favourite mug. 'I doubt it will even start, and I have no interest in finding out.' I swept a tea towel over the puddle of spilled water. 'I have a perfectly good washing machine you're welcome to use for Amala's things, and yours too if you need to, and the local shop will absolutely have nappies and wipes. I'm sure the walk and the fresh air will do you and the baby good,' I added, my voice firm and inflexible as I stirred the fragrant dark brown liquid. 'And you might as well look in at the community centre while you're there. They have a support group for young mothers that runs every week, though I'm not sure which day it's on. I remember a leaflet coming through the door a while back. It might be helpful.'

She bit her lip, and I could tell she wasn't happy. 'Will you walk down with me?' she asked quietly. 'To the village? I... I'm not sure I can do it alone.'

I met her hopeful stare, shaking my head before she'd even finished. 'No. I can't do that. I *won't* do that.' I offered no further explanation, letting the silence grow until it became uncomfortable.

She bowed her head. 'Okay... Well, is there anything you need while I'm there?'

'You can pick up some bread and milk if you can carry it. If not, my neighbour will do that later. I'd ask him to get your nappies, but I don't want to put him out. He already does such a lot for me. It's not fair to ask for more.'

'Right. I understand. I'll wait for Amala to wake up from her nap and then we'll go. We won't be long,' she added, as if she was afraid I might bolt the door and ignore her knocks on her return. I couldn't deny that the idea was more than a little tempting.

She left the kitchen, and I heard her quiet footsteps on the stairs. I took my coffee over to my chair by the fireplace and slumped down into it, exhausted. I was shocked that she had even asked the question. Wasn't it enough that I'd let her, a complete stranger, into my home? Did she really expect me to leave her unattended, free to snoop through my private things? I shuddered at the thought of it. I wished I could find that bloody photograph. The more I looked at her, the more I was convinced I was right. That she was the woman who had married the man who'd made my life a living hell for far too long. I should throw her out, but she looked so vulnerable. And that poor baby deserved a safe place to rest. If Ryan *was* her father... if he found her... It didn't bear thinking about.

I glanced up at a sound in the hallway, and a moment later, Jade appeared in the doorway, Amala strapped into the carrier on her chest, the empty changing bag slung over one shoulder.

'Are you sure you won't come for the fresh air?' she asked, her voice soft, pleading.

I shook my head. 'I'll get plenty of that in the garden this afternoon. Don't forget to look in at the community centre to find out about that mothers' group.' I winced internally at the sound of my cool, clipped tone, wishing I could find it in me to offer more warmth, especially when she looked so in need of empathy. But my fear, my discomfort at her presence here was making me tense and snappy. I longed to be rid of her.

She gave a resigned nod and turned away. I waited to hear the front door close, then jumped up, slamming my mug on the table as I rushed into the hall. I could see from several feet away that she'd left the door on the latch. Was the reason simply so she could get back in on her return? Or, I thought, my blood running cold as I slid the bolt across, was she leaving it open for someone *else* to get inside? To sneak up on me when I wasn't looking. Had she been so insistent on my joining her because she was trying to warn me... to protect me?

The things I'd done at Ryan's bidding flashed bright in my mind. The way he'd sweet-talked me, so persuasive, and, on the occasions I had refused to bend to his will, forced my hand by violence, terror. I could imagine how torn Jade would be between doing the right thing and protecting herself and her tiny daughter.

My shaking fingers gripped the smooth brass handle, testing it, my forehead pressing against the ancient wood as I tried to breathe through the panic that was pulsing frenetically in my veins. The sudden knock on the other side of the door reverberated through my skull, making me lurch back in horror.

'Annie?' Aaron's familiar voice called, and I pressed my palm to my chest, collecting myself. 'Annie, are you there?'

For a moment, I considered not answering. Retreating to my seat by the fireplace and pretending I hadn't heard him. But I was certain his timing was deliberate; he'd seen Jade leave and now wanted to grill me. There was no point prolonging the inevitable. I sucked in a shaky breath and stepped forward, slowly sliding back the bolt and opening the door, though it felt like opening the gate into a tiger's enclosure.

'Hi,' I said, trying to summon what might look like a natural smile as I met his brown eyes. They were narrowed, taking in every inch of my face as if he was looking for answers to a question he'd yet to ask. His dark-blonde hair was falling over his tanned forehead, and he pushed it back. 'Thanks for dropping off that shopping last night,' I blurted. The bag had been left on the step, just as I'd requested, and he'd added a big bar of my favourite chocolate to the collection, which had made me come over inexplicably tearful.

'You have someone staying here.'

I pressed my lips together, offering a silent nod, the thought of having to explain the situation I'd found myself in wholly unappealing.

'I met her when I dropped off the strawberries. And I just saw her leave.'

'Right.'

'Is she gone now? Or will she be returning?'

I raised my face to meet his probing stare, straightening my spine. 'She's just gone into the village. She's coming back.'

'I see.' He hesitated, his eyes piercing as they burned into mine. 'I didn't realise she had a baby.' The words were delivered slowly, his tone accusatory.

'Yes. A little girl.'

He stared at me, silent for too long. Finally, he spoke. 'Why is she here, Annie? Who is she to you?'

I couldn't hold his intense eye contact. I looked past him, hoping Jade wouldn't change her mind about going to the shops and reappear. 'She's an old friend. She's just staying for a few days,' I lied, unwilling to get into the complicated mess, the answers I still didn't have. I didn't *want* to lie to him, but he'd given me no choice. I wasn't about to bring up who I thought she really was, her link to the past I'd fled. I didn't want to remind him of the state I'd been in when I'd arrived here... the awful things that had happened in those harrowing few weeks after I arrived at the empty house. 'She'll be gone soon,' I added, hoping that would settle his fears a little.

He folded his arms, his usual smiley face and carefree demeanour conspicuously absent. It was clear that he didn't believe me. '*Annie.*'

'What?' I replied innocently, though I felt my cheeks flush.

'What are you *doing*?' he whispered, his tone suddenly urgent. 'They can't be here... you shouldn't have let them stay. You know that!'

I shook my head. 'It's just a few days. It's fine. It will be fine.'

'That baby—'

'Is perfectly safe here,' I snapped, folding my arms tightly across my body. 'As is her mother.'

He opened his mouth as if to argue, then sighed, shaking his head, his eyes trained on the ground as if he was ashamed of not being able to find the right words. 'I'm right next door. Remember that, okay? If you need me... if you want to talk – about anything. I'm not on shift for the next few days, so I'll be there. Day and night.'

'Well, maybe you can find the time to do as you promised and get my bloody birdhouses off the internet. I saw the website! Jade found it in minutes when I asked her to look. And there's a Facebook page too, with my name plastered all over it! Thank God Ron doesn't have a photo of me, or that would no doubt be on there for the whole world to see too!'

'I think you're being a bit dramatic, Annie,' he replied, his tone dismissive.

'Oh really?' I snapped back. 'Why do you suppose she was able to discover it so easily? She literally typed in "Annie, hand-made wooden birdhouses", and there it was! He must have been running it for weeks without my knowledge! Are you telling me you didn't know before? Or were you hoping to sway me by waiting until you had the sales logged? Do you think I'd sell my safety, the life I've built here, for a chance at making more money?'

He blinked. 'I don't know what you mean...'

'Think, Aaron! Think about the position you've put me in. You should have made it clear to Ron that he wasn't to do anything of the sort when he put forward the idea. You should have watched him take the site down before you promised me it was sorted. It makes me wonder whose side you're on. How I can possibly trust you when you can be so flippant about my safety! You know better than anyone why I don't want the world knowing where I sell my stuff. How easy it would be to track down my location from there. I should never have let you talk me into working with Ron.'

Hurt flashed in his eyes, but I didn't allow myself to care.

'I'll sort it,' he said, his voice gruff. 'I'll go to the shop today and make sure it's down.'

'But don't you see? It's too late for that!'

He frowned, confusion clouding his eyes. 'What do you mean?'

I glanced over his shoulder to the lane behind him, checking again that Jade hadn't returned. I didn't want to admit to him who Jade really was. His face was creased with worry, and I couldn't help but think that even now, despite the breach of my privacy, the way he'd risked everything I'd built for myself by being so careless with my wishes, it wasn't me he was worried about but Amala. He didn't like me flying off the handle like this, acting unhinged. He was worried what it might lead to – what I might do out of fear, self-preservation. He couldn't have made it more clear that he didn't think I was fit to have a baby in my home, even with her mother watching over her.

I wanted to ask what he was so afraid of, why he looked so intense, but I already knew, and I wouldn't open that can of worms now. I couldn't cope with that on top of everything else. 'Make sure you get it taken down,' I said sharply. 'And don't worry about me having guests. I'll be fine,' I repeated.

'But will *they*?'

I snapped my head up, my eyes wide at the implication behind his words, but he'd already turned for the gate. I didn't wait for him to walk through it before I shut the door on him, bolting it tight.

NINE

JADE

I slumped down in the chair beside the big stone hearth, exhausted from the sweltering walk into the village, grateful that the thick stone walls of the house worked so well at keeping the heat out. I was used to modern new-build houses and flats that became a sauna at the first sign of spring, and this quality, this *craftmanship*, was a welcome change. They didn't build them like this any more.

I leaned my head against the high-backed, sun-faded patchwork chair, shuffling Amala in my arms and latching her on to my breast before picking up my phone from the small round coffee table beside me. The sight of the unopened messages made tension swell inside me, constricting my throat. I hadn't been prepared to leave, hadn't been ready, and now, finding myself out of my depth and floundering about how to proceed, I couldn't help but be aware of everything that could go wrong. If he found me here... if he knew...

I shook away the thought, steeling myself and clicking on the notification button. I couldn't keep putting it off, and besides, I wanted to know what was going through his mind right now. What he planned to do next.

I read through the messages, not surprised by the way the tone changed so quickly with each one. The first had come just an hour after I'd caught that train, and the last had been sent early this morning. There were voicemails too, but I deleted those without listening to them. I wasn't about to put myself through that.

One by one, I erased the texts, feeling my shoulders lift as his words disappeared from the screen. Finally, there was nothing left. As if he'd felt me pulling away, known he was on the verge of losing my attention, another popped up, and I gripped the phone, swallowing thickly as I read.

For fuck's sake, Jade! What are you playing at? If I don't hear from you today, I'll—

There was a gasp behind me, and instinctively I flipped the phone over on my lap, pressing the button on the side to lock it. I turned to see Annie standing there. She must have tried to sneak up on me. There was no other explanation for it. You couldn't walk across the flagstone floor without making a noise unless you were really going out of your way to be sneaky.

'Mr *Tenacious*?' Her voice quivered, and I shook my head, pretending I didn't know exactly what she'd seen. The nick-name I'd saved his number under, spawned from the moment I realised just how stubborn he was.

'It's nothing. He... he just wants to know where I am. I'll block him.'

Her eyes were wide, and I could see she had more she wanted to ask but couldn't find the words. Instead, she turned, and this time I heard the slap of her bare feet as she rushed out of the kitchen, leaving me alone with my daughter, wishing I'd had the foresight to wait until I was back in my room to read his messages.

This was going to complicate things for me, and that was the last thing I needed.

TEN

ANNIE

I sat hunched on the closed lid of the toilet in my en suite, gnawing at my thumbnail, my eyes trained on the locked door. The nickname – Mr Tenacious – rushed through my mind, and I felt a wave of nausea ripple through my belly, bile searing the back of my throat. I'd been so sure of who Jade was from the moment I saw that bruise on her arm. Her confession that she was running from someone dangerous had only cemented the certainty – though I couldn't be sure how involved Ryan was in her disappearance, what games he might be playing. But that text... that *name*... it had stirred a memory that had long been buried in the depths of my mind.

Kenna. I had never met her, never even spoken to her, but I had known what she meant to him. Ryan had talked about his cousin, ten years his junior, with reverence, and in the early days of our relationship, I'd thought it was sweet. How she would call him late in the evening to talk over a problem she was having, or send him care packages in the post. She still lived in Edinburgh, and though I'd made it clear to Ryan that she was welcome to visit us in our home, hoping to gain more insight into who he was and discover whether she'd seen the emerging darker side to his personality too, he had always refused, getting the train up to visit her instead. Later, when he'd become too paranoid to leave me home alone for fear that I'd escape, he'd stopped going to visit, but still she'd never come to us. Somehow I had sensed her dislike for me even without having spoken to her, and I couldn't help but wonder what Ryan had told her about me. And, when I let myself go down a darker path, whether there was an element of jealousy at play.

There had been something in the way he spoke about her, the warmth in his tone, that had made me uncomfortable, as if their relationship was more than just cousins. I'd never been able to put my finger on it, but there had been little comments that felt off to me. He'd once said she was the only woman in his life he could rely on, and when I'd asked him to elaborate, he'd told me she was family, something I would never be. He'd told me that when he'd fallen out with his previous girlfriend, an eighteen-year-old fresh from sitting her A levels, and she'd accused him of beating her badly after an argument, Kenna had provided an alibi, sworn she was with him and made sure the charges were dropped.

I'd wondered when I'd first heard that whether Kenna felt any sort of guilt over that claim, or whether the Ryan *she* knew was so different from my version that she simply took his word without question. But it had become clear over the years that she would do anything for him. Lie to the police. Believe his stories. And love him no matter what he did.

I bit down on the tip of my thumb, tasting dirt and blood, a hiss escaping my clenched teeth. *Mr Tenacious*. I'd heard him repeat it on the phone, followed by his deep, rumbling laugh – a sound reserved almost exclusively for her. 'Why did you call me that?' he'd asked, his face cracked wide open in an unfamiliar, genuine smile. There was a pause, and he laughed again. 'Because I always get what I want? Yeah, you're damn right, babe, I do.'

I felt stupid, *careless*, as I recalled those words now. I'd been so single-minded about protecting my ex's vulnerable new wife that I hadn't stopped to consider that the woman in my home might be someone entirely different. She was the right age, pale and pretty – that was what he'd always said when I asked what Kenna looked like. He'd said she had dimples, and I was sure I'd seen them on Jade's cheeks too. Had I made a terrible misjudgement? Was it in fact Ryan's cousin, the woman who would lie, perhaps even kill for him, sitting downstairs in my kitchen playing the victim in order to draw me into her web? His game of cat and mouse. Kenna would do it, I knew without a shadow of a doubt. She would do *anything* for Ryan and their odd relationship.

I felt like I'd swallowed a lead balloon, goose pimples rushing up my arms at the thought of what that would mean, the danger I could be in. She would do everything he asked of her and more. Anything to impress him. No doubt he had woven some story casting himself as the victim, just like he had when the police came looking for him for battering that poor girl.

My heart was racing, panic fizzing through my body, threatening to explode out of me in a primal scream. I pressed my hands to my face, forcing myself to slow my breathing. I was being ridiculous. Making up stories in my mind because I was afraid, because I wasn't used to having anyone here under my roof. I was jumping to conclusions *again*.

Jade had confirmed who she was, hadn't she? And she couldn't fake the things I'd witnessed – the enormous purple bruise on her arm, the fear in her eyes. The love she quite obviously had for her baby girl. She wasn't Kenna. She was nothing like her. She was quiet, vulnerable, the polar opposite of the brash, obnoxious voice I'd overheard on the phone countless times. And there was no hint of a Scottish accent there. She *couldn't* be Ryan's cousin.

The poor woman had fled from abuse – abuse *I* could have stopped if I'd gone to the police three years ago to report what Ryan had done to me – and now, instead of helping her, I was letting my anxiety lead me into a fantasy fuelled by my own damn PTSD. *I* was the reason Ryan had been able to find another victim. I'd failed her, and I wouldn't make the same mistake again.

I stood up, going to the sink and splashing cold water on my face before meeting my blanched reflection in the mirror, determination flaring in my eyes. She was his wife. Simple as that. I'd seen the photo. The bruise. I would not let myself be driven to madness by fear. Not again.

ELEVEN

I tossed aside the novel I'd been trying to focus on, leaning my head back against the squashy sofa cushions and sighing heavily. I could hear Jade moving around in the kitchen, and just the knowledge that she was out there made me fidgety, unable to relax, to enjoy the hobbies I usually relished. The door to the living room creaked, and she popped her head round, smiling. She'd been in a strangely good mood since she'd got back from the village, completely glossing over the message I'd read over her shoulder in the kitchen – almost as if it hadn't happened. Now she was annoyingly chatty, as if she thought she could make me forget what I'd seen if she made enough inane small talk.

I'd refrained from encouraging her as much as possible. I didn't want her to think this was some holiday retreat. That we were going to become friends. Anything that might make her stay longer than absolutely necessary was to be avoided as far as I was concerned. Twice, she'd asked me to hold the baby – an offer I'd instantly recoiled at, finding flimsy excuses for why I couldn't. I should have never touched her in the first place, and now that I'd volunteered once, it seemed she was determined to make a habit of it. It made me uneasy, and yet it also brought me more certainty that she couldn't be Kenna. Ryan would have poisoned her against me long before sending her here – there was no way *she* would trust me enough to hold her child.

'I hope I'm not interrupting?' she said now, stepping into the room bearing an old plastic tray laden with two steaming mugs and two plates stacked with sandwiches. 'I don't want you to think I expect to be waited on,' she said, lowering the tray to the low walnut coffee table. 'I was making myself some lunch and thought you might like some too.'

She straightened, unclipping the straps of the baby carrier across her chest and easing the scrunched-up newborn out. I couldn't help but watch the way the baby's tiny limbs flailed involuntarily as they met the air. Jade sighed. 'Ah, that's better. This damn thing really cuts into my shoulders. You wouldn't expect a baby so small to cause such neck ache, would you?'

'Well,' I said, trying to find something to contribute, aware that to remain silent would be unbearably rude, much as I might like to, 'I imagine your body is still adjusting to not being pregnant. Recovering from the birth. It will take a while before you're back to your full strength.'

She smiled, and I looked away, feeling uncomfortable. She continued to speak without showing any sign that she'd noticed my stand-offishness. 'You might be right. I didn't do much in the way of exercise while I was pregnant. Too tired all the time. Too stressed out by everything...' She looked down at Amala, who was still fast asleep despite being moved – a talent reserved for newborns – then glanced back up as if remembering something. 'Oh, did you want milk and sugar in your coffee? I wasn't sure.'

I'd made no move to take the offerings from the tray. Wasn't certain I wanted to eat or drink anything made by a stranger.

'I take it black,' I said. 'But I've already had two this morning. I'll get heart palpitations if I have any more caffeine.'

'Oh, sorry, I should have asked.'

I waved away her concern. 'It's fine. I was about to pour myself a glass of water anyway.'

'I'll get it. Here.'

Before I knew what was happening, I found the baby being lowered into my arms. The weight of her made me want to flinch, to let her drop to the sofa. I felt my whole body stiffen as Jade turned, rushing back to the kitchen, leaving me alone with her child. It was as if her mothering instincts were entirely absent. What other reason could there be for her to be so reckless with her daughter's safety? To leave her with me, blissfully unaware of what had happened to the last baby I touched. The torment she was causing in her thoughtless actions.

Amala shuffled against me. Slowly, I lowered my gaze to her face. Her eyelids were closed, flickering as she dreamed. I pursed my lips, turning my head away, pushing down the terrible feelings that seemed to rush to the surface like a tsunami, choking me, drowning me. I listened for the sound of the water running out in the kitchen, then counted the footsteps as Jade made her way back to me.

'There you go,' she said, handing me the glass.

I took a tiny sip, sniffing surreptitiously, then put it down on the table. 'You can have her back now,' I said stiffly.

'Would you mind giving her a cuddle while I have my coffee? I like it scalding hot, and I don't like to drink it while I'm holding her in case I spill it. It's been ages since I had a really hot drink.'

I opened my mouth, then closed it, realising I didn't know how to refuse. It would seem churlish to deny her something so simple, especially when I could hardly claim to be busy. I sighed, then, despite my crawling desire to hand her baby back and rush from the room, gave a short nod.

'Thanks.' She sank into an armchair, picking up her mug and sipping her drink, her eyes half closed in pleasure. She looked at me over the rim. 'This really is a beautiful house. You're so lucky to live in such a lovely place. Have you been here long?'

'I grew up here,' I said, talking to distract myself from the feeling of the baby cuddled into my body. 'It was my parents' house, but they died three years ago, and I moved back then.'

'They both died at the same time?'

I nodded. 'It was a boating accident.' I glanced at the photograph of them on the mantelpiece, both tanned and grinning, my dad's arm slung casually round my mum's shoulders. It had been a shocking death. Some inexperienced university students had hired a massive speedboat and taken it out for the day, got stupidly drunk and crashed headlong into the little yacht my parents had been sailing off the coast of Hampshire. They'd both been down in the cabin and had got trapped in there, the speedboat having cracked clean through the hull, the front end slamming up hard against the only door: the only escape. The yacht had begun to sink fast, and the students had been too drunk – too stupid – to help them get free. The boat had gone down, taking my parents with it.

'They drowned?' Jade's face was pale.

'Yes.' I didn't like to think of it. To remember the panicked phone call my mother had made in her final moments. There had been no sweet goodbyes. She was begging to be saved, my father bellowing and hammering at something in the background, trying to get them free. And I'd been helpless – less than useless – stuck indoors, miles from the coast, hiding from Ryan in the bedroom, black and blue, my eye swollen shut, listening as my parents – the only people who might have helped me – fought for their lives. The memory of my mother's screams still tore me from sleep in the middle of the night. The echo of her terror, followed by that unbearable silence as the phone cut out, the awful knowledge that they were still alive, their lungs slowly filling with water. I'd held on to that phone for hours afterwards, waiting for a miracle, for them to call, tell me they'd got free, been saved. But it hadn't come.

'I'm so sorry,' Jade said, and I blinked, remembering she was watching me.

I shrugged. 'Life can be cruel sometimes.'

'Yes.' She looked over to the photo of my parents, then pointed to the one beside it. 'Who's that?'

'*That* would be my brother, Thomas. I haven't seen him in a long time. Years.'

'Did he come to your parents' funeral?'

'No... he wasn't there.' I didn't admit that I hadn't been either. That I'd been in no fit state to go anywhere at that time. 'They weren't close. He wasn't their biggest fan,' I admitted. 'He always felt they were too hard on him.'

'Oh... Did you agree?'

I shrugged. 'He was a strong-willed boy, and an even stronger-willed man. He had very different ideas about the world. How to live. They just clashed.'

'You must miss him, though?'

I looked down at Amala, surprised to realise I no longer felt so tense. Her hand had wrapped around my thumb, holding it tight for comfort, and I couldn't help but smile as I watched her. 'Sometimes,' I said, looking up. 'But I'm better off on my own. I prefer it that way.'

'It must be lonely.'

'No.' I smiled. 'It's just how I like it. I never was much of a people person.' I looked over to the photo of Thomas, thinking of all the ways he'd let me down. All the terrible things that had happened to me, all the awful things I'd done in return... things my brother might have been able to prevent if he hadn't turned a blind eye, looked out for himself. But that was what people were like. They didn't see what was needed. Didn't want to trouble themselves, get involved. We'd had a conversation on the phone in the weeks following our parents' demise, and the things he had said, the assumptions he'd made about me, had left a bad taste. I doubted I'd ever see him again.

Jade gave a sigh, then took another sip of her coffee. 'Family can sometimes be more trouble than they're worth. Mine certainly were,' she added darkly.

'You don't see them?'

She shook her head. 'My dad was never in the picture. And things were... complicated with my mum. I have a sister, but we were never close. The only person I really felt any connection to was my cousin. He helped me out of some difficult situations.'

I felt my stomach twist at the words. Since I'd read that message, seen that horribly familiar nickname on her phone, I had refused to let myself go down that path, berating myself for even considering that Ryan had sent Kenna here to play games with me. I had forced myself to put the idea from my mind. Jade's revelation now undid every speck of my efforts to hold those fears at bay.

I held her gaze, wondering what the look in her eyes meant; if she was enjoying this.

'He's been through a hard few years himself, but I've been there for him too. It's been a good opportunity to pay him back for all he's done for me. But the rest of them...' She shrugged, gulping back the last of her coffee, then placing her empty mug on the table. 'They can go to hell.'

I felt like I was going to vomit... like I would drop the baby. I gave a sudden start, then stood in a rush, carrying Amala to her mother, not giving her the option to push me further out of my comfort zone. I shouldn't be holding her. Hosting them here. Aaron was right. They should never have made it through the front door.

I left the sandwiches uneaten on the tray and, without

another word to Jade, walked outside to the garden, my mind racing. Who the hell was this woman, and why was she doing this to me?

I would never be able to relax with her under my roof. I wanted her gone. For good. And I was going to have to figure out the best way to make that happen – soon.

TWELVE

I'd had no intention of digging a new pond this afternoon, but with each back-breaking shovelful of heavy clay soil, I felt the tension dissipating. The sun was hot on my back, the string straps of the vest top I wore providing no protection from its rays, but I didn't care. I needed to be busy. I needed to feel the burn in my muscles, the sweat trickling between my breasts. I reached for the water bottle I'd left in the shade of the cherry tree I'd planted with my father when I was just five, spinning off the top and gulping back the tepid contents, wiping my mouth on the back of my hand and tilting my face up to take advantage of the light, barely there breeze.

What had Jade meant when she said she and her cousin were close? Had she known what she was doing? How those words would make me react? Had that been her goal, to see me squirm, knowing she could so easily backtrack and deny the suspicions swirling through my mind? The idea of Ryan's cousin here, under my roof, the two of them laughing together at how after all these years I was still naïve enough to fall for a sob story, made me sick with fear. And more than that – it made me angry. Made me want to defend myself, my home, the life

I'd fought too hard to lose now. It was bad enough when I'd thought she might be his wife, doing as he instructed out of fear, her desperate need to protect her child. But Kenna would do it just to hear him laugh. She'd do it for the fun of it...

I closed my eyes against the injustice, the cruelty. The truth was, I couldn't reconcile the image of Jade's wide, terrified eyes, the way her hands had trembled that first day here, with the brash confidence of a woman who meant to hurt me just for the hell of it. I couldn't make it make sense in my head. And even if it were at all possible, there was still that photograph of her in a wedding gown. I *knew* it was her in the picture. I would stake my life on it.

I dropped the drained water bottle back on the grass, pressing my hands to the base of my spine with a groan.

As if he'd been waiting for me to straighten up and take a break, the front door to Aaron's house opened, its distinctive creak giving him away, and I tensed, not turning to look in his direction, hoping he wasn't going to cause a scene. My front gate opened, and I leaned heavily against the handle of the shovel as I watched him approach.

'You look like you're in your element.'

I smiled, knowing it was true. 'Thanks.'

'Not everyone can make shovelling look so...' He wrinkled his nose and laughed. 'Even covered in mud and sweating buckets, you still manage to look gorgeous. It's a talent.'

I shook my head, blushing. This was our normal. We'd always been friendly, but over the past year it had become more flirtatious between us. I was sure that if I wanted it to, our relationship could easily become something more than just friendship. But Aaron understood me. He knew I had walls he would never be able to break through. Even so, I enjoyed the easy banter we shared. I just hadn't expected it from him now – not after the accusations he'd thrown my way on the doorstep this morning. I braced myself, waiting for the real reason he had come over so soon. He was checking up on me... on *them*, and I didn't like it.

'Annie!'

I turned, seeing Jade emerging from my front door. 'Oh, sorry,' she said, stopping short as she clocked Aaron. 'I didn't realise you were talking to someone.'

I glanced between the two of them, hyper aware of the lie I'd told Aaron to keep him from delving too deep. I didn't want them having a conversation, revealing my deception. It would only make things worse. Jade was looking at Aaron with unveiled suspicion, dislike even, and I frowned as she walked up the path towards us.

'It's fine,' I said, hoping to find out what she wanted and get her to go back inside as quickly as possible.

'I just wondered where the towels are kept? I used the ones you gave me, and Amala needs a bath. She's exploded through her nappy again.'

'Oh, right. They're in the airing cupboard on the landing – it's the door beside my room.'

'Okay, thanks.' She nodded, taking a step back. I held my breath, hoping that was the end of the awkward encounter, but Aaron moved in, extending a hand.

'I think we got off on the wrong foot,' he said. 'Jade, isn't it?'

'That's right,' she replied, looking at his hand without taking it.

Aaron shrugged. 'Annie's friend, right? How long are you staying?'

Jade glanced at me enquiringly, and I met her eyes briefly, then looked at the hole I'd been digging, wishing I could climb into it and cover myself in dirt, hide from this awful situation.

She broke into a smile that was too stiff for her pretty face. 'That's right. I'm not sure how long I'm staying.' She looked at me again. 'Sorry, I better get back to Amala. I've left her on the changing mat.'

I nodded, watching her rush back up the path, wondering why she'd gone along with the lie. She had done me a massive favour by not landing me in it. Aaron would have been on my case so much worse if he learned that I'd fabricated my story.

I turned back to Aaron, seeing his expression of deep thought as he watched Jade close the front door, and wondered if he'd been hoping to catch me out.

'I'd better go in and help her,' I said, wiping a soil-streaked hand across my sweaty forehead. He looked at me, then gave a nod. I didn't wait for him to question me further as I picked up my water bottle and walked briskly up the path.

Once inside, I watched Aaron through the peephole, standing where I'd left him, his eyes trained on the bathroom window. He stood motionless for a full two minutes before finally leaving. I leaned my head against the door and let out a sigh of relief.

'Here,' I said, passing the soft white towel to Jade as she lifted a squirming Amala from the shallow water. Amala had been crying when I'd gone up to offer assistance, feeling reluctant but obliged, but the moment her tiny body had touched the warm water, she'd been stunned into silence, her dark eyes wide. Now Jade wrapped her in the thick towel, bringing her to her shoulder and rubbing her back. I stood in the doorway, blocking her path to the bedroom. 'Why did you lie for me?'

I watched her face closely as she raised her eyes to meet mine. There was no need for me to explain my question. I could see she knew exactly what I meant.

'I didn't want to make you uncomfortable. I could tell he was prying, and I wanted to end the conversation.' She shrugged. 'Your neighbour is a busybody. And who you have staying with you is none of his business.'

'I only told him you were a friend because it would worry

him to know the truth.' I paused, wondering how to phrase my next question. 'Would he be right to worry? Should *I* be worried?'

She shook her head. 'I don't know what you mean.'

I folded my arms. 'What I mean is, why have you come here? What do you *want* from me, Jade?'

She stared wordlessly back at me, and I could see fear in her eyes, panic at having been put on the spot. I couldn't help but feel bad for having pushed her. She was so vulnerable. But that made it all the worse. If anything were to happen to her, to Amala, *I* would be in the spotlight. I couldn't have that.

She gave a shaky sigh. 'I wish I could tell you. I really do. But... I just can't. I'm sorry, Annie. I do realise what an imposition we're being. If you could just give me a few more days, a little more time...'

'Time for *what*?' I asked, my voice turning angry as the frustration of having my questions go unanswered bubbled up in my gut.

She shook her head, her face blanching. 'Amala's getting cold. I need to dress her.'

I remained in the doorway, blocking her path from the bathroom, determined to force her into telling me the truth, but she walked towards me and I felt myself stepping back, allowing her to pass, unwilling to get physical with a young mother holding her child. She walked around the bed, placing Amala on the duvet, and I hesitated, then left the room. I was certain that if she was unable to speak about her reason for being here, it was because she knew I wouldn't like the answer.

I fought between my need to protect her and my own self-preservation. If Ryan found me, if she led him to me, he would kill me. But if I kicked her out now, would she and Amala take my place?

I paused halfway along the hallway and leaned back against the wall, my limbs heavy with dread. I had no idea what to do.

THIRTEEN

The whittling knife slipped against the soft wood, my thick protective glove the only thing stopping me from taking a nasty hit from the blade, and I gripped it harder, willing myself to concentrate on the little frog I was carving beside the already finished lily pad. I could already feel the bruise forming on the side of my finger from the impact of the knife. I needed to eat, sleep, but with my stomach churning and my mind racing, those things seemed pretty much impossible right now. I couldn't help the quick, furtive glances I kept shooting across the wooden workbench. I shifted on my stool, trying and failing to look away from the glint of silver, the freshly sharpened metal catching in the ray of sun streaming through the open workshop door.

I hadn't known what had come over me when I'd found myself in the back of the rickety garden shed earlier, delving into the piles of dust-coated tools to find the axe I knew to be there. Hadn't let myself think about why I was carrying it into the workshop, casting nervous glances over my shoulder as if I was afraid of being caught.

But now I couldn't avoid the thoughts. The need to defend

myself had overcome me. I was just sitting here waiting for what I knew was coming for me. A victim, just as I'd always let him believe. Just as *I* had learned to believe too, if I was honest. And if I did nothing – if I was too scared to make a change, take control for once in my miserable life – it would carry on as before. Until he killed me.

I looked back down at the tiny half-carved frog, biting my lip as I tried to focus on whittling his back legs, a detailed, intricate process I usually adored, saw as a meditation, an escape from all worry, all fear. The knife slipped again in my shaking hands, and I watched, numb, as his head was severed from his little body, falling with a soft thump onto the workbench. In a rush of blind anger and frustration, I swept the nearly finished birdhouse to one side with a furious slash of my hand, watching as it fell to the hard stone floor below, the huddle of blue tits snapping from the base, the curved pillar that held up the roof shattering in two. I stared down at the ruined mess, my eyes flicking back to the axe, and wished he would come soon. That I could end this now.

The waiting was unbearable.

FOURTEEN

Then

My thighs burned with the effort of squatting in the cramped, stifling darkness. How many hours had passed since he'd locked me in here? He never allowed me to wear a watch, enjoying the knowledge that each minute would feel like twenty. I shifted, the metal hanging rail he'd drilled in halfway up the old wooden wardrobe, placed intentionally to reduce my head room, digging against my skull. My neck cracked as I tried to stretch, finding myself boxed in.

I was hyper aware of the danger of toppling over, the long metal spikes he'd driven into the wood on the opposite side, the silver gleaming in the darkness, reminding me not to move. I'd had to go to hospital after the last time I'd been shut in here. Not because I'd been caught by the lethal spikes, but because my left leg had swollen and I'd realised I had a blood clot in my calf, brought on by dehydration and staying in this unbearable position for so long. I'd hoped some part of him might feel guilty. Remorseful. That he wouldn't put me through it again. And for three months, he had resisted. But today I'd known it was coming. Known it would be my punishment for failing the task he'd set for me.

The games were an intrinsic part of our relationship. The limits I set being continuously pushed, barrelled through, smashed to oblivion. He'd started so slowly I hadn't realised what was happening, though in hindsight I could look back and see how he'd trained me like a dog wanting to please its master.

The first time, it had been merely a comment, delivered in an offhand, casual tone, about my wearing flats to dinner. I had never been one for stilettos, placing comfort over style. He'd said, 'I expect you don't wear them because you're afraid you'll fall flat on your face.' Then he'd stared pointedly at a group of beautiful women, all dressed elegantly, all wearing sky-high heels. He'd looked them up and down, appreciation shining in his dark eyes, then turned his attention to me, his gaze lingering on my flat sandals, a sneer marring his handsome features. And like a fool, I'd fallen for it. Ordered a few pairs of the painful but sexy shoes he clearly favoured. Taught myself how to walk in them. And when we'd next gone out to dinner, I'd strutted by his side, feeling his smile of approval with every step I took. Somehow I'd let myself believe that it was *me* who'd manipulated *him*. Learned the way his mind worked and won him over by watching and adapting.

But I'd been a puppet. And when I'd resisted, I'd been punished. The comments. The comparisons. The little digs and insults. And so slowly I didn't realise, it had morphed to the physical.

The first time I'd made a meal with blue cheese, not realising he hated it, and he had slapped me. He'd never apologised. Only said that next time I'd do better. I couldn't explain to myself why I didn't walk away then. I could reason that he was wrong, he should never have raised a hand to me, but somehow he twisted everything so that I ended up blaming myself. And now... I winced, rubbing my palms up and down my thighs, trying to encourage the blood back into them as I held my position in the darkness, listening for his footsteps and hearing only silence. Now the tasks had mutated from my needing to become exactly what he desired, to cater to his every need, into something far more twisted. His sick need to control me, to make me do things that made me recoil in horror.

The person I was becoming at his insistence was someone I could no longer look at in the mirror. I'd stolen for him. I'd manipulated. I'd lied. And this morning he'd asked me to look at those images on the computer – violent, terrible photographs he'd sourced on the dark web of women being bound, broken, naked and vulnerable. He'd told me to organise them into files for him, and I had thrown up.

I'd tried to switch my mind off, just carry out the task, knowing he was only making me do it out of his own desire to rule me in every regard. But I hadn't been able to. Like an idiot, I'd started crying, unable to stop myself from wondering where those women were now. If they'd survived. If they had started out like me, trying to placate a partner who could never be satisfied.

My emotional breakdown had been unacceptable to Ryan. And now, as a result, I was back in the place I dreaded more than anything, my knees screaming in agony, my head pressed into the solid metal rail. It would have been better if he had just hit me again. Taken his rage out in a few agonising minutes of violence, as he so often did. But when it came to his tasks, his *lessons in humility and obedience*, as he referred to them, the punishment was always long. To allow me to reflect. Reconsider. Become better.

I closed my eyes, trying to block out the pain, the fear of what would come next, and wished I'd just done as he said. There was no place for morals, boundaries in my life. Not any more. I would do better next time.

FIFTEEN

Now

I woke with a start, hearing sounds in the ancient house that had me instantly on edge, the creak of the wooden floorboards outside my bedroom door making me sit bolt upright, straining my ears for a sign of the man who had destroyed the girl I'd once been. It had been three days since Jade's arrival, and still I had no answers. It had been clear after our conversation yesterday that she had no intention of revealing her secrets, and despite searching high and low, I still couldn't find the photograph my aunt had sent of Ryan's new bride. Enough was enough. I couldn't go on like this. Wouldn't allow myself to fall victim to one of his traps again, become that stupid, naïve girl who he'd manipulated, controlled – broken.

I'd thought I was stronger now. What my delightful ex hadn't bargained for during those years of playing with my mind, forcing me time and again to extend the boundaries of what I believed to be morally right, was that I would lose my empathy. Not just for the people he wanted me to hurt. But for *him* too. For the whole damn world. In the end, it had been his sick games that had given me the means to come up with my escape plan, had made me cold enough not to care that what I had done was wrong.

It was hard to even think of it now. Something about living alone, with nothing but my own conscience for company, had shone a light on the terrible things I'd been forced – and had chosen – to do in those years with Ryan, and despite myself, the guilt had been inescapable.

In order to live with myself, I had let myself believe that I'd had no choice. Forgiven myself. But with Jade and Amala here, my past was screaming at me once again, and the urge to bury it all somewhere deep and inaccessible was all I craved.

I got out of bed, dressing quickly in the denim shorts I'd tossed on my dressing table stool the night before, pulling on a cotton T-shirt and scraping my hair back into a ponytail without bothering to brush it. When I opened my bedroom door, it was slowly, cautious of what – *who* – might be lurking in the corridor beyond. I longed to break into a run, the closed doors to either side of the long, wide corridor making my heart beat faster, my imagination running wild with the terrible possibilities that might be waiting to catch me off guard. I walked quietly through the house, edgy, my ears pricked, and found Jade in the kitchen. Her back was turned to me as she poured orange juice into a tall glass, then gulped it down in one go. She put the empty glass on the counter, breathing heavily.

'You okay?'

She turned as if startled and wiped her mouth with the back of her hand. Amala was asleep in the carrier on her chest, and I marvelled at how few times I'd seen her with her eyes open. She seemed to always be napping. I realised that in another lifetime, a better version of myself might have known that. Might have known a whole lot of things about babies, their habits, how to take care of them. I shook off the thought, looking away from her, focusing instead on Jade's freckled nose.

'Oh, hi, Annie,' she said, smiling. She nodded to the glass. 'I can't stop drinking. I think it's the breastfeeding. I'm constantly craving juice.'

'I'll ask Aaron to pick some more up later,' I said, glancing at the near-empty bottle.

She followed my gaze, looking guilty. 'Sorry. I should have saved some for you.'

'It's fine.' I walked over to the kettle, filling it with fresh water, trying to find the right words to begin as Jade chopped some honeydew melon into slices, her back towards me again.

'I want to talk to you,' I said suddenly, knowing there was no easy way around it.

She turned, biting into a slice and chewing slowly. 'About what?'

I folded my arms, feeling horribly vulnerable. 'About Ryan.'

I watched her face as she gave a convincing frown of confusion. She was good. She really was. Just as *I* had learned to be.

'We were together for ten years. And he was abusive from very early on.'

'I'm sorry.'

I ignored her. 'He beat me. He raped me. He locked me up and he broke my soul, over and over, until I wasn't sure I even existed any more. He broke me completely.' I realised I was digging my fingers into the soft skin of my upper arms so hard I knew I would leave bruises.

'Why are you—' She broke off. 'That sounds awful, really awful. But why are you sharing this with me, Annie?'

I felt a wave of anger, sure that she was playing dumb. I'd done it myself, under his tutelage. Pretended to be stupid to gain access, information, do his bidding. It made me livid that nothing but the partner had changed. I hated remembering how good I'd become at playing the role of innocent, loved, happy, just as *she* was now. As if she didn't understand why I was spilling my secrets to her.

'You told me you were running from someone. Someone *dangerous*. Obviously my mind went straight to him. Why else would you have come to me if it wasn't because you knew I would understand? That was why I let you stay. But now...' I shook my head, frustration making me want to scream until there was no air left in my lungs. I met her eyes. 'It's not lining up in my mind. I deserve the truth, Jade. I've let you into my home and put myself at risk in order to do the right thing, but you're not making it easy for me. Did he make you do it? Is he planning to come for me now that he's tracked me down?'

She dropped the slice of melon back on her plate, shaking her head. '*Come* for you?' She raised an eyebrow as if the idea was entirely outlandish. 'Annie, stop. You've got it wrong. I... I've had my issues in the past with men, though nothing like what you've just described. But Amala's dad has never been in the picture. I'm not here because I'm fleeing abuse.'

'*What*? You said you were in danger! That's the only reason I let you stay! This isn't a fucking hotel!'

She was lying. Either now, or when she'd turned up. I knew what I'd heard, and I'd believed it because it had made perfect sense. Why else would she have looked so terrified when she'd rushed into my garden? Why had she looked so uncomfortable when she'd had to go into the village to get nappies? She was protecting him. Regretting telling me the truth early on and trying to backtrack now. It made my blood boil. She clearly had no intention of telling me his reasoning for sending her here. I would have to get hold of her phone, search through it to find out what was really going on.

'No, I said I was in a difficult situation, and I am. I'm sorry I gave you the impression I was fleeing abuse. I'm not sleeping well and I'm under a lot of stress. I muddle my words a lot lately. If I'd known your past... I can imagine how triggering that would have been for you,' she said softly.

'I don't understand.' I shook my head, trying to recall her

exact words. Had I let my own fears fill in the blanks? I'd been here on my own for so long. It was possible I'd let my imagination run away with me. Seen my worst fears coming to life. I took a deep breath, clenching my fists and releasing them, trying to dispel the tension fizzing through my veins. 'If you're not running from abuse... if you're not here at his behest,' I said, spitting the words as if she'd give herself away, blush and look guilty, 'then what *are* you doing here?'

She sighed. 'I wish I could tell you. But it's complicated. I'm sorry, Annie. Look, just give me a couple more days and then we'll be gone. There are just a few things I need to sort out... Please, can you give me that?'

I stared at her, unable to speak, unable to know what to think, what to believe. The memory of her face, pale and terrified, when I'd told her to leave that first night came to mind, and I swallowed, wishing she would just confide in me, let me help her. Whatever was going on, I could cope if I knew. This secrecy was driving me mad. I didn't know what I might do...

I let my gaze travel down to Amala's sleeping face, those cherubic cheeks, her little pursed lips, and thought I couldn't bear to have her here... couldn't stand it.

'I'll go to the shops now. Get that juice for you,' she said quietly, reaching for her bag.

Silently, I watched her go.

I would have to get that bag... the phone, her purse too. I needed to delve inside it at the first opportunity and take the answers she was too afraid to give.

I picked up my mug of coffee and gulped deeply, my fingers trembling as I listened for the sound of her fading footsteps on the flagstone floor.

SIXTEEN

The bed – the fresh mattress atop the polished brass frame that had once belonged to my parents, where I could still remember happy childhood mornings climbing in between them, listening to them talk about what we'd do that day – felt strangely unfamiliar, too hard as I lay in the glow of the lamp, looking up at the ceiling.

I had tried to switch off the light, but the instant I had, I'd found myself picturing nightmarish images lurking in the dark and had quickly flicked it back on. The clock read 2 a.m. now and I was sure I wouldn't sleep tonight.

Jade had avoided me after returning from the shops with three bottles of juice, complaining that the heat had worn her out and heading upstairs to the bedroom with Amala. She'd taken her bag with her, and I'd watched her go, trying to figure out a way to get access to it, to find out what I needed to know. Now that I was conscious of it, I had become aware of the fact that she never left it unattended. Never provided an opportunity for me to snoop. A deliberate decision, no doubt.

I'd had another awkward conversation with Aaron in the garden, the hole I was digging for the new pond getting quite deep now – though not nearly deep enough. It was back-breaking work, and the few minutes I'd stopped to rest had been laden with probing questions. He'd seemed overly involved in my situation, my guests. I'd made an excuse, heading indoors, feeling his gaze on my back again, a pattern forming.

There'd been no opportunity for me to talk to Jade over dinner either. She'd been distracted by Amala's fussing, not seeming to hear me when I tried to ask questions, and had taken herself off to bed as soon as she finished her meal. And now I found I couldn't relax. Couldn't stop thinking of how to get that bag. If I went to her room now, could I sneak it away without her waking, without disturbing Amala? If I was caught, I could always say I'd come in because I heard the baby making noises and was worried. She'd have to believe me... I'd *make* her believe me.

I lay flat on my back, listening hard, no desire to be caught. I was summoning the courage to move when I heard it. The distinctive sound of the front door opening. The house was old and had moved over the years, and now the door always scraped a little on the tiles in the entryway. It was unmistakable. Someone was coming inside.

The terror was instant, my heart thumping like a wind-up toy, my bowels churning, a desperate need to run to the bathroom as cramps shot through my gut, fear making my whole body break into a sweat. My bedroom door was locked from the inside, but would it be enough? It hadn't been in the past...

I tried to suck in a breath as I lay frozen, a statue on the hard mattress, and felt like I was breathing through a straw, the air refusing to fill my lungs. There was the sound of a door opening below – the living room, perhaps? Then, as I tried to gasp at another breath, there was nothing but silence... an eternity of horrifying silence. I balled my hands into fists, wanting to throw myself out of bed and storm through the house, my sanctuary, my home, and demand the intruder leave at once. I wanted to be courageous, to be fierce. But still I couldn't move.

And then there was another sound... Footsteps. Slow. Intentional. Heading up the stairs, the floorboards creaking beneath the thick carpet. I stifled the scream that rose unbidden from my body, pressing my lips together to contain the sound.

Jade had told me she wasn't who I thought she was. But I remembered the advert online and I felt certain. He had come. It wasn't as if I hadn't pictured this moment over the past three years. I had imagined myself being stronger if I ever had to face him again. Braver. Standing up to him and telling him I was no longer under his control. I wasn't afraid of him. But now I was petrified. I couldn't move a muscle as I waited for the man who'd been my tormentor for so long, the man I'd escaped from, to come smashing through my door, smile that awful, knowing smile he'd always had. I couldn't stand myself as I gripped the covers. The footsteps reached my door, pausing outside, and it was all I could do not to cry out, beg him to leave me alone. He'd always made me beg. Enjoyed the power over me.

A long, agonising moment passed, and then, to my surprise, the footsteps retreated, heading back down the stairs.

I didn't understand. What was this game he was playing? Of course it wouldn't be a simple confrontation. *That* would provide no entertainment for Ryan. No sport. He always had to push the boundaries. So *what*? He was letting me know he was here; he'd found me after three years of blissful freedom? Building the fear so I went mad with the anticipation of what he might do next?

The realisation, the memories of how he'd done just that time and again throughout our relationship hit me, and I pressed my hands to my mouth. He was going to torture me... break me. And as strong as I'd let myself believe I'd become, I couldn't feel an ounce of that strength now. I was just the pathetic girl who'd nodded along to his commands – who'd lost herself – and when he came for me, I wouldn't be able to fight. I would surrender just as I always had.

Unless... I thought as I lay in the dark, my heart racing, listening for a clue to his next movement, unless I could find a way to summon my courage and end his hold over me once and for all.

My body ached, my muscles cramping as I stomped down the stairs, the first rays of dawn casting soft beams of light across the wooden floorboards. I hadn't moved from the bed all night, too afraid of what – or *who* – I might find if I went searching in the dark, and now the circles beneath my eyes were as black as my mood. I was exhausted, my nerves hanging by a thread. The thoughts that had spun uncontrolled through my mind in the wake of that unwelcome night-time intruder had made me sick, terrified of what I was considering, what I might be forced to do. I couldn't let him take me back to that place, that hell he'd kept me in, his prisoner, his slave. I wouldn't go.

I made no effort to soften my footsteps as I walked past the front door. It was closed, but the deadbolt was slid back – not how I'd left it when I'd gone up to bed. Jade had passed me in the hall at midnight, said she was heading down for a glass of water. She must have opened it then, leaving it on the latch. I seethed at the thought of her deception. After all I had done for her...

I glanced down at the heavy brass doorstop I was clutching in my palm, shaped like a terrier, a little Westie, like Charlie, my childhood pet. I squeezed it tighter as I rounded the corner and walked into the living room.

Something had moved. I felt it more than saw it, the second I walked in. Something was different. I cast around trying to work out what was wrong, and my gaze landed on the display cabinet to the right of the fireplace. On one side were my dad's old ornaments – blown-glass yachts, wrought-iron anchors – but on the opposite side were papers. Nothing of importance, but I could see instantly that someone had been looking through them.

I walked slowly across the carpet, reaching for the little silver key in the lock, my fingers grazing it as I stared at the evidence, as clear as day. The piece of paper that had floated down, a corner now sticking awkwardly out of the side of the door, as if someone had shut it in a hurry and rushed away without checking. I turned the key and slid the paper out. It was just an old bill from the electricity company. Nothing of interest. I frowned, placing it back on top of the stack and locking the cabinet door, turning to survey the rest of the room.

I sniffed, trying to detect a whiff of his aftershave, that horrible, overpriced stuff he had always worn, the smell that had made goosebumps rise on my arms, knowing he was close, that he had found my hiding place. It wasn't here. All I could smell was the lilies drooping in their vase, flowers Aaron had presented to me more than a week ago, before this mess had kicked off. I clutched the sturdy brass dog against my chest, my stomach churning.

'What are you doing with that?'

I glanced towards the voice, seeing Jade watching me from the doorway, Amala lying in the crook of her arm, her dark eyes open for once as she stared up at her mother's face.

I looked down at the doorstop. 'Oh, um, I was going to polish it... It's dusty.'

'Right.'

I stared at her, desperate to confront her but suddenly realising how unhinged my accusations would sound if I had somehow got it wrong. 'Did... did you come in here last night?'

She shook her head. 'No... Oh, wait, yes, I did. I came down with Amala for a little while when she wouldn't settle.'

'What time?' My tone was curt, demanding, but I didn't care.

She shrugged. 'I really don't know. It was dark. I think she's getting trapped wind at night.' She walked across the carpet towards me, and I felt myself tense, my grip on the doorstop tightening.

'I hate to ask,' she said, 'but would you mind holding her while I have a shower? She brought up some of her milk in my hair, and she doesn't seem to want to be put down for even a second.'

I gave a slow, reluctant nod, placing the doorstop on the coffee table and holding out my hands for her to pass the baby over.

'Thanks, Annie. You're a lifesaver,' Jade said, smiling. She turned and headed out the room.

I waited for the sound of the creaking old pipes, then, with Amala wriggling against my chest, I walked slowly to the front door and pulled it open, listening as it made that same distinctive scrape on the tiles. I knew I hadn't imagined it. But if it hadn't been Ryan, if Jade wasn't at the bottom of this, then *who*?

I stepped out into the front garden, the sun still low in the sky, though I could already tell it was going to be a sweltering day, and let my gaze move to Aaron's house. He always seemed to be watching these days. I wondered if *he* might have seen something. Heard something suspicious. I stared up at his bedroom window, assuming he was still asleep. The curtain seemed to move, and I wondered for a second if he was there, but though I continued to wait, there was no sign of him. My imagination was clearly running wild. It was hardly a surprise.

I swallowed, feeling nauseated, the exhaustion making me dizzy, and turned, heading back inside.

SEVENTEEN

JADE

I retied the towel around my wet hair, walking as softly as I could manage past the closed living room door. I could hear Annie in there talking softly to Amala. I needed to be quick. There was something unsettling about her, the way she looked at me, my child. Something off. She was nothing like I'd imagined – expected. When he had spoken of her, it had been clear that despite himself, his wish to distance himself from what he called his past, there was still a lot of feeling there. Reverence almost. It hadn't made sense, his story of why they no longer kept in touch, but when I'd tried to push it, I'd been shut down. I'd expected a softer character. Someone warmer, but there were times when frankly she seemed a little unhinged.

I knew she wasn't sleeping. Could hear her moving around at night. The creak of the floorboards. The opening and closing of her wardrobe, as if she was searching for something, or squirrelling something away. I shivered, thinking of her cold, flat eyes when she watched me. He had mentioned none of this. Nothing that might suggest Amala and I wouldn't be safe here. Did he intentionally miss that out, or was I just a victim of my hormones? Seeing danger everywhere?

I couldn't deny they had been brutal in the wake of Amala's birth. Made everything so much harder to cope with. And the bleeding was wearing me down, making me feel weak and vulnerable. Surely it should have stopped by now?

I had to be strong. Keep going. I didn't have a choice, and besides, things would be easier soon. I had to hold on to that thought to get through the next few days.

I walked quietly through the big kitchen, past the enormous fireplace, the morning light streaming through the windows. It was a beautiful house. I couldn't help but wonder if Annie was blind to the privilege she had, the gift of living somewhere like this. The village was quintessentially English, and surprisingly, unlike so many, was still thriving. I'd seen people gathered outside the post office, chatting as they waited to go in. The local shop assistants had been warm and curious about what I was doing here, and cooed over Amala, congratulating me on becoming a mother. It had felt like I'd gone back in time, into a better world, a kinder place, but Annie, it transpired, never set foot outside her house. Never took the time to get to know them all. It was a shame.

I slipped my feet into the flip-flops I'd left by the back door and, pressing down on the handle, opened it slowly, stepping outside and heading across the lawn to the old shed. Testing the door and finding it unlocked, I glanced over my shoulder, then slipped inside.

I was in there for less than three minutes before, dejected, I re-emerged into the bright sunlight, squinting after being in the dark. I was just closing the door when I felt myself forced forward, a hard body pressed into my back, my chest squashed against the splintered wooden door.

'You lied.' The man's voice was gravelly, his breath hot against the bare skin at the back of my neck.

I tried to twist free, but he held firm. I'd managed to glimpse his face, though. It was that awful neighbour again.

'Get. Off. Me,' I demanded, flinging my head back, hoping to headbutt him in the face but meeting only air.

'Not until you explain who you are. I know the name you gave me was false. I looked it up. There's no such person as Jade Ashton, at least not one matching your description. So,' he went on, pressing into me again, 'I'll ask you once more. Who are you, and what the hell do you want with Annie?'

I gritted my teeth, my wrist aching as he twisted it tighter against my spine. 'Is *this* how you were trained in the police force, Aaron? Because I have a feeling your supervisors would be interested to hear how you conduct yourself when not in uniform.'

He released his hold in an instant, stepping back just far enough that I could spin to face him. 'I've been expecting you to show your face,' he said.

'*What*? I don't know what the hell you're talking about, you weirdo!'

He dipped his head, and when he looked back up, his eyes were twinkling with inexplicable laughter. 'I knew you'd come. Sooner or later. I was surprised it took so long, to be honest. The baby was a nice touch – very clever. Who doesn't trust a mother, right?' He flashed a wink, though his mouth morphed into a cold sneer.

He stepped closer, and I turned my face to the side, trapped against the shed door, panic racing through my veins.

'Whose is she?' he asked, his voice silky, as if he was in on a secret I hadn't shared with him. 'Don't tell me she's yours – I don't believe it for a second.'

I shoved him hard in the chest, snapping my head round and jutting out my chin, a sick dread pooling in my gut. 'I have no idea what you're talking about,' I spat, my voice low and vehement. The last thing I wanted was Annie to come out and find me here with him. 'What makes you think you're entitled to know my business?' I demanded. 'What gives you the right to harass Annie's guests?'

'She's my friend. And she's... vulnerable.' He said the word slowly, as if he meant something quite different. He shook his head. 'I don't want you here. You *or* your borrowed baby. It would be best if you left. Today.'

'Best for who?' I asked breathlessly.

He glanced over his shoulder as if he was afraid she might hear, then lowered his voice. 'Take my advice and move on. And get that baby back to her mother before it's too late.'

'She's *my* daughter!' My chest heaved with conviction, and I met his shocked gaze, challenging him to argue otherwise. I would not have him claiming Amala wasn't mine. How dare he!

He stared silently back at me, then shook his head sadly. 'Then you're a bloody fool to have brought her into this. What kind of mother *are* you?' He didn't wait for me to offer a response as he turned and strode away, heading through the side gate towards the front of the house.

I realised I was shaking. Squaring my shoulders, I rushed back across the lawn and slipped indoors, turning the key in the lock, securing the back door. I couldn't help but feel he would come back, come *inside*.

My wrist throbbed, and I looked down, seeing the red imprints where his fingers had pressed so urgently. Who *was* this man? And why was he so wrapped up in what Annie did, who she had under her roof? The two of them were as strange as each other. They were unsettling.

Trying to compose myself as best I could, I took a deep breath and headed through the kitchen to the living room. 'Thanks, Annie,' I said, holding out my arms for Amala, relieved that she didn't put up any resistance. I needed her back in my arms after that awful encounter. I felt like his words had been a warning – one I hadn't bargained for when I'd made up my mind to come here. 'I appreciate your help.'

'You're welcome,' Annie said stiffly. She walked out of the room without another word, and I heard her by the front door. A moment later, I watched as she walked down the garden path, picking up the shovel and setting to work on the ominous hole she'd created. As I watched her dig, I pictured myself being tossed into that pit, buried alive as she dumped soil over me, suffocating, silencing. Had all these years alone sent her mad? It certainly seemed that way.

I shivered, lowering myself as Amala rooted, offering her a nipple. I tried to shake off the goose pimples that had rushed over me at the hideous premonition.

My gaze landed on the metal doorstop sitting on the table, and I suddenly remembered the way Annie had been clutching it so tightly when I'd come in earlier. What had she been planning to do?

I looked down at my daughter and felt a wave of uncertainty about having come here. The sooner I got what I came for, the better. Annie and her creepy neighbour had made me quite sure of that. This house wasn't safe.

EIGHTEEN

ANNIE

I stood under the hot stream of the shower, rinsing the soil and sweat from my hair, the old pipes creaking deep inside the thick wall behind me. I'd spent the morning in the garden, hoping the physical activity would trick me into feeling awake after the shocking night I'd just had, but it hadn't worked. I was unable to switch off the chatter in my mind, the memory of the sound of the front door opening in the dead of the night.

Jade had admitted to being out of bed, and I couldn't deny that she had given a perfectly reasonable explanation for going downstairs, but it didn't stop me from spiralling, turning over the worst possible explanations for the sounds I'd heard in my mind. It was just like me to do this... to ignore the most simple answer: that the sound I'd heard outside my bedroom door was simply Jade passing, trying not to wake me, and the rest had just been my imagination telling stories.

The more I thought about it, the more I was convinced I'd worked myself into a frenzy, imagined the sound of someone entering my home out of a heightened state of anxiety. I had spent every waking moment since she'd arrived expecting Ryan to show his face. It was hardly a surprise that I'd begun hearing things that weren't really there.

I had to keep reminding myself of her words. Her confusing confession. That she wasn't connected to my ex at all. I'd been angry, baffled when she'd told me, but the more I let it sink in, the more I realised I could breathe again. It was clear that she was hiding from something – some*one*. But not him. Not the man I'd feared. He wasn't coming.

Jade would figure out a plan, and I would go on with my life, safe just as before. I tilted my head back under the hot water, my chest no longer tight and painful as I let out a long, slow sigh. I was going to be okay. I wouldn't have to face him.

I climbed out of the shower, wrapping my wet hair in a towel and flinging the window wide. I wiped the steam from the huge oval mirror, then slapped a dollop of thick moisturiser on my face, frowning at the pinkness of my nose and cheeks, noting the deepening sun damage and lines that had formed since leaving Ryan.

It had been a conscious decision to let my beauty fade. I'd left the expensive make-up behind, the hair-styling products and gadgets, the beautiful clothes he'd liked to dress me up in when he took me out in public. His trophy. His prize. Only he and I knew what bruises were hidden beneath the expensive silk and cashmere. He'd controlled what I ate, weighed me every Sunday and adjusted my diet accordingly when I'd let him down by gaining even a pound. He liked me to be underweight – said it was more feminine. The freedom I'd felt at hacking my waist-length hair up to my shoulders, putting on an old pair of jeans I'd found in my teenage wardrobe, accompanied by a slobby long-sleeved striped T-shirt, a burn mark front and centre on the hem, had been exhilarating. In the three years I'd spent here, I'd gained a stone and a half, I'd shunned heels and make-up. I'd done my own hair, to my own preference. And I'd let my face turn brown in the sun, the smile lines brought on from my growing sense of serenity deepening with each summer that passed.

He would hate what he saw now. Perhaps so much that he wouldn't bother with me. That thought had been with me with every choice. Systematically making myself into the kind of woman I'd heard him talk about with disdain – invisible, no longer worth his time. God, I hoped he would think that. That he'd be so disgusted by the steps I'd taken to leave him that he wouldn't want me. But I couldn't let myself believe that he might give up so easily. That he wouldn't take me back, lock me up, starve the weight from me and set about restoring the woman he'd lost so that he could begin all over again. So that it could be exactly as though I'd never left.

'Stop it, you stupid woman,' I muttered under my breath, meeting the frightened reflection of my eyes. 'He isn't coming. She's not his wife! You're perfectly safe!'

I pulled on a pair of worn cotton pyjamas, despite the sun still shining high in the sky, and opened my bedroom door. Jade was just coming out of her own room, and her eyes met mine, guilt flashing across her features for half a second before she offered a warm smile I tried to return.

'You going down?' she asked, shifting Amala into an upright position.

I nodded, walking ahead of her to the stairs, wishing I was better with people – that I knew what to say. My parents, my grandmother, they'd all been so good at it: small talk, hosting, making people feel welcome. It was a skill that had clearly passed me by, and despite the knowledge that Jade wasn't here to hurt me, I still felt stiff with her, an issue that was wholly mine to defeat.

We made our way in silence to the kitchen, and she slumped down in the chair by the hearth as I went to the cupboard, pulling out a packet of pasta and a jar of pesto. I tipped some into the pan on the stove, then, reminding myself to be more accommodating, added an extra portion for Jade, noting the way her eyes lit up.

'You must be sore?' she said.

'Huh?' I glanced over, frowning in confusion.

'After all that digging, I mean. Is the hole going to be a pond?'

'Oh... yes,' I said, nodding.

'It's big,' she commented.

'Yes.' I saw her look down at Amala and sighed, hating myself for being like this. Years living as a recluse certainly hadn't helped.

She was struggling, trying to make conversation to dispel the awkward energy between us. Maybe even trying to make a friend of me. I could understand that – how alone she might be feeling right now, a new mother relying on a stranger for the roof over their heads. Poor girl to land herself with a woman like me.

I waited for her to look back up, then smiled, though it felt unnatural. 'Yes,' I repeated, more softly this time. 'I love being out there, working the soil. It's the one place I feel truly at peace.'

'What about the woodwork stuff?'

I tilted my head. 'Yes, I suppose there's that too. I *do* enjoy it, and I find myself in a state of flow sometimes, but it's different when you earn a living from it. The garden, that's just for me. No incentive other than seeing the bees and butterflies multiplying with each new plant I add.'

'That makes sense. But do you *need* to sell the birdhouses? I mean, you're hardly living in a slum here,' she joked, glancing around the big stone kitchen.

I gave a wry smile and nodded. 'You're right. And I'm not ignorant of that privilege, though it's good to be reminded of it every now and then. It's a beautiful place to live.' I stirred the pasta, forcing myself to think of something else to say to show I was making the effort. 'What about you? Do you have a job to go back to when Amala's old enough?'

She wrinkled her nose. 'Nothing at the moment. I did a law degree, but I never went on to do anything with it. Life sometimes has other plans, doesn't it?' she said softly, and I nodded. It made sense. Ryan had never let me work either. He hadn't wanted me out of the house, influenced by other people, mixing with men. A law firm would be the last place he would want his pretty young bride to spend her days, with all the vibrant, ambitious people surrounding her, showing her a different path available to her. Only she *wasn't* Ryan's bride, was she? I had to keep reminding myself of that. Every time I thought his name, I felt my muscles seize up in terror.

I let out a long, silent breath and waited for the tension to leave my shoulders, chanting a mantra in my head. *You're safe, you're safe, you're safe...*

'And,' I continued once I could speak again, 'what about living arrangements? Do you have somewhere you plan to go when you leave here?'

She glanced down, fiddling with Amala's vest. 'Not yet.'

I looked at her, waiting for her to tell me more, wondering if this might be the moment she confessed the real reason for coming here, but instead she said, 'You never considered selling the house? I can't imagine living in my childhood home. I think I'd feel like I never got away, never grew up.'

'I liked my life here. I had a good childhood. Well, as good as the next person,' I added. Up until I'd escaped Ryan and finally dispelled my naïve, rose-tinted illusions, I'd always been one to look on the bright side. Brush aside people's faults. The ways they let you down. I shrugged. 'Although if you asked my brother, *he* might have quite a different version of events.' In fact, I *knew* he would. He'd called our parents narcissists, and if I was willing to examine their behaviour closely enough, perhaps I might have agreed. Thomas and I might have had a very different relationship now.

'Really?' Jade frowned. 'How come?'

I shrugged, not keen to get into it. Families were complicated, and the last thing I wanted was to air my dirty laundry with her now. I'd called my brother a few weeks after moving in here, hoping to find the words to ask for his help, to explain the dark place I'd found myself in, the horrors I'd been living through. I'd never been more alone, more afraid, in my life. I had needed him, needed someone to speak up for me, defend my character after the way I'd left Ryan, the consequences that I'd found myself facing. I needed him to tell the police I wasn't what they thought. But the moment he saw the phone number I was calling from and learned that I'd moved back here, he'd shouted me down, refusing to let me get a word in. He'd accused me of having no scruples, of caring only for what I could get from our parents. He'd said it was clear I was just like them.

Of course, he hadn't known the escape this place offered me. The reason for my hurry to claim it, make it into my safe house. I hadn't felt I could trust him enough with the truth after his explosive accusations, and we hadn't been close enough for me to confess any of the things I'd endured during my relationship with Ryan, so I supposed, from his perspective, it might indeed look as if I was out for all I could get.

It was clear that he didn't know me at all. I shouldn't have been surprised. He'd never bothered to check in on me while I was trapped living with a monster. Hadn't cared enough to ask if I was okay. I had ended the call, let him believe what he wanted, and we had never spoken again.

I met Jade's expectant expression and shook my head. 'We were very different people, that's all. And he was quite unforgiving when it came to our mum and dad. He cut them out of his life once he was old enough to leave home. It's hard for me to understand what went wrong between them, between *us*, because from everything I saw growing up, they treated us the same, despite the many challenges he gave them. They were always fair, though he wouldn't necessarily agree.'

'I don't have siblings, but I imagine it's a complicated relationship,' Jade replied, a sadness lingering in her tone.

'You can certainly say that.'

'It must have been hard for your parents that he wouldn't speak to them. Your mum especially.'

I nodded, though the truth was, she'd never said as much. I'd assumed she was being stoic, having never been a particularly open book when it came to her emotions, but I'd sometimes wondered if I'd pushed my own feelings onto her, if maybe Thomas had been accurate in his view of their failings. 'They weren't perfect parents, but who is? Everyone has their flaws. And even with all that going on, they never reciprocated, never closed the door. They split everything equally between the two of us in their will. I think they hoped that they'd have a chance to speak to him again one day – I just wish they'd got that opportunity.'

Jade was looking at me as if she was stunned that I'd said so much after days of barely speaking a word, and I couldn't blame her. Amala began to fuss, and she shifted in her seat, adjusting her top to let her latch on for a feed.

I swallowed, disgusted at myself for having given so much away. I couldn't seem to get the balance right – it was either rude one-word replies or this totally inappropriate oversharing. My cheeks burned with embarrassment at having gone on about my life so much – as if she would care. It was a credit to her manners that she hadn't got up and walked out.

I stirred the pasta again and put a lid on the pot to let it simmer, feeling a strange sense of sadness at the thought of my brother, the hole his absence had left in my life. We had been close as children. That much I remembered. We'd played together. Shared toys and secrets. Made dens in the bushes in the garden. I couldn't pinpoint the exact moment we'd started to drift apart, but I was sure it was during the teen years, when I'd naturally been forced into the role of mediator between him and our parents as he had grown more abrasive towards them, making everything more difficult than it needed to be. I wished I'd been able to rely on him when I needed him most.

Amala let out a cry, thrashing her head back, refusing to latch, and I averted my eyes from Jade's bare breast. 'I'll give you some privacy,' I said, dropping the wooden spoon on the counter and rushing out of the kitchen.

Amala let out an angry bellow that made my insides churn, and I strode briskly into the front garden, closing the door behind me, dulling the sound of her screams, squashing down the discomfort they brought with them. The memories I had sworn to myself I would never revisit.

NINETEEN

The baby was quiet in my arms as I walked through the hallway to answer the front door. She had squirmed and fought all through dinner, and finally, needing to put a stop to the unbearable sound, I had offered to take her under the guise of enabling Jade to eat her meal. The look of relief on Jade's face had been instant. As I'd held Amala against my chest, she'd let out an almighty burp and then settled. Jade had commented that she had smiled at me, but I'd brushed it off, sure it couldn't be true.

I peered through the peephole and saw Aaron waiting on the step. I hesitated, not wanting another uncomfortable conversation, but I needed a few things from the shop and didn't want him to stop offering once Jade had gone. I relied on him, despite my reluctance to lean on a man. He was my only lifeline. And despite his reaction to Jade being here, the hurt I'd felt at his harsh words, I missed him. Missed the way he looked at me, the awareness that he wanted more from me than we'd previously explored. My skin felt like it was too tight for my body whenever his eyes met mine like that, and I wished I could let myself give in to the pull of him, to sink into something that I already knew would be exceptional.

I took a breath, shaking off the thought, knowing I was flushed from picturing it, then opened the door slowly, unsure of what to expect.

His eyes narrowed the instant he saw Amala. 'Where's her mother?' he asked, his tone far more demanding than I was used to from him, making me step back instinctively, my hand spreading protectively across the baby's back. There was no flirtation in his expression today, and the heat turned to ice as if he'd thrown a bucket of cold water in my face.

'She's in the kitchen.'

'I want to talk to you, Annie.'

I raised an eyebrow at his tone, and he held up his hands as if in apology. 'Please? Will you step out here for a second so we can speak in private?'

I glanced over my shoulder. 'She can't hear you from the kitchen, but fine.' I stepped out, pulling the door closed on the latch. Aaron stared at Amala as if she were some alien creature. 'Go on,' I said, needing it to be over with.

'That woman isn't an old friend of yours. You lied to me.'

I'd expected as much. I'd seen the curiosity in his expression when they'd met in the garden, known he would worry. Would dig deeper. 'Aaron, I know you're only being like this because you care. But please, I need you to back off.'

'How *can* I, Annie? How can I just stand by and watch while you—' He broke off, pointing to the baby. 'What are you playing at?' he hissed. 'Acting like some doting auntie to that child. Are you even thinking straight? I don't know who that girl is, but she's clearly vulnerable. And she's lying for you.'

I tensed. 'So?' I replied, silently daring him to continue.

He stepped closer, and I squared my shoulders, refusing to break eye contact, to be cowed by a man as I'd been so many times in my past. 'We both know what happened to the last baby you brought here,' he whispered, his words conjuring memories I'd failed to slice from my mind. 'You *cannot* play mother to this baby, Annie. It isn't right. It's not good for you.'

'How *dare* you!' The words came through me like a breath of fire, and I shoved open the front door, stepping back inside. I turned to slam it in his face, but he held out an arm, preventing me from shutting him out.

'It's not healthy, Annie. And if she doesn't know the truth, you're playing a dangerous game.' He stepped back, clearly satisfied that he'd said what he'd come to say.

I swung the door closed, bolting it from the inside and breathing heavily. I was shaking, my stomach churning, the pasta I'd just eaten threatening to come back up. How dare he suggest I wasn't fit to care for this baby. That I might be a danger to her, to her mother. How fucking dare he, of all people. I had thought he was on my side!

I wrapped my trembling arms tighter around Amala, looking down at her sweet little face to find her dark eyes staring back at me. I let out a long, shaky breath, pressing a kiss to her forehead. I was doing just fine. And Jade didn't have a right to know any of my secrets when she'd been so careful about sharing hers. Aaron might be right about a lot of things, but *this* wasn't one of them.

I wasn't going to tell her a thing!

TWENTY

JADE

'Is this all you have for her?'

I glanced over my shoulder to see Annie standing in the bedroom doorway holding a white plastic laundry basket. She walked over to where I was changing Amala's nappy on her little travel mat, placing the basket down on the bed and reaching into it, holding up a handful of baby clothes as she screwed up her face in disapproval.

'Oh, yes, that's all, aside from what she's wearing today. I didn't have time to pack much,' I added, not meeting her eyes.

I felt her stiffen beside me, as if she was remembering how frazzled I'd been the day I turned up here, though I didn't turn to look her way. She hadn't mentioned her past again, her escape from abuse, since that one uncomfortable conversation, and I was glad. It was easier if she didn't. Even so, I couldn't be sure she believed me when I denied that he was the reason I was here. She'd been kinder to me, warmer, and the conversation we'd had where she'd opened up had been very insightful, but I could sense that there was a part of her that was still afraid of what might be coming. Even so, it was clear that she also felt responsible for me somehow. I hoped she wouldn't ask about him again.

A moment of silence passed, and then she dropped the meagre collection of sleepsuits back into the basket. 'No wonder you need to use the washing machine so often. You don't have enough to get by – especially given how often she's bursting through her nappy.'

I shrugged, not sure what she wanted me to say. She'd told me I was free to use it, and she'd refused to drive into town to pick up more clothes for Amala. I was perfectly aware that the situation was far from ideal. If I'd had more time to plan – if I'd known in advance what *his* plans had been – I could have prepared so much better. My own clothes were creased and haphazard, my outfits mismatched. I hadn't anticipated the heatwave we were experiencing, and only had the one skirt and the jeans I'd been wearing when I left. I couldn't wait for an opportunity to go home and pick up the rest of my things, but it wouldn't be easy. I wasn't sure it would even be possible, not for quite some time at least.

I wondered if Annie had any idea of the daily struggle I was going through right now. If she could fathom just how exhausted I was, how I was constantly on edge, the clock ticking at a rate I couldn't seem to outrun. Every instinct in my body was to protect my daughter, and yet I'd been forced out of my own home to come here, to this madwoman's house, knowing I was wholly unwelcome, with no idea of when I'd be able to leave. It was the last thing I wanted so soon into my time as a new mum.

I'd barely slept since I'd arrived here, on constant alert for a sign that Annie had figured out why I had come, or that he had arrived before I could do what I'd come here to do. I shivered, thinking of how bad things would be for me if that happened. I *couldn't* fail. The timing wasn't what I would have chosen, but it didn't matter. He'd given me no choice. It *had* to be now.

Through the open window, I heard the hedge trimmer start up in next door's garden. I refused to turn my head and look, not wanting to see the man who had threatened me. Annie and Aaron had clearly grown too used to their own strange ways. It was obvious I was interrupting the unusual set-up they had going here. It was somewhat surprising to see how involved Aaron was in Annie's day-to-day life, given how private a person she was. I couldn't help but wonder when that had started and why she had chosen to let him get close to her, especially considering her past.

She sighed, that same familiar noise she made every time she wanted to let me know how much I was inconveniencing her. 'I think most of my old baby clothes are up in the loft. My mum liked to keep the best ones in case they were needed again. She hated wasting money on things that were only used for a few months, or weeks in the case of the newborn stuff. We could go and have a look up there if you like? They'll be dated; they're from the early nineties, but they'll do for now,' she added.

I nodded, wondering if she was trying to make amends for her coldness. She looked stiff, as if each word was costing her a monumental effort, but perhaps she was trying, and if she was, I should take the olive branch. I might not get another opportunity. I hadn't known how to respond when she'd confided in me about the abuse she'd lived through before coming to this house. Hadn't been able to find the right words. I'd wondered if she expected me to share my own story, but of course that hadn't been possible, and I'd felt a prickly sense of disappointment radiating from her every time I'd entered the room ever since. But now it seemed she was offering an icebreaker.

'That would be wonderful, thank you,' I replied, smiling as I tried to make eye contact with her.

She gave a short, businesslike nod. 'If I remember correctly, there might even be a bassinet and a bouncy chair up there. I should have thought of it sooner. Pop Amala on a blanket on the floor and we'll go and have a look.'

I frowned, looking at the carpet beside the low chest of drawers. 'You think that's safe? To leave her alone?'

'Safer than climbing a ladder with her, I should think. We won't be a minute.'

I pressed my lips together uncertainly, not sure I felt right leaving my newborn daughter down here alone. But I didn't want to miss the opportunity, and having got to know Annie a little over these past few days, I was sure the offer wouldn't be extended a second time. I nodded, and she laid out a fleecy blanket on the carpet, gesturing for me to put Amala down on it. 'But we should be quick,' I added.

'Oh, we will be,' she said with a rare smile.

I followed her out of the room, past her bedroom door to the far end of the hallway, where she took a long stick from against the wall and used the hook on the end to pull open the hatch to the loft. A fitted ladder lowered smoothly down, and she stepped back. 'Go ahead,' she offered. 'The light switch is to the left.'

I glanced back down the hall to the open bedroom door, hoping I'd be able to hear Amala if she cried. For some reason, the look on Annie's face, the unfamiliar smile, made me uneasy, and as I stepped onto the first rung, I felt a cold wave of dread wash through my belly. I swallowed, suppressing it, then began to climb into the darkness of the cavernous loft space. The ladder creaked as Annie stepped onto it behind me, and I reached hurriedly for the switch, grateful when the fluorescent lights overhead illuminated the enormous room. Boxes lay piled in every direction, a hoarder's paradise, and as I straightened, waiting for Annie to ascend, I wondered how on earth she would know where to begin searching. I certainly didn't.

She groaned as she stretched out her back, her spine cracking loudly as she pressed a palm to it, arching.

'Are you okay?' I asked.

'All that digging. It's good for me, I'm sure, but I really feel it these days.'

'Maybe you should have a rest day. Go and have a picnic somewhere,' I suggested, but she walked past me as if I hadn't spoken, heading through the stacks as if she knew the path by heart. I followed, glancing back every few seconds at the open loft hatch, my ears pricked as I listened for my daughter, but I heard nothing. She was probably just staring at the ceiling rose, or an interesting pattern in the wallpaper, but I wished she would make some little sound to reassure me.

Annie stopped by a pile of red cardboard boxes and tapped a fingertip on one. 'Ah, just as I thought.' She flipped it open and pulled out a plain purple babygrow that looked well made and unstained. 'It still has the tag on,' she remarked. 'C&A. I suppose you're too young to remember that shop. It closed down years ago.' She looked into the box. 'Most of them still have tags actually. I suppose I grew too fast to wear them.'

'Perfect,' I said, looking around. Annie turned to reach behind her for a much bigger box, *BASSINET* written in capital letters across the side, and I moved to the stack behind me, opening the one on top and peering into it. As I stared at the contents, I froze, not sure what I was looking at. Then slowly I reached down. The box was barely half filled with a few teddies and baby clothes, but these were clearly worn. And as I lifted the minuscule poppered vest from the top of the pile, I stared at the rusty brown stain across the front of the soft white cotton and knew it could only be one thing. *Blood.* A lot of blood. This wasn't just a smear from a cut... A shiver ran down my spine. What had happened to the baby who had worn this? Who had done this?

I heard a gasp and looked up to see Annie staring at the vest, eyes wide, the bassinet clutched in her hands, her knuckles blanched against the brown wicker. She dropped it on the dusty floorboards, then strode across the gap, swiping the vest back into the box and slamming the lid closed. As she turned wordlessly and picked the bassinet up, she knocked into another box, its contents spilling to the floor. There was a sharp intake of breath as she stared down at the photograph on the top of the pile of papers. For a terrifying moment, I thought she might faint.

Slowly, cautiously, I walked forward and bent down, though I kept my gaze trained on her, picking up the picture of Annie and a tall black-skinned man, his thick, muscular arm curled tightly, proprietorially, around her shoulders, a busy pub garden in the background, wooden picnic benches dotted on a verdant lawn. Her mouth was smiling but her eyes, as she stared into the lens, were wide and frightened, as if pleading for help from whoever was behind the camera.

She met my stare, her top lip trembling. 'Burn it,' she said, her voice filled with venom. 'Get that man out of my house. Out of my sight!' She swept past me, and I heard her feet clomping down the ladder.

I looked around at the overwhelming piles of stuff in every direction, then hurriedly followed her, not daring to hesitate a moment longer. Not wanting to be away from Amala while Annie was down there with her. What had Annie done to that baby? Was *this* what Aaron had been warning me about?

I tucked the photograph into my pocket, and, hands shaking, lowered myself down onto the ladder, away from the horrors of the loft, wondering what on earth I'd dragged my daughter into.

TWENTY-ONE

ANNIE

I had been gnawing at my fingernails for so long I could taste blood, and yet even with the metallic tang hitting the back of my throat, making me want to vomit, I couldn't stop. I was wrapped into a tight ball, my arms cocooning my body as I sat on the edge of my bed, unable to relax, despite the locked bedroom door protecting me from the outside world. I couldn't get the image of that baby vest from my mind. The crusted brown stain, the sheer tininess of the garment. It had taken every ounce of my willpower not to scream, the memory making me recoil, sick to my stomach over what had happened. What *I* had done.

And now that Jade had seen it, there would be questions. Ones I had no intention of answering. I'd seen the look in her eyes, the fear at what she'd walked into, who she was living with, what I'd been through before her. It had been as if she'd suddenly seen me for the first time. She'd been terrified. For herself, but more so for her baby. And I had done nothing to quell that fear. It might not be Ryan she was fleeing, but there was someone she was trying to escape, someone like him. It was better that she saw the reality, the situation she had let herself be forced into. Better that she was forewarned. That she didn't have to relive my past. Leave herself behind and become someone wholly new in order to escape.

That photo of him – seeing his face again – had shaken me. What if I was wrong to trust her? If she was lying? If this whole thing was one of his games? I pendulated back and forth between wanting to help her and wanting to lock the door and hide in the dark until she left for good. I wanted to believe that she was too clever, too strong to fall victim to him, but *I* had once been an intelligent woman, and it hadn't stopped him from preying on me. If Jade was here because of Ryan, there was no point in sugar-coating what lay ahead if she continued to do his bidding, play his sick games. No guarantee she'd have the strength *I'd* had to do what was necessary.

I heard the front door opening and rushed to the window, breathing a sigh of relief as I watched her walking to the gate, Amala tucked against her body. She'd mentioned going to the village shop, though this time she hadn't invited me to go with her. I watched her stride away, shoulders stiffer than usual, her purse clutched in her hand, and realised that she wasn't carrying the changing bag. She'd finally left it unattended. All my resolve to try harder, take her word that she wasn't connected to the man I'd escaped, faded into vapor, and I spun from the window, my heart pounding against my chest. I didn't have time to waste.

Wiping my raw, throbbing fingertips against my top, I slid back the bolt, opening my bedroom door and heading into the coolness of the hallway. I went straight to her room, stepping inside without a trace of guilt. I had every right to know why she was here, what she wanted from me. And if she wouldn't tell me, I would damn well find out myself.

There was no sign of the bag, but I seized the opportunity to snoop, yanking open the dresser drawers, finding them all frustratingly empty. I turned, hurrying down the stairs, first darting into the living room and seeing nothing, then making for the kitchen. The dark green changing bag was slung over the back of a chair, and I didn't stop to question myself as I darted towards it, pulling it onto the table and emptying its contents.

Nappies, wipes, Sudocrem, nipple cream, spare dummies and, to my relief, her phone. I grabbed it, determined to get my answers, but found the screen locked, a generic background staring back at me. But wait... there was something else. An ICE number. Her in-case-of-emergency contact. No name, just a number. If I called it, would *he* answer? Did I even dare?

I didn't recognise the phone number, but that meant nothing. He could have easily changed it since I had lived under his rule. I cast around, looking for a piece of paper to write the number down, for once wishing *I* had a mobile, not to mention an internet connection to look the number up.

'What's going on?'

I froze, my fingers damp with nervous sweat as they gripped the phone, unwilling to let go of the only clue I'd managed to clutch hold of this past week. Slowly, I turned to face Jade. She was standing in the kitchen doorway, Amala in her arms, a strong smell of milky poo emanating from the baby and a give-away stain seeping up her back.

'I knocked into your bag,' I lied, my tone clipped and annoyed as I turned from her to face the table. 'I was just picking everything up for you. The strap was dangling off the side of the table. I nearly went flying. You really need to be more careful.'

'The bag was on the chair.' Her words were slow, accusing. 'Just there.' She pointed, and I shook my head.

'You're mistaken.' I held her stare, and she walked towards me, holding out her hand for the phone. I wanted to refuse to give it to her. At least until I'd had time to write down the emergency number. It might be my only opportunity. In fact, I was sure it would be. But it was too late. I couldn't keep hold of it without making a scene and letting Jade see how rattled I was by her being under my roof. Biting my tongue, I handed it back to her.

I shook my head, feeling suddenly tearful. The stress had all but broken me, and I couldn't cope with it any longer. I had to know who she was and why she'd come here.

'I can't have you here if you won't tell me the truth, Jade,' I said softly. 'You said you're not Ryan's new wife, but that's not enough.' I pressed my hand to my forehead, trying to steady my breathing. 'Why won't you tell me? Given everything I've shared with you, why won't you trust me enough to explain what's going on?'

Her eyes were still narrowed in anger as she pocketed the phone. Her chest heaved as she composed herself, and I could see the effort it cost her.

Finally, she met my eyes. 'I have to change Amala. This isn't good for her skin.' She scooped the pile of nappies and wipes back into the changing bag, then, slinging it over her shoulder, strode to the stairs, her footsteps heavy.

I stood, frustrated and angry, staring at the empty doorway, and felt sure, if she wasn't telling me her story, it could only be because she knew I wouldn't like it.

TWENTY-TWO

JADE

'I want you to leave. *Today.*'

My head snapped up, my free hand hurrying to adjust my top to give myself some privacy as Amala fed ravenously at my breast, her mouth making noisy sucks that indicated she was taking far too much air in with her milk, though I had no idea how to fix her latch. Annie stood in the bedroom doorway, her blonde hair tangled and wild, mud streaked across her red, sweat-glistening cheek.

'Annie,' I said, my tone already desperate, pleading. I couldn't go. I just couldn't. And yet there was no way for me to explain why. I knew I'd already pushed my luck, already reached the limit of her charity. I'd never felt like I was welcome, but I knew she had an intangible need to help me, her own story forcing her hand. '*Please*,' I said, meeting her determined stare. 'I... I don't have anywhere—'

'Stop. It's not going to work. I'm *not* your family. Not your friend. I'm nothing to you. And you are nothing to me. I don't know what I was thinking letting you into my home. Aaron was right. It's ridiculous. I must be losing my mind to have thought

—' She broke off, shaking her head, and I felt panic coursing through me.

'Annie, *please*,' I whispered. 'I just need a few more days; I need time...'

'For *what*? What the hell do you plan to do? Because as far as I can see, you're not making any arrangements to leave. You seem to be waiting for something. *Someone*,' she spat, her eyes narrowed, suspicious. 'And I get the feeling you have no intention of telling me who that someone might be.'

Amala released my nipple, her head lolling heavily against my arm, her dark eyes focused sleepily on my face as if she was listening to every word. Couldn't Annie see that I was doing this for my daughter? Her future. I had to make her change her mind. 'Why did you let me stay?' I asked softly. 'After I left that first day. What made you come outside and invite me back in?'

'You know exactly why I let you back in. Because of my ex, *Ryan*. Because I thought you'd come at his bidding and a part of me couldn't bear to turn you away. I wanted to help you! It was stupid of me, careless to let the snake into the rabbit's nest, but you looked so afraid, so desperate, and I couldn't live with the thought of what might happen if I didn't help you. But it's clear to me now that you're not here for my help. You obviously have some other agenda. So I want you to go. This isn't a refuge; it's my *home*, and I want it back.'

My chest tightened as I took in her words, saw how deeply she meant them. Shaking, I placed Amala gently down on the bed beside me and leaned forward, my head dropping to my hands. I hadn't wanted to have this conversation, had hoped it wouldn't be necessary, but I could see now that I had no choice. I had to give her something... tell her what she needed to hear in order to convince her. Her anger was palpable, and I glanced down at Amala, knowing there were no limits to what I'd do to protect her. I swallowed.

'You were right,' I said softly. I took a shuddering breath and looked up, meeting her eyes. 'You were right,' I repeated. 'I *do* need your help.'

'What do you mean?' Her face was cold, stiff, and I couldn't help but think of that bloodstained baby vest in the loft, the guilt I'd seen in her eyes up there. Instinctively, I repositioned myself so that Amala was shielded behind me. 'I lied to you before. I thought you were going to make us leave, so I panicked... I was scared. But you had it right all along. I'm married to your ex. And all the horrible things you said he did to you...' I bowed my head, unable to meet her eyes. 'He did the same to me. I couldn't get away from him, and then I had his daughter and became even more trapped. To begin with, I thought becoming a father might make him change, but it only got worse. He... he's jealous of her,' I said, my voice barely a whisper. 'He hasn't taken the changes well. You know what he's like...' I met her eyes. 'You remember.'

Her hand flew to her mouth, and she stepped back as if she might make a sudden break for freedom, her eyes darting down the hall in terrified expectation. 'I was right? You *are* his new wife? He sent you here to spy on me? Play some sick game with me?' All the colour drained from her face, and despite her deep chestnut tan, she looked sallow and pale.

'No...' I shook my head. 'That's not why I'm here. He has no idea I've come. He speaks about you all the time. Compares me to you. He's *obsessed* with you,' I added, watching as she gripped the door frame as if to steady herself. 'So I knew your name, knew what you looked like, but not where you lived. He hates that he doesn't know where you are. He never talks about how you left – I can't imagine he'd want to give me any ideas,' I added wryly. 'But last week, a letter came through the door with your name on it, and I opened it. It was a school reunion invite. I called the organiser and told them you didn't live there any more, and the woman, Jessica, said she would send a copy to your parents' address instead. She was in a hurry and seemed really overwhelmed, irritated at the extra task, so I offered to send you my copy to save her a job. And she gave me this address.'

'A school reunion?' Annie repeated, her tone doubtful. 'I don't remember a Jessica.'

I nodded. 'I had no idea if you'd be here, but I knew I had to try. That *you* would understand what I'd had to do to leave. You're the only person who knows what it feels like to be in my shoes. My family have all given up on me. He made sure of that,' I added, looking down at my lap. 'I meant to ask for your help in getting free from him. And I guess I forgot what I told you the day I got here. I was in such a state, I wasn't thinking straight. But when you brought it up again, I suddenly felt terrified that if you knew the truth, you might not let me stay. Or worse – that he might somehow find out I was here and come for me. I just wanted the anonymity for a few days, you know? The freedom to just be with my daughter while I figured out my next steps – to be safe for once.'

She was shaking her head before I even finished speaking. 'I asked you outright. I told you my story. You should have known I'd never give you up to him.'

'I know... I'm sorry.'

'Doesn't he track your calls? Your phone? He always did mine.'

'I... uh...' I shook my head, shocked to hear that. 'No. I don't *think* so. I meant to check when you said the other day, but I really don't think he tracks me. He'd have come for me by now if he knew I was here.'

'You don't *think* so?' Her voice was low, dangerous as she stared at me. 'Are you stupid? You could have led him right to me! After three years, three fucking years of being free of him, you could have led him right to my door! I heard someone come into the house the night before last. I managed to convince myself I was mistaken, but now...' She sucked in a breath. 'Oh my God, Jade. Do you have any idea what you've done?'

'I don't think he tracks me... I really don't.'

'Then you're a bloody fool!'

There was a long moment of silence as Annie gathered herself, her breathing jagged as she stood fidgeting in the doorway, as if unsure how to proceed.

'I'm sorry... I shouldn't have dragged you into this. That wasn't fair to you,' I said, my tone apologetic though my heart rate steadied at the sound of her panic. She believed my story. Of course she did – it was everything she'd feared from the moment she saw me standing in her garden. 'I just wanted to protect Amala. Give her the future she deserves,' I said, though the realisation that I might have put my baby in danger just by being in this house, being near Annie, was impossible to ignore.

Annie looked past me, her gaze falling on my daughter. She gave a slow, thoughtful nod, then walked purposefully across the carpet towards us, reaching over and picking Amala up, holding her against her chest. I wanted to scream at her to put her back down, to hand her to me, but I couldn't. I couldn't risk her throwing us out, not when she seemed to be softening.

'I'm glad you told me the truth at last,' she said, her hand spread across Amala's rounded spine, her fingernails embedded with soil, reminding me of that ever-deepening pit in the front garden. 'We can prepare now... we can be ready.'

'What do you mean?' I whispered, half afraid to hear the answer.

She levelled an assessing glare at me, then, as if deciding I wasn't ready to hear the answer, turned towards the door, my daughter still clutched in her arms.

'Um, actually, Annie, I was about to get her down for a nap,' I said, panicked at the idea of her taking my daughter anywhere without me. I didn't trust her. Not one bit. When I'd arrived here, she'd seemed like a woman who was used to her own space. Isolated, yes, and socially awkward. *Rude* even. But I'd taken her for someone harmless. Someone who would never be more than a background character, even in her own life. It was hard to believe I'd misread her so badly. I could see now that she was far from the victim I'd taken her to be. How stupid I had been to leave this woman alone with my baby. It was a testament to how distracted I had been in my hurry. And a mistake I would never repeat.

She turned, a frown forming a deep crease between her eyebrows. Amala's fingers were wrapped tightly around Annie's thumb, and I wanted to unfurl them, to snatch her back. I sat perfectly still, though my heart was racing, as I waited for Annie to respond. Her expression was glazed, as if she was deep in thought, plotting, planning, and it made me uneasy to my core.

'She's tired,' I added softly.

She seemed to hear me then. She glanced down at the baby in her arms, as if she was reluctant to let her go, then, to my relief, handed her back to me without meeting my eyes. 'Of course,' she said matter-of-factly. 'She should rest. As should you,' she added.

She turned, walking out of the room, pulling the door closed behind her, and I wondered what on earth I'd unleashed in having that conversation.

TWENTY-THREE

ANNIE

The church bells were striking 11 p.m. I stood just outside the back door, listening to them as I stared up at the clear night sky, the stars bright overhead. Jade hadn't come down to dinner, and I hadn't taken anything up to her, grateful for the solitude to consider all she'd told me.

I felt a sense of relief that had been absent ever since she arrived. The constant chatter in my head had grown quiet now that the question of who she was, why she had come, had finally been answered. And beyond that was the knowledge that I had done the right thing in taking her in, no matter the risk it had presented to me.

What that poor girl must have endured at the hands of my ex was unthinkable. No wonder she was subdued, jumpy, flitting from skittish energy to hiding in her room. I could well remember the monumental high that had come in the first hours after I'd escaped his clutches, followed by a dark depression I'd been sure I'd never claw my way free of. How she'd managed to get out with Amala unharmed was a marvel to me. I owed her an apology. I would have to make amends and help her however she needed now. I could only imagine what might have happened to *me* had I not had this house to hunker down in in the aftermath of my escape. I'd been only vaguely aware of the privilege it afforded me back then. But it was clear Jade had no sanctuary to call her own, nobody on her side. She'd been brave to come, not knowing the reaction she would get. So very brave.

I breathed in the night air, the scent of jasmine heady after the long, hot day. There was no choice to be made – I would tell her she could stay. For as long as she needed. I'd get over my discomfort at sharing my space. At hearing the baby cry. I'd find a way to move past it so that she could have somewhere safe to begin again and get back on her feet in her own good time. I owed her that much.

I'd gone into that room earlier with every intention of making her leave, give me my home back, and yet not only was she still under my roof, but I knew for sure now that she was exactly what I'd initially suspected. I couldn't be entirely sure that she wasn't here at Ryan's bidding, but the fear in her eyes had indicated that she was telling the truth – that she'd come in desperation, wanting my help to escape him, and despite my fears that he might have tracked her, might be plotting this very moment to come for us, I believed her.

I only wished I'd thought to get rid of the phone the moment she set foot inside my front door. I'd left my own behind when I'd made my escape. But hers... hers had been under my roof for almost a week. He *had* to know she was here. The question was, why hadn't he come for me yet?

I sighed. Today hadn't gone at all how I had anticipated. Her confession had shocked me. This morning, whilst digging outside, I'd reflected on her reaction when that box of photographs had been knocked over in the loft. She'd already sworn to me that she wasn't running from abuse, from Ryan, but a part of me – my gut, I supposed – couldn't accept her story. At the time, up there beneath the dusty rafters, I'd been so shaken by seeing that baby vest, so sickened by the sight of the photograph of the man who had stolen the best years of my life, that I hadn't stopped to consider *Jade's* reaction. It was only as I'd replayed the scenario in my mind that I'd thought about her total lack of reaction. As if she didn't recognise him at all. As if she might have been telling the truth when she denied their connection.

It had made me question everything I'd been thinking since she'd arrived here. Made me wonder who she really was, what the hell she wanted from me. She'd had her chance to tell me the truth, and as far as I could see, she had no intention of spilling her secrets to me. So I'd made up my mind to send her away. Let her be someone else's problem.

I hadn't been ready for the confession that proved I'd been right all along. That my worst fears weren't all in my head. *And* that Ryan more than likely knew exactly where to find me now.

I blinked up at the stars, then heard a sound behind me and spun to find Jade standing there.

Slowly, I stepped back inside, closing the door on the balmy night, turning the key in the lock and facing her.

'How are you?' I asked, smiling with more warmth than I'd offered up till now.

'I... I'm okay,' she replied, her tone cautious.

'Did Amala go to sleep quickly?'

She nodded wordlessly, and I could see how tired she was. 'I could listen out for her while you have a soak in the bath?' I offered. 'I imagine you're feeling drained by everything. The stress. It can't have been easy for you since leaving him.' I pressed my lips together, summoning my courage. 'I wanted to say... I'm sorry for how I've been. And I don't blame you for not telling me everything straight away – why would you trust me when you didn't know me? I remember just how vulnerable you become, how every stranger is someone to suspect.'

I gave another tentative smile, though she didn't return it. 'Honestly, Jade, I won't hold a grudge. You were protecting

Amala. And now that I know who you really are, I want you to know that you're welcome to stay here for as long as you need. If there's anything I can do, anything that will help you get back on your feet, just say.' I tried to meet her eyes, but she glanced away, and I followed her gaze to the mess by my feet, my fingers tightening around the smooth wooden handle of the hammer in my fist. I couldn't remember how long I'd been holding it, but my knuckles throbbed, my forearm aching against the weight of it.

'What did you do?' she asked, her voice jagged.

Her phone was lying on the slate floor, smashed to pieces. I'd made no effort to conceal my hunt for it this time, no effort to be discreet as I upturned her bag, shaking her things out onto the table after our conversation upstairs. The ICE number was conspicuously absent, the screen still locked, and I'd wasted no time in smashing the thing with every ounce of my strength. I'd hit it so hard I'd cracked one of the ancient tiles beneath it, but I didn't care. I wanted it gone. Obliterated.

'It's probably too little, too late,' I said, switching the hammer to my other hand, wincing as I cracked my aching knuckles one by one. 'If he's been tracking you, he already knows you're here. The signal might be bad, but it's not completely absent.' I shrugged. 'But just in case...' I let my words drift off, stepping over the debris towards her.

'You smashed my phone?'

'I had to. You can get another one. It's for the best, Jade. A fresh start.'

'That wasn't your decision to make.'

Her eyes were narrowed, and I considered apologising in an attempt to placate her, but I wasn't sorry. She'd realise soon enough that it was the right thing to do. 'So do you want to go and run that bath?'

'No. I only came to grab something to eat and drink.'

'Do you want me to go and sit with her while you get what you need? You probably shouldn't leave her alone. It's not safe.'

'No!' she snapped, and I glanced at her, surprised by her tone. She gave a stiff smile. 'No thank you. She's fine. I'll go back up in a sec.'

I paused uncertainly, wondering if my sudden change in attitude had caught her off guard. I tried to put myself in her shoes, remind myself how unreasonable I'd been with Aaron when he was just trying to help me. How much I'd resented him for being in my space, tensed at the sound of his voice. It was all still so fresh for Jade. She had every right to her emotions now. I wouldn't let myself be offended. I walked past her towards the fireplace, placing the hammer on the sideboard and settling down into my chair. 'If you're sure?'

She nodded, pouring a tall glass of water without bothering to run the tap to let it cool, then grabbing a few slices of bread from the chopping board. 'Annie...' Her voice was uncertain, nervous, and I waited for her to go on. 'That baby vest... the one in the loft. What happened?'

'What do you mean?'

She looked down, busying herself with slicing cheese from the block. 'Why was it covered in blood? What happened to the baby?'

'*Blood?*' I gave a choked laugh that sounded too high-pitched to my ears. 'It wasn't blood. It was coffee, wasn't it? It looked like coffee to me. I expect my mum spilled a cup on it whilst ironing or something.'

She looked up, frowning. 'The label said it was from Frugi.'

'So?' I shrugged.

'That company wasn't around when you were a baby. It was founded in 2004.'

I pursed my lips. 'How do you know that?'

She blushed, dropping the cheese onto a plate next to the bread. 'I... I looked it up last night.'

Anger surged inside me, and I was certain it showed in my face. What justification did she have to question me? After the lies she'd told! What right did she have?

I sucked in a slow, steadying breath, reminding myself of my promise to be kinder to her. 'I don't know what to tell you,' I said, holding her gaze. 'And right now, we've got bigger issues to tackle, wouldn't you agree?'

She pressed her fingertips against the chopping board, and I was certain she was thinking about saying more, but I didn't give her the chance. 'You'd better go back up. Like I said, it's not safe to leave Amala alone.'

She sucked in a breath, as if I had threatened her rather than helped her, then picked up her plate and left. I waited a moment, then heaved my exhausted bones from the chair. I walked back across the kitchen, looking out of the glazed back door, and saw Aaron's familiar silhouette in his bedroom window. And I could have sworn he was staring right down at me.

TWENTY-FOUR

I pressed my hand to my mouth, stifling the yawn that felt as if it would split my head in two. I'd hoped to sleep better last night after speaking with Jade, getting my questions answered. I'd felt so much better having got the secrets out in the open – not to mention dealing with her phone – but as it had turned out, the moment I laid my head on the pillow, I had been hit with a thousand memories of Ryan, and a thousand more imagined scenarios that Jade might have lived through over the past few years.

She was a nervous wreck. I could see that she was still uneasy around me, and the conversation about that baby vest had done nothing to ease her anxiety, but I was determined to make her comfortable here. She'd gone out on a limb to tell me the truth, and I was grateful for it. It was going to take time for her to feel like she could really confide in me about all she'd been through, but I would wait.

There *was* something that might help her to trust me. I had a secret of my own I could share. But no... she might not understand, might not see my side. The thought of her hearing what I'd done and taking it the wrong way, *blaming* me rather than seeing my confession as the olive branch it was intended as, made me instantly tense, and I knew I wasn't ready to go there. Might never be.

He's obsessed with you...

Her words from yesterday had played on a loop in my mind ever since she'd told me. I hadn't even been surprised. I'd known he would never forgive me for the way I left. For winning, because I knew that was how he would see it. But to have her confirm my worst fears had set my heart racing, my senses on high alert.

I picked up my mug of coffee, the fourth or fifth of the day, breaking my own rule of stopping after two, the caffeine keeping me going in lieu of sleep, and grabbed one of the chocolate muffins Aaron had dropped off yesterday. Then I headed out to the back garden, down the stepping-stone path, past the array of bushes filled with songbirds and their chicks, to the little secret garden hidden right at the far end, where I planned to eat before heading out the front to resume my digging.

There was a wooden bench that ran in almost a full circle around the eight-foot clearing surrounded by tall golden privet, an ancient oak behind the hedge providing dappled shade – a respite from the blistering June heat. As a child, I'd come here every day after school, sprawling out on the smooth wooden planks to learn my spellings and read, decompressing after too much noise, too many people. And in part, I thought now, to get away from my parents for a while.

It had been years before I'd seen that my brother might not have been entirely unreasonable in his judgement of them. That the reason I'd fared better than Thomas, avoiding the rows and conflict, was not in fact because they loved me more, but because I'd learned more quickly to shape myself into what they needed me to be. Quiet. Unobtrusive. Agreeable. As a young girl, I'd flinched at the sound of raised voices and wished Thomas would fall in line, stop provoking the arguments that could be so easily avoided. But where he had gone his own way, cutting Mum and Dad off the second he got the chance, I had stayed. I had tried to make them happy. And I had studiously avoided the glaring fact that they were both textbook narcissists.

It was patently obvious to me now that all those years of people-pleasing had made me the perfect target for a man like Ryan. It had been so easy for him to step into the role of my boss, my dominator. To set me tasks he knew I couldn't complete and get his entertainment out of watching me try nonetheless, the desperate need to please him fuelling my every choice. I'd been putty in his hands.

Sometimes I wished I could confront my parents with my accusation, explain to them how they'd turned me into a victim, stolen my voice and made me weak. But they would never have accepted it. They would have turned it on me. *And*, I thought, biting into the chocolate muffin, crumbs dropping onto my lap, *I* would have been the one to apologise in the end.

I envied Thomas his ability to hold his head high, keep his sense of self despite all they had done to erase it. Even now, even knowing all that I did, I couldn't help but miss our parents. *Love* them, though I was sure they didn't deserve it. I *was* weak. Fundamentally broken. At least I had been until I'd reached rock bottom...

I thought again of that vest, the blood splattered over the cotton, stiff and rusty. The mouthful of muffin wedged itself in my throat, and I coughed, then gulped back half the mug of coffee in one go. *Of course* Jade hadn't believed my story. It was too ridiculous for words. I balanced the muffin on the paper case, pressing my hands to my face as I thought of the guilt I carried with me, and knew with every fibre of my being that he was dead because of me. That *I* had killed that baby.

TWENTY-FIVE

JADE

It had been impossible to drift off to sleep after Annie's haunting warning in the kitchen last night. I'd felt like Amala was too exposed, too vulnerable sleeping in the bassinet beside my lumpy double bed. I'd been unable to stop myself from imagining Annie creeping into the room in the dark, snatching my sweet girl from the basket and making off with her – to do God knows what. Had she been warning me about herself? What *she* might be capable of? It was as if she was trying to keep control of some long-hidden part of herself, and our presence here was somehow unravelling her hold on the chain. These dark thoughts had made me sick to my stomach, dread churning up the meagre supper I'd managed to grab.

I had brought Amala into my bed, tucking her into the crook of my arm, holding her close as I kept watch over the locked bedroom door, waiting uneasily for the smooth brass doorknob to turn.

I wished with all my heart that Annie would just leave. Pack a case and go, disappearing into the night without a word. That she would put the puzzle pieces together and come to the conclusion I could see she was battling with, leaving me and Amala to finish what we had come here to do. It would make it all so much easier, and I was running out of time. I could only outrun him for so long before he caught up with me. And if that happened, this would all have been for nothing.

I dressed blearily, my heart racing from sheer exhaustion. I couldn't cope with much more of this. And yet I had no choice. I couldn't walk away now. It would ruin everything.

I stifled a yawn, a shudder working up my spine, bringing a fresh wave of nervous adrenaline with it. Every time I closed my eyes, I saw that bloody vest, the look of guilt on Annie's face when I'd asked her outright what had happened. She'd been lying. Of that there was no doubt. The stain was no more coffee than it was jam. I'd seen dried blood before, and it was unmistakable. The way it flaked, the uneven splatter pattern. She hadn't been able to meet my eyes, her cheeks flushed as if she'd been caught out, her tone high and unnatural as she tried to talk her way out of what we both knew to be true. Why was she so determined to protect her secret? What was she hiding? Perhaps I should ask to go back up there, to see it again. Surely an innocent woman would have no objection to putting her guest's mind at ease?

I wished I could stay in this room all day, but doing so would achieve nothing. Leaving Amala sleeping in the bassinet, I unlocked the door, swearing under my breath as the bolt squeaked. If only there was a key I could use to lock it behind me, to keep my daughter safe.

I hurried down the hall, pausing outside Annie's bedroom door and hearing nothing from behind it, then turned to the small window on the landing overlooking the front garden. I wasn't sure if I should be relieved that she was already out there, digging away. For a moment, I stood still, deliberating. But then I made up my mind. This might be my only opportunity. Annie was always nearby, always popping up when I least expected it. But if I was quick...

I didn't stop to reconsider as I rushed towards the loft hatch. The long wooden pole was exactly where I'd watched Annie hang it, and I hooked it through the catch, holding my breath as the ladder descended noisily.

I ran back to the window and peeped out to check the coast was clear. Annie was still digging. Heart thumping wildly, I sprinted back to the ladder, clattering up it as fast as I could manage. I flicked the light switch on, then, not stopping to let my doubts creep in, rushed into the maze of clutter, intent on finding the right box.

I couldn't understand how Annie had navigated through this sea of mess as if she were following a well-worn path. It all looked the same to me, and though I knew I should leave no trace of my snooping, I didn't have time to be tidy, careful. I flipped open lids, rifling and tipping out contents, heedless of the chaos as it piled up around me. I upended yet another box and sucked in a breath. Was this it? Was this what I'd come for? I hoped so.

As I reached down, the awful sound of the front door opening echoed up the ladder, chilling me to the bone. She couldn't find me up here. Amala was alone...

After grabbing what I needed, I shoved it into the back of my jeans, yanking my top over the lump, then, my palms dripping with sweat, took wide, silent strides towards the ladder. My mouth turned dry as I heard footsteps on the stairs below. She was coming up. I reached the hatch and practically slid down the ladder, my feet barely touching the rungs, spinning to shove at it forcefully, watching it retreat into the hatch. But I'd left the light on. *Shit...* And then the ladder ground to a halt, the rusted hinge jamming firm, leaving the hatch gaping open, making it clear what I'd been doing.

I couldn't let her know I'd been up there. Grabbing the pole, I gave a frantic shove, gritting my teeth against the resistance. I felt the ladder give a tiny bit, and then, without so much as a squeak, it slid back into place, the hatch closing beneath it. I didn't have time to let myself feel any sense of relief. The footsteps reached the landing, and I glanced around, trapped, then ducked into a bathroom to the left, flushing the chain and stepping out the door just as Annie rounded the corner.

She stopped, frowning, an expectant look on her face, and I knew I had to be drenched in sweat, red and shaking. 'I hope you don't mind,' I said breathlessly, pulling my shirt lower and keeping my back to the wall to hide my contraband. 'I didn't want to flush the toilet in the en suite. Amala had an unsettled night, and I didn't want to risk waking her.'

Annie pursed her lips. 'Is she feeding?'

'What?'

'Is she still feeding regularly? Are you engorged?'

'*Excuse* me?'

She pointed a dirt-covered finger at my face. 'You're sweating. You look like you have a fever. Could be mastitis. You need to make sure you keep feeding her. Unblock your milk ducts. You're supposed to massage the breast while you feed.'

'Um... right. I'll do that.' I wiped a shaking hand across my forehead. 'How do you know about that? I thought you said you didn't know anything about babies?' I said, recalling the conversation we'd had my first day here. I'd asked for her help, said I knew nothing about raising a baby, and she'd said neither did she. Where had this come from?

She shook her head, turning for her own room. 'I need a shower. Aaron usually comes around this time. If he does, will you take the shopping from him and put it away in the kitchen?' Her eyes met mine, a challenge somehow, and I didn't dare to refuse. I nodded, and she walked away without a word of thanks.

I let out a long, slow breath, then reached behind me, my hand gripping tight to the package I'd secreted away, and wondered if I had finally found the answers I so desperately needed.

TWENTY-SIX

I could hear the boiler working hard, creaks and rattles reverberating through the old house – a clear indication that Annie was still in the shower in her en suite. The whole system was ancient, in desperate need of replacement, but she seemed not to notice the many things she'd neglected to tend to over the three years she'd spent living here.

The fact that the hot water took so long to warm up that by the time it started to come through the tap, you'd already finished washing your hands. The strange wiring that meant if you turned on the dining room light, the lamps in the living room switched themselves off. I wasn't sure if it was simply a quirk of the house or a safety issue, but when I mentioned it, Annie just shrugged and said her parents had lived with it this way for years and it didn't bother her a bit.

I'd waited to hear the bolt slide across her bedroom door, then rushed back to my room, relieved to find Amala still sound asleep in the bassinet. I'd stashed what I'd snatched from the loft in the inner zipped pocket of the changing bag, attaching the little padlock I'd picked up in the village hardware shop as it had become obvious that I needed a deterrent for Annie. I still couldn't believe she'd gone through my things and smashed my phone. I'd been so stunned that I had barely reacted, but in the aftermath, the consequences of what she'd done had hit me.

That phone had been my lifeline. My only way of contacting the outside world. And under the guise of being fearful that I was being tracked, she had destroyed it, cutting me off. Had she *meant* to do that? To make me feel quite so vulnerable? As if it hadn't already been difficult enough. I had no choice but to order a new one, but how? Annie lived like it was the bloody dark ages, and I had hoped not to have to use my bank card. But I couldn't risk leaving. Not with him looking for me... not until I had what I had come for.

I glanced out of the bedroom window at the sound of the gate opening, and felt my shoulders stiffen as Aaron sauntered up the path, a shopping bag slung over his shoulder. I knew I couldn't ignore Annie's instruction to take the shopping from him, but another encounter with that man was the last thing I wanted. Then again, I thought, looking at the remains of my broken phone on the dresser, he might be the only hope I had. But would he help me?

I bit my lip. Amala was still sleeping, and I knew she wasn't likely to wake any time soon. Leaving her in the bassinet, I sucked in a deep, courage-giving breath and headed downstairs to get it over with.

I opened the front door just as he was reaching for the bell. 'My daughter is asleep,' I said quietly. 'Annie said to take that.' I reached for the bag, and he passed it to me.

'I'm glad it's you,' he said, his eyes soft, friendly, though I stepped back instinctively at his words. 'I wanted to apologise.'

I frowned, instantly suspicious.

'No, I mean it. I was heavy-handed. It's only out of concern. Annie... she doesn't have guests. Especially not—' He broke off, then gave a smile. If I hadn't known better, I might have believed him.

'Not what?' I pushed, curiosity getting the better of me.

He shrugged. 'She doesn't have anyone to stay. She's not had the easiest time of it, and she likes her space. That's all I meant.'

I nodded, meeting his eyes. 'I get that. She explained about her ex... how she's still afraid of him coming for her.'

His eyebrows shot up. 'She told you about Ryan?'

I nodded.

He let out a long breath. 'And what are you planning to do with that information?'

'*Do* with it?'

He twisted his mouth. 'I'm just saying, morals go out of the window when it comes to money. Wouldn't you agree?'

I bit my lip, glancing across to the house he'd somehow managed to afford on a policeman's salary. 'Did *yours*?' I bit back. 'What morals did you have to bend to buy a house like that in this pretty little village?'

He glanced towards it dismissively. 'It was a wreck. Practically derelict. I bought it at auction for next to nothing and did it up myself. Took years.'

I gave a shrug. 'Sure you did.' I sighed. 'I thought we were getting somewhere, Aaron, and yet here you go again, tossing out outlandish, nonsensical remarks and accusations. What is it you think I'm planning to do? Hmm?' He looked at me, considering, and I went on. 'Annie's business is her own. I have no intention of sharing it with anyone else. Okay?'

He was silent for a moment, folding his arms across his broad chest as he regarded me, analysing me like a bug under a microscope. Finally, he gave a resigned nod. 'Okay. I—' He broke off, rubbing his palm over his face as if he were suddenly exhausted. 'Sorry,' he mumbled. He had the grace to look sheepish, his eyes softening again. 'I'm just protective of her. And this' – he gestured to me in the doorway – 'it's out of the realms of normal, and it makes me uncomfortable. I'm sorry,' he repeated.

I screwed up my face, unsure what to think. 'Fine. But if you could just stop jumping down my throat, I'd appreciate it.'

'Got it.'

I put the shopping bag down by my feet and folded my arms. 'Did she—' I broke off, not wanting to continue the conversation but knowing there was nobody else I could ask. I could hear the desperation in my voice, the fear, and I didn't want him to pick up on it too. I tried again, though the second attempt was not much better. 'Have you seen other babies here?'

His face blanched, and he quickly shook his head. 'What do you mean?'

'I... I just wondered. Did *Annie* have a baby?'

'Is that what she told you?' he whispered.

'She didn't tell me anything.'

He stepped back as if he'd been caught divulging secrets he shouldn't share, then swallowed, glancing up at the window above as if he might find her looking down at us. 'Annie doesn't have a baby.' His words were firm. 'She's fragile. Her mental state is... She's been through a lot. I won't tell you her business. It isn't for me to say. And I get that you don't mean to cause issues, but you being here... your daughter being here... You really should go. *Soon.*'

'What do you mean? Is she dangerous?' I asked, thinking of that mad glint in her eye as she'd held the hammer in the kitchen, the moonlight streaming down behind her, the complete lack of remorse or apology as she stood over my ruined phone. The way I could hear her walking around her bedroom behind the bolted door at all hours of the night. The pit she was digging with a level of obsession that was impossible to ignore.

A high-pitched creak sounded above us, and I looked up to

see her bathroom window opening wide, steam bellowing from it, her shower clearly finished.

'Tell Annie the plums are divine!' Aaron said in a loud, jovial voice. His eyes met mine, full of warning, and I wondered if I'd got him all wrong. If he'd been trying to help me see what was right in front of my face. He turned for the gate, calling a too-friendly goodbye.

I shut the door, realising I'd got more than I bargained for when I came here. But even knowing that, I couldn't leave. I glanced up the stairs and felt my insides turn to ice. There *had* been a baby here. I'd seen the truth written all over Aaron's face. I'd known he was hiding something horrible. And I was certain I didn't want to know what it was.

TWENTY-SEVEN

ANNIE

I felt like a trespasser in my own garden as I lurked awkwardly beneath the magnolia tree, waiting for Aaron to go on his evening stroll through the village. I knew he wouldn't be popping by again today, having already dropped the shopping off with Jade earlier, but I had to speak to him. I'd wanted to ever since Jade had admitted the truth to me, and yet each time I'd seen him coming up the path, I'd avoided him, unable to bring myself to voice the terrible words.

I knew how he would react, what memories it would bring back – the past we'd both glossed over in our desperation to forget. But I couldn't keep this from him any longer. I needed him.

It was my shame, my longing to leave the past where it belonged, that had made me hesitate, lie. And more than that, my doubt. The worry that years of isolation had made my imagination overactive, made me jump to conclusions that nobody else would think of. But now Jade had admitted the truth herself. I'd been right. She *was* Ryan's new wife, and she had come here needing my help. And after days of carrying the fear that my safe place was about to be invaded by a man who still had the power to make me sick with terror, I knew I couldn't keep it in any more. I needed Aaron's help, his advice. It was ridiculous that I couldn't bring myself to walk through the garden gate, take the ten steps up the lane and knock on his bloody door, but the idea of heading out there made my legs turn to granite, my chest tight and panicked.

I just couldn't help it. The memory of the last time I'd been out there – carried, not walking, stinking of death and dried blood, barely conscious of what was happening around me, what I was being accused of – stopped me in my tracks. Here, in the house and garden I'd grown up in, I was safe. Hidden. I could do no harm. Cause no distress. It was best for everyone – me most of all – that I stayed tightly within my boundaries.

The sound of footsteps jolted me from my thoughts, and I stepped out from beneath the tree, standing just inside my front gate. His gaze as he passed rose to my house, trained on my bedroom window. I cleared my throat, and he stopped short as he saw me waiting there.

'Annie, hi!' His face broke into a wide smile despite the way we'd left things when we last spoke. I was relieved, I realised, that he was still on my side. I'd been more upset than I wanted to admit at his reaction, though I knew it had been my own lies that had caused it. But the way he was looking at me now, there was no trace of that anger. He nodded towards the shovel propped against the tree behind me. 'Still gardening at this time?'

I shook my head, clasping my hands together as I stepped towards him. 'Can I talk to you?' I murmured.

His smile faded as he took in my expression. 'Of course. Look, I'm sorry about how I spoke to you. I was just—'

'It's not that. You were being a good friend.'

He raised an eyebrow. 'What's happened?'

I glanced over my shoulder to the house, not wanting to be seen by Jade. 'Not here,' I whispered. 'Come with me.'

I turned, heading for the narrow path that ran alongside the house, leading him towards my secret garden out the back, emerging into the circle of hedges. He raised an eyebrow, clearly confused, but lowered himself onto the bench beside me, waiting in expectant silence for me to speak.

I took a deep breath, not meeting his eyes. 'I lied to you,' I said, my voice thick with shame. 'Jade isn't an old friend. She turned up here looking terrified and begged me to let her stay. I didn't want to. You *know* how I feel about letting anyone into the house.' I could feel his gaze on my face, though I couldn't bear to look up. 'But I remembered a letter from my aunt...' I gave a shuddering sigh, knowing I was rambling, not making things clear, and raised my eyes to meet his at last.

'She was so afraid, Aaron. Clearly running from someone. She said as much – that she was escaping abuse – and I knew it had to be him she was running from. Why else would she come *here*? It's no coincidence – she meant to seek me out.'

'*Him*?' Aaron's brow creased in confusion.

I took a deep breath. 'My ex.' I met his eyes meaningfully, knowing what memories the word would dredge up for him.

'What makes you think he has anything to do with this woman?' he asked softly.

'My aunt told me last year that Ryan had got married. There was a photo – not that I can find the bloody thing now, but I was sure it was Jade.'

He nodded, then pressed his lips together, taking it all in. 'You should have told me what you were thinking, Annie. You don't have to deal with every challenge alone. You're allowed to ask for help.' His brown eyes met mine, and I held his gaze, feeling the swirling guilt in my belly at having got it wrong again.

'I've been so afraid,' I whispered. 'She admitted it. She *is* his wife. She married that monster!'

He frowned. 'She said that?' His tone was incredulous.

'I should have warned her. Done something when I received that letter and found out he was getting married. But I let myself hide away here, and now she's discovered for herself what kind of man she's shackled herself to.'

He reached for my hand, his fingers linking through mine, cool and strong. 'It's not your fault, Annie. You know you could have told me this earlier. I would have helped you.'

My heart stuttered, a current of electricity I wasn't strong enough to resist passing through me, a rush of heat chasing up my neck, warming my cheeks. I wasn't ready for this. Didn't know if I ever would be. I slid my hand from his, leaning back to create some space between us, ignoring the flash of disappointment in his eyes.

I reached beside me to pick a tiny yellow leaf from the hedge, ripping it in half, rolling the pieces between my fingers in an attempt to dispel the nervous energy pumping through my veins. 'I didn't want to talk about him... to remind you of the person you'd met back then. You hated me,' I reminded him quietly. 'You were disgusted by me.' I closed my eyes, picturing the first time he'd seen me. The cold, blank look of a professional trying to keep his composure. He'd been in uniform, surrounded by his team. Blue flashing lights everywhere. A perfect nightmare. The weeks that had followed had been a blur.

He didn't deny my accusation, and I felt sure he was thinking of that time too. 'It's taken a long time for us to get to this place... this *friendship*,' I said, risking a quick look at his eyes, surprised to see them still warm, open. 'I didn't want to ruin that.' I bit my lip.

'I'm glad you told me. I wish you'd done it the day she showed up. I don't know if she's being totally honest with you, Annie. Don't trust her blindly, and don't share your secrets with her.'

'My secrets?'

He took a deep breath, his nostrils flaring. 'I'm not going to call you naïve, because I think you see things in a person that everyone else would miss. But as much as I admire that about you, it's also your downfall. You look for the good in people whilst glossing over the red flags. It's how you found yourself in that toxic excuse for a relationship, trapped, being taken advantage of, and still walked away blaming yourself.'

I ran my tongue over my teeth, then chewed my lip. 'I'm different now,' I said softly.

He looked at me as though he wasn't sure about that, and I felt the stubborn desire to prove it. To show him he had got it wrong. I *had* been weak, pathetic, but there was a fire in me now – a darkness I couldn't squash, casting shadows on the very fabric of my soul. And though I knew I should be afraid of it, try to eliminate it, I wouldn't. It brought me comfort. Made me sure that if it came to it, I could delve into those dark spaces in my mind and somehow come out as a victor... because the alternative was unacceptable. I would never be a victim again.

Aaron sighed. 'I googled her. Jade. I couldn't find any trace of her online, but I never went further than that. I knew you would tell me who she really was when you were ready. It makes sense that she'd give a fake name if she was afraid of a man like that looking for her.' He paused. 'Here's what I'm going to do. I'll pop into the station first thing tomorrow and get the team to run some checks on her, confirming she is Ryan's new wife.' Something in his expression made me think he still didn't believe it, but I didn't want to focus on that – not when he was offering to help me.

'You don't need to do that.'

'For my own peace of mind. And then we'll get her into sheltered accommodation. As much as you might want to help her, you shouldn't put yourself in a vulnerable position to do it. You have to protect yourself.'

'The baby, Aaron, that baby...'

'We'll get her somewhere safe, okay? Far away from here. Away from *you*. She's going to be gone before you know it. She's going to be fine.'

I shook my head, unable to believe him, unable to stop myself picturing another baby who hadn't survived. The tiny, helpless newborn who'd been dragged from my arms, blue and cold... who'd never had a chance. Because of *me*.

'They can't stay here,' I whispered.

'I know.'

He put his arm around me, pulling me close, and just for a moment, I let myself sink into his warmth, knowing I didn't deserve his comfort.

TWENTY-EIGHT

JADE

I hadn't had the chance to ask Aaron to help me get a new phone before he'd rushed off yesterday. He'd left me feeling shaken, afraid, and I had made up a plate of food and taken it to my room before Annie emerged from her shower, needing the safety of the thick wooden door to let me breathe freely. But I *had* to have a phone. And I couldn't leave to go into town. I was sure that once I did, I wouldn't be allowed to set foot back inside. Annie would come to her senses and lock the door behind me. And if I was spotted... if he found me... I couldn't risk it.

The rushed foray into the loft had turned out to be a waste of time. I hadn't picked the right box, it had turned out, though I'd been so hopeful I'd finally got what I'd come for. I knew there was a more likely option. I needed to go into her bedroom. I'd seen all those papers spread out on every surface when I'd walked in on her frantically searching for something the day after I arrived. I didn't know if she'd found whatever it was, as she'd given no clue as to the outcome. But *that* was where she kept the things that were most important.

I paced back and forth, watching my tiny daughter sleeping,

her jet-black hair already long enough that it was curling into tiny ringlets, framing her perfect face. I wondered if I'd made the wrong choice. If I'd already failed her. I couldn't relax as I waited for Annie to go outside, as she always did, to pick up that shovel. My nerves felt frayed, my heart constantly racing, the ticking of the grandfather clock in the hallway a persistent reminder of how long I'd already been here – how little time I had left.

I heard a door opening and rushed to the bedroom window, but it was Aaron, not Annie, I saw heading outside. Scooping Amala into my arms, I rushed down to meet him, letting myself out just as he opened his car door, parked up on the lane outside.

'Aaron,' I said breathlessly, rushing through the gate to intercept him. 'Where are you heading?'

He paused, straightening as he looked at me, confusion written all over his face. 'Um, into town,' he replied. 'I have some things to attend to.'

I nodded, feeling stupid, vulnerable, but knowing he was my only option. 'I really need a favour. My phone got broken, and I need a new one urgently. I know it's a massive ask, but do you think you could pick one up for me?' I reached into my pocket, pulling out a wedge of cash. 'I'll pay, of course. I just… I really need one – *today*. Anything they have; it doesn't need to be fancy. I have a SIM,' I added, grateful that I'd been able to retrieve it from the debris Annie had left on the kitchen floor. 'Just any Android phone. Please?'

He stared at me, and I waited for the onslaught of questions, the moment he would tell me to go and get my own phone and leave his friend in peace, but instead he reached for the money in my outstretched hand. 'I'll see what I can do,' he said, his voice almost gentle.

I blinked in surprise. He'd made it clear I was unwelcome

here. I'd expected him to argue. What had changed? Where was the warning in his tone that I'd learned to anticipate?

I nodded, stepping back as he climbed into his car. I watched him drive away, then headed back inside, hoping he wouldn't let me down.

The floorboards creaked under my bare feet, and I tensed but kept moving forward, knowing it might be my only chance. Annie's door had been closed, but like mine it had only a bolt on the inside, no key. I'd feigned tiredness after sharing a plate of tuna sandwiches with her in the kitchen, heading up to nap with Amala as she finally went outside to take up her shovelling. She should be a while. Hours. But I had to leave no trace. I couldn't let her suspect I'd been in here.

I tiptoed across the thick carpet to the dresser, sliding open the drawers one at a time, pausing after each one to listen, for both Amala and the sound of Annie coming back in. I didn't want a repeat of yesterday, when I'd cut it far too fine.

The light coming through the window cast soft buttery beams on the pale cream duvet cover, and with the window flung wide, all I could hear was birdsong and the occasional flutter of the curtain rustling against the wall in the breeze. It felt like the middle of nowhere out here, even with the little village a short walk away. I'd barely seen a car this whole week, aside from Aaron's. The ramblers took a path at the bottom end of the lane, and I'd yet to see any venture up this far. Annie and Aaron were in their own private world up here, and it was clear that I was interrupting.

I turned back to the drawers. They were filled with all manner of trinkets, diaries and old letters, and I rifled quickly through them, putting everything back just as I'd found it. I walked over to the wardrobe, twisting the handle, only to find it locked. I cast around for a key, sure that it must be close. Why would she lock her wardrobe? What did she have in there? Hope surged inside me, and I twisted the handle more roughly, frustrated when it didn't budge.

I spun, looking around, my gaze falling on the bedside cabinet. Moving quickly, I pulled open the drawer, hoping to see a tiny key to grant me access. There was nothing but notes, scraps of paper covered in sloppy, disjointed handwriting, a purple ballpoint pen tossed on top of them, an inky blot marring the words. Looking closer, I saw a list of plants, no doubt her upcoming plans for the garden. I sighed, sliding the drawer back into place, but it jammed on something stuck behind it.

Bending low, I reached into the gap, prising out a rigid A5 cardboard-backed envelope. I was sure it wasn't what I was after, but I glanced into it anyway, wanting to be thorough. And suddenly I realised what Annie must have been searching for that day. I also knew that there was no way she had found it. Because if she *had*, she would have known instantly who I was. I held the photograph pinched between my fingers, my own eyes staring back at me. I was wearing a classic white satin dress, my long light-brown hair curled around my face, a bouquet of pale pink roses clutched in my white-lace-gloved hands.

I held my breath, shocked to find it here. I'd had no idea Annie might have known about the wedding. Why hadn't she said anything before? It didn't make sense! She'd told me she was suspicious of who I was, that she wanted me to admit my connection to her ex, but if she'd seen this picture, the accompanying card, she would have known the truth. Known exactly who I was the moment I walked through that gate. Had she forgotten the details? Had she *really* lost her mind?

I pushed the drawer closed, checking that there was no evidence of my snooping, and, casting a frustrated glance at the impenetrable wardrobe, straightened up, shoving the photograph back into the envelope. I would take it to my room to hide away. I couldn't risk her finding it while I was still under her roof.

TWENTY-NINE

ANNIE

I wished I hadn't told him. Hadn't opened the floodgates to the outside world. The fight I'd had when I'd come here three years ago had been the hardest of my life, and I had let that influence me, let Aaron steamroll me into agreeing to send Jade away, though deep down, I knew it was wrong.

I curled into the armchair, my tanned bare feet tucked beneath me, the chunky blanket I was halfway through knitting draped over my lap, cosy despite the warmth of the evening. I let my fingers work fast. I wanted to finish the blanket for Amala and give it to Jade as a peace offering, a signal that I really meant what I said when I'd told her she was welcome to stay here. Now that I knew the truth, I was regretting my behaviour, the coldness that I was perfectly aware had been far from welcoming. I would tell Aaron I'd made a mistake. That I wanted her here with me.

There was a part of me that was actually excited about the idea of Jade and the baby staying longer. I hadn't realised how alone I'd been before now, but the thought of having a friend here, someone who understood me, my past, who had her own demons to battle too, was something I could learn to embrace.

She was going through such a lot right now, but I could see that in time we could be close. It surprised me to realise how much I would like that.

And Amala... what a blessing it would be to have the opportunity to watch her grow. She'd already changed in the short time she'd been here, her expressions more alert, her wide brown eyes taking everything in. The image of a little girl toddling round the place, asking me about the flowers in the garden, breaking the silence I'd grown accustomed to, was far more warming than I could have anticipated. I *wanted* them here. Wanted to make up for my own failings in not making sure Ryan couldn't hurt another woman.

I placed the knitting needles on my lap, unwinding the ball of yarn, then dropping it by my feet and beginning another row.

When I'd first come here, it had made perfect sense to cut him off and never speak his name again. Aaron had pushed and pushed, determined to find out what had happened to me, but I'd steadfastly held my tongue, refusing to speak his name for fear that it would lead him right to me. I'd risked everything to keep my connection to Ryan a secret – risked *prison* even. In the end, it hadn't come to that. I'd been released without charge, though I knew they were wrong to let me go. That I deserved to have the book thrown at me.

But I'd been sent back here to this empty house, labelled a victim, piteous and pathetic, and the only saving grace had been that my location was still uncompromised. It had taken a long time before I'd felt able to open up to Aaron about what had really happened in the lead-up to those awful first months here.

The living room door creaked, and I stopped knitting, looking up to see Jade in the doorway, Amala upright in her arms, her little head bobbing around as she stared at everything with fascination. The sight of it, her curiosity, her development in just the space of a week, made my stomach twist with an emotion I wasn't ready to face, but I pushed it aside and smiled, determined to make Jade comfortable. 'I hope you like yellow,' I said, holding up the soft square in my lap to show her. 'It's for Amala. I'll have it finished in the next day or so. I know that room sometimes gets a draught.'

She didn't reply, didn't return my smile, and I tried not to let it offend me. Instead, I looked down at my needles, resuming my task.

'It wasn't coffee.'

I froze, my eyes wide as they rose to meet hers.

'On the vest. You and I both know it wasn't coffee.'

'No,' I said softly. 'It wasn't.'

She stepped into the room, pushing the door closed behind her. 'I don't have a right to know your business. But I have to think of Amala. To know she's safe here.'

I frowned, confused. Jade had given no indication that she was afraid Ryan might turn up, and despite my initial fears that he would, the more time that passed, the more I had begun to relax. Surely, if he knew where she was, if he was going to come, he would have done so by now? He'd never been a patient man. I could only assume her location had been turned off on her phone – that he wasn't aware of her being here – a fact that made my fear dissipate.

'All I can think about is that vest... that blood.' She closed her eyes as if remembering, disgust flooding her pretty features. Then she opened them and set her jaw. 'I want to know what happened. No, actually,' she corrected, her mouth twisting, 'I don't want to know. But I *have* to know.'

I knitted silently, the needles clacking together as I worked towards the end of the row. The rhythmic movement steadied me, prepared me. I could see she had no intention of letting it go. I'd been waiting for this moment. Reaching the last stitch, I clutched the smooth wooden needles in one hand and gave a single nod.

'Sit down,' I said softly, gesturing to the sofa. 'But I warn you, it's not a pretty story.'

She crossed the room and lowered herself onto a cushion, her arms a cage around her daughter as she positioned her on her lap.

And then I began to tell a story I'd hoped never to speak of again.

THIRTY

Three years earlier

'Annie?' The soft Scottish accent came down the phone line, and as I always did when I spoke to Ryan's mother, I wondered at how easy it was to fall for a facade. She seemed like the sweetest woman you could imagine. The kindest mother figure you could dream up. Her church group would be stunned to learn the truth. The terrible things she had done to her only child during his most vulnerable years.

He'd sobbed to me in the wake of his violent outbursts in the early stages of our relationship, spilling his trauma like lava spewing from an active volcano, as I alternated between the roles of punchbag and therapist. It had been so long since he last broke down, bothered to make excuses for why he was the way he was, why his core was made up of pure rage, but I hadn't forgotten the stories. His father had been no better than his mother; wearing a suit to Sunday service, putting on the show everyone in their close-knit village expected to see, then coming home to take out his frustrations on his young son.

Ryan hadn't shed a tear when his dad died three years into

our relationship, had never been able to forgive him for the abuse, but when it came to Gloria, he couldn't walk away. Even now, nearing forty, he still craved his mother's love. Jumped at her call. Pretended not to remember why she didn't deserve him, how she'd ruined him for the rest of the world, me most of all.

I had only once tried to ask for her help. It had been a stupid mistake on my part, but since she was the only woman he really listened to, I'd thought she might be able to step in, stop the horror I was living on a daily basis. Help me *leave* even. But it hadn't gone well. She'd been silent as I'd whispered the reason for my bruises, after a Christmas dinner I'd prepared single-handedly whilst never letting my smile falter. Ryan and his grandma had been distracted playing cards, and I'd caught Gloria in the kitchen, making sure to bend low as I reached for an oven tray so that she couldn't miss the purple bruise the size of a house brick across my hipbone. When she had studiously turned away, I'd grabbed her wrist and breathlessly begged her to help.

She'd made some muttered comments – *That won't do... Not acceptable to treat you this way* – and then the party had gone on as planned. For three days I'd waited, tense at the thought of what I'd done. Ryan's reaction if he found out. I think I'd known instantly that I'd made a horrible mistake.

I'd been right. He'd dragged me from our bed in the middle of the third night, and the beating had been so intense I was sure he meant to kill me. By the end, I *wanted* him to kill me, just to make it stop. He'd been angrier than I'd ever seen him, before or after, and the trigger was that he didn't want his mother to have any reason not to love him. I'd bad-mouthed him to the only person whose opinion he cared about, and *that*, he told me, was unforgivable. He'd not held back after those floodgates had opened. I'd thought life was bad prior to that Christmas, but I quickly found it could get so much worse.

Now I held the phone with my left hand, cradling my heavy pregnant belly protectively as I shuddered at the memory. 'Hi, Gloria,' I said, keeping my tone light, friendly.

'Is the man of the house there?' she asked, her voice girlish, giggly.

I shook my head. 'He'll be back in a few hours. He's at a meeting today.' I swallowed, looking over at the bars he'd installed on the windows. The front door was alarmed and would alert him if by some miracle I figured out how to get past the intricate set of locks he'd fitted. Aside from outgoing calls to Ryan and his mother, this phone only allowed incoming calls – and only from phone numbers he had pre-approved. And I had to pretend this was all perfectly normal. That I wasn't a prisoner on the verge of giving birth.

I had my mobile phone, of course, the Christmas gift he'd surprised me with a few years back, having conveniently lost mine, but it hadn't taken me long to realise that it was entirely for his benefit. Not only was it used to track my every movement – well, when he bothered to let me out of the flat – but he would go through every number that was listed in my call log, interrogating me over them, calling them himself and telling them not to contact me again.

I was dreading the moment he discovered I'd had a call from my mother's number three weeks ago. It had been the first time we'd spoken in several years, Ryan making it clear that the punishment would far outweigh the benefit of trying to keep up a relationship with her. I'd been shocked to see her name on the screen, a flash of hope igniting in my belly that perhaps I wasn't entirely alone.

That harrowing call had been on my mind every moment of every day since; the screams, the roar of water. I'd been terrified he would find out my parents had both drowned in that horrific accident, that he'd want to go after the fortune they'd left behind, but he was too wrapped up in himself to notice my grief, my trauma.

'Oh well, no trouble,' Gloria said, breaking into my thoughts, her voice conveying nothing but kindness, patience, honed by years of practice. 'I just wanted to let you know that there's a new company who've installed this superfast broadband in the village. It seems a massive inconvenience, but everyone says it's excellent.'

'Right...' I said, not understanding why I needed to know that.

'I'm getting the man round tomorrow to fit mine. Madge said he's very good. So I've cancelled my internet, and that means my phone won't work until he's been.'

'*Does* it?'

She gave a tinkling laugh. 'Yes, dear, because it's run off the internet. I'm expecting it to go off sometime in the next thirty minutes, and then I won't have it back until tomorrow. I wanted to let Ryan know so he doesn't worry if he can't contact me. You know how he loves our nightly chats.'

I opened my mouth to explain that there was no need to cancel one service before getting the other. That if she'd left it, the switch could have been instant and there would never have had to be a gap. But then an idea – a *terrible* idea – hit me. 'I understand. I'll let him know,' I said, trying to keep my voice steady. 'I'm sure he'll be disappointed. He *does* love your calls.'

I hung up, my eyes fixed on those ugly iron bars on the window, seeing past them to the chink of blue sky beyond. The freedom I'd been denied for so long. It wasn't right. Wasn't sustainable. The walls had seemed tighter, more suffocating with each inch my belly grew, as if my dormant instinct to fight back, do something, was waking up, roaring at the injustice. I could feel myself spiralling into a black hole, and if I let myself slip too deep into the numb comfort of its embrace, continue to detach from reality, I might not be able to find my way back. This was a gift, a chance... but could I really sink that low?

The baby nestled snugly within my womb gave a slow turn, almost as if encouraging me, agreeing with me. I bit down on my lip, wincing at the split that had yet to begin healing, the burning ache in my shoulder from the sick game he'd forced me to play, the too hot shower he'd made me endure whilst critiquing my changing body, heedless of the impact on the baby – *his* baby – and as I swallowed, making up my mind, I found that I was trembling. I sucked in a few deep breaths, reminding myself of the importance of keeping calm so I didn't trigger labour. That would ruin everything...

Thirty-five minutes later, I pressed speed dial number two – Gloria's number. I was immensely grateful she'd never taken to her mobile. She'd had one back when Ryan's father was alive but got rid of it not long after he passed – said she wouldn't buy another one for fear of a brain tumour, as she'd watched a documentary linking the two. The wait was unbearable as I held the phone tight against my ear, the silence stretching on. Then, at last, I heard the long, dead dial tone. The phone was off. It was really off!

I didn't waste time. I knew Ryan well enough to predict exactly what his response would be to my story, and I needed to be prepared. I packed a case for each of us, stashing my mobile phone right at the back of a cupboard, not daring to actually switch it off in case it triggered some alert on Ryan's own phone.

Whispering a low apology under my breath, hoping what I had to do wouldn't harm the baby, I rushed to the kitchen, pouring six heaped tablespoons of salt into a glass, then mixing the still warm kettle water into it, stirring it and watching it dissolve. I held the glass tightly in both hands, watching the seconds tick by on the wall clock. At ten past five exactly, I heard Ryan's car pull up below, on the shared gravel car park. I took a deep breath, pinched my nose and gulped down the salty concoction. Then, eyes watering against the urge to throw it instantly back up, I washed the glass and put it away in the cupboard still wet. I was standing by the front door, ready and waiting, before he even reached it.

I never deviated from the routine he insisted on. Always met him with a smile, hands clasped modestly in front of me, make-up refreshed, hair washed and styled. I wore the three-inch heels he found sexy, even though my swollen ankles protested; the dress that he'd picked himself in a simple yet flattering style that was now stretched uncomfortably around my bump. I longed for baggy tracksuit bottoms and loose-fitting T-shirts. Comfort. The opportunity to relax in my own body for once.

Usually his dinner would be ready, though he would often find some fault in what I'd cooked, despite the fact that it was always something he'd pre-approved. He would launch his plate at the wall and fold his arms, watching as I rushed to clean up the mess and start the meal from scratch. It was humiliating. I was no more than an entertaining pet to him. I would never be worthy, human, equal.

There was no meal ready tonight, though. Every muscle in my body tensed as I heard his key slide into the lock. I took a shuddering breath, then launched into the role I had to play – my last-ditch attempt at survival.

'Ryan!' I cried, rushing forward, a break from the norm. Usually I didn't dare to speak until he'd assessed me from top to bottom and given the nod. I saw his surprise, his confusion, but didn't give him a chance to react, to punish. 'I just got a call from your mother's neighbour, Madge. She was calling from Gloria's house.' I pressed my hands to my face, willing the tears to come, the emotion he needed to see in order to believe me. 'I'm so sorry, Ryan. She... she said your mum had had a heart attack. The paramedics took her in, but Madge said it was really bad. She doesn't know if... if she'll...'

I let my words trail off, allowing Ryan to piece together his own horrific conclusion. His face turned ashen, and for once, he didn't look like someone to fear. Despite his towering frame, his broad, muscular shoulders and wide neck, he was suddenly a frightened little boy. I gripped his wrist, though every part of me screamed at the contact, wanted to flinch away. 'I didn't know what you'd want to do. I packed bags in case you want us to go up there right away?'

His expression hardened in an instant, and he yanked his hand away, striding for the phone. I watched him dial, checking the last number to call, hearing Gloria's familiar area code being relayed by the automated voice. He pressed to return the call, then looked at me. 'Her phone's dead.'

'Maybe it got knocked off the hook in the commotion.'

He slapped the handset to the ground, reminding me of a toddler starting a meltdown. 'She can't die. She can't!' His voice was almost pleading as he stared at me. He pressed his hands to his face, breathing deeply as he tried to contain himself. Then he looked up and exploded. 'What the fuck are you waiting for? Get the fucking bags! We're going. *Now*!'

I nodded, rushing into the bedroom, returning with the two small wheeled cases. He made no offer to help me with them as he opened the front door. I knew he would never agree to leave me here. He didn't trust me not to figure out an escape. I dragged the cases down the hall in the direction of the lift, but he yanked me by the hair, jerking me back. 'I'm not waiting for the lift. We'll take the stairs.' He set off in the opposite direction, and I followed him, my lower back crying out against the strain, my stomach churning in protest at the salt water I'd chugged back.

I made it down the first flight of stairs, the cases heavy and awkward, bashing into my ankles, leaving scrapes, then paused, seeing Ryan reaching the bottom, completely focused on his phone. 'I just got tickets. There's a train leaving in fifteen minutes. Hurry up. I'm not going to miss it.'

'Ryan, *please*, slow down,' I begged. 'The baby… I'm not feeling well…'

He snapped his head up, then, seeing me unmoving, sprinted back up the stairs towards me. For an unfathomable moment, I thought he actually intended to help. That in his desperate hurry he was going to take the cases. But even as he reached me, his hand was ricocheting across my cheek. I stumbled back, grabbing for the banister.

'It always has to be about *you*, doesn't it?' he spat. 'Even now! Pull yourself together, Annie, or I'll do it for you.'

I swayed; then right on cue, as if I'd set an alarm, I bent double and vomited all over the floor. It didn't stop. It kept on coming, the retching agonising, burning my throat, making my belly contract. I couldn't straighten, saliva and tears dripping from my face as the contents of my stomach emptied over and over onto the tiles. I glanced up, seeing the pure disgust in Ryan's expression, then retched again, bile exploding with such force that the liquid spurted out of my nostrils. I was perfectly aware of how awful I must look – a complete state. Exactly as I'd planned.

Ryan couldn't bear illness. He'd once told me that his parents had made him sleep in the shed at the bottom of the garden whenever he was ill. Even as a baby. His earliest memory was of struggling to breathe, shivering in the dark, surrounded by cobwebs and spiders, looking out of the tiny window at the pitch-black night and believing his mum and dad were never coming back. They'd had no tolerance for weakness, and he'd inherited the same trait.

'I'm sorry,' I said, casting around for a tissue to wipe my face with and finding nothing. 'I'll be fine. Let's go.'

He cringed away as if I was contagious. 'You selfish *bitch*... What the fuck am I supposed to do with you now?'

'I'm sorry,' I repeated, making my voice as pitiful as I could manage. 'It's the baby, the pregnancy... I can't help it. It's nothing catching, I swear.'

He sneered at me, the disdain he'd collected over our ten-year relationship undisguised as his hard eyes met mine. 'That baby...' he spat through gritted teeth, 'is not your fucking priority. *I* am. And you need to remember that.' He turned as if to leave, then spun back. His fist collided with my belly, and I screamed. I tried to duck into a ball, to protect the tiny life inside me, but he kicked out, again and again, madness clouding his face.

I'd pushed him too far, made him too angry. I should never have—

My head collided with the tiles, my own vomit seeping into my hair, ruining the dress he'd cared so much about, and I realised he had stepped back. His black irises seemed to narrow as he checked the time on his phone. 'Fuck!' he muttered. He threw a key at my face, smirking as it hit my eye, the skin splitting open, fresh warm blood gushing out, blurring my vision. 'Get yourself back inside the flat and lock the fucking door. When I come back, I'm going to show you exactly how you're going to keep your priorities straight. I'll call you tonight, and you better pick up on the first ring.'

'Yes, Ryan... I'm sorry, I will,' I said, not daring to break eye contact. He grabbed his case, leaving me lying on the floor, my arms cradling my throbbing belly as he dashed down the stairwell, muttering furiously about what he would do to me if he missed his train.

'*Now*!' he bellowed from down below. 'Go back to the flat, now!'

I heard the door bang, the car starting up, the skid of tyres on gravel, and then he was gone. Hauling myself to my feet, heedless of how I looked and smelled, I slid my hand through the handle of my case and slowly, body aching, descended the stairs. I walked out of the fire door into the fresh air and flinched at the brightness, the freedom. I didn't look back.

THIRTY-ONE

Now

I was trembling, I realised. I had curled myself into a tight ball on the armchair, and as I'd talked, I had unpicked half the blanket I'd been knitting without even noticing. Jade's pale face had turned sallow, her lips devoid of colour as she clutched Amala tight against her chest, a statue of pure horror. I wondered how much of what I'd told her was her own experience. Had Ryan changed at all in the past three years? If he had, I couldn't imagine it was for the better. She had to have known what she was going to hear. Even so, the undiluted disgust was written on her face clear as day.

She glanced down at Amala, and when she looked back up, her eyes were glistening. 'What happened to your baby?' she choked out, and I knew she was thinking of the blood on that vest.

I winced, shaking my head, my own throat thick with emotion. 'I went into labour in the early hours of the next morning. I was here, in my bedroom. Alone, but that felt safer. I couldn't stand the idea of being in a position of vulnerability whilst giving birth. Couldn't let myself be in that situation ever again.'

'That must have been terrifying.'

I nodded, remembering the pain, the fear, the sensation of ripping in two, knowing it would all be worth it if I could just get through the night. I closed my eyes, picturing that final agonising push. The silence that had followed. 'He was still-born,' I said softly, the words barely a whisper. 'He had... injuries. Broken bones.' I swallowed back a sob. 'I let it happen... let that monster beat me time and again, even knowing he was harming our son. I couldn't get free. I tried, but I couldn't find a way, and my ineptitude... my inability to escape cost my baby his life.'

'Oh, Annie...'

'I should have found the courage to call the police, but I told myself they wouldn't help me. I didn't trust that I'd be safe. And the things he would have done to me... I was too scared. Too fucking weak...' I swallowed. 'Did he do it to you too? Did he hit you while you were pregnant?' I didn't want to know, to picture her going through the same, but I couldn't stop myself from asking.

She bowed her head, a silent answer that spoke a thousand words, and I felt the urge to scream building inside my chest. I should have found a way to warn her. To *help* her. The moment I'd got that letter from my aunt, seen Jade smiling and innocent in a white dress, oblivious to the trap she was walking into, I should have risked my anonymity, my safety to tell her the truth.

I could remember the fear that had erupted in me at the knowledge of what I was obligated to do. The instant response, shoving the letter back into the envelope and putting my head in the sand, not wanting to know. I'd allowed myself to turn my face away, and it was only by sheer luck that Amala had survived. If she hadn't, *I* would have been responsible. Another baby I could have saved. *Should* have saved. I pressed my hands to my face, trying not to throw up.

'But the blood...' Jade whispered. 'There was so much of it. How—'

'The blood was mine.'

I looked down, picking at the blanket again. 'I stayed up in the bedroom for a whole week after he was born. I couldn't let him go... couldn't bring myself to call anyone and have him taken from me, have him be erased from my life for ever. I couldn't bear the loss... the guilt.' I twisted my mouth, the darkness of that time swirling through my mind. 'I wasn't thinking straight, I know that, but some part of me thought...' I heard the quiver in my voice as I fought against the tears that were dangerously close to the surface. I would not cry. I would not permit myself that release. I swallowed back the emotion, balling my hands into tight fists.

'I thought that if nobody found me, nobody knew I was here, I might keep him. That I could care for him, love him as he deserved, and that he might somehow take some of that love with him. I never had the chance to show him how much he meant... how deeply I wanted him. All he ever knew was fear,' I said softly, picturing the screams I had tried to hold in as Ryan beat me, hurt me, knowing every emotion pulsing through my system was filling *his* little body too. 'I wanted him to experience something different, something pure and good, though clearly it was too late for that. I missed my chance to be a good mother.'

Jade was silent, and I couldn't help but cast my gaze to Amala sitting in her lap, remembering the visceral pain that had flooded through me at the feeling of her tiny warm body in my arms – the way my son should have felt. That first time holding her had served as a stab in the heart, a reminder of what I had lost. It had broken my heart to know I never got to smell the milk on his breath, see his eyes open in wonder, feel his heartbeat reverberating against my palm as I rocked him to sleep. It had been torture to hold Amala and know I had to give her back.

'I hoped I might contract a postnatal infection – that I might suffer the way *he* had, go with him, but it wasn't to be. I suppose I didn't deserve it to be so simple. So, on the seventh night, I dressed his little body in a fresh vest, wrapped him in a blanket and took a blade to my wrists.' I kept my hands facing down as I spoke, not wanting to see the glistening silvery scars. 'But I fucked it up, as I do with everything.'

'What do you mean?' she murmured, her eyes wide.

'I didn't cut deep enough. The blade was too dull. And I was afraid... such a coward. But it *did* bleed, and I panicked. I ran outside looking for help, my baby in my arms, and there was Aaron. The moment I saw him, I knew I should have stayed in the house. I could see myself through his eyes. A madwoman. A *murderer*. That's what I heard him say when he called in for backup. I ran back indoors, but he followed, and I collapsed. Not from the blood loss. They said it was dehydration. I had severe mastitis too. My milk had come in, but of course I couldn't feed my baby. I *was* mad,' I said with a wry snort.

'You must have been in so much pain,' Jade said softly.

I shrugged. 'I don't know... I honestly can't remember. I was only focused on my son. Aaron took him from my arms as the paramedics arrived. I was struggling to stay conscious, begging him to give him back, but he wouldn't.' I swallowed, the hazy kaleidoscope of memories flitting across my mind making me shiver. 'I never saw my baby again. I was carried out by paramedics, treated in hospital and then arrested for infanticide.'

'But you didn't kill him!'

I wrapped a thread of yarn so tight around my fingertip that it began to tingle. 'I may not have inflicted the injuries, but I didn't save him, did I? I didn't protect him as a mother should.'

She frowned, shaking her head. 'But they discovered the truth?'

I nodded slowly. 'The post-mortem revealed the injuries had happened before birth and the baby never breathed. The blood on the vest was tested and found to be mine. It was returned to me, along with the little socks he'd been wearing. And since I wouldn't name the person who'd attacked me, wouldn't press charges, they dismissed the investigation.'

'But Ryan killed your baby! Why wasn't he arrested for murder?'

'In the eyes of the law, until a baby is born, it doesn't count as a person. They used the word foetus. I think in some countries they see it differently, but not here. It would complicate things too much with abortion laws, take away the right of the mother to choose. Besides, Aaron said it would have been near impossible to prove without my testimony. Who's to say I didn't fall down the stairs and cause the injuries myself? It would have been an impossible battle.' I pressed my lips together, filled with shame that even then, even with the death of my own child, I hadn't had the courage to speak up, fight for justice. I'd slunk away with my tail between my legs, hoping to never hear Ryan's name again.

I sighed. 'The police sent me home, and I haven't set foot beyond my front gate since. You're the first person I've let into this house since Aaron and the paramedics came inside that day.'

'In three years?'

I nodded.

'But I thought you and Aaron were friends?'

'We are, I suppose,' I admitted, though *friend* seemed too weak a word to describe the relationship we'd built. I wished I was brave enough to offer him more, but it was *because* I knew it would be so good that I held back. I was afraid of losing myself in wanting, loving him. Afraid of losing control. I'd created a world that was safe, regimented, predictable. Letting him get closer risked all of that. It could be something incredible if I'd let it, but I couldn't risk it.

I sighed. 'It took a while to get there. I didn't tell him the real story for a long time, and I could tell he thought I was unhinged. I imagine it would be hard to move past an image like that, the memory of how I'd looked the day we first met, covered in blood holding a dead baby. He didn't like me... didn't trust me, but I think he felt responsible for taking care of me somehow. Like I was incapable. He was right. I bloody proved that,' I muttered.

I remembered how he had watched the house, noticing that I never left. He'd realised I wasn't eating, wasn't buying food, and had taken it upon himself to start dropping meals round. I'd been so rude to begin with, terrified of his presence, not even bothering to open the door, instead sneaking out to pick up the bag from the doorstep once I was sure he'd gone. It had only been my hunger that had made me take his offerings, but over the months, I'd gradually grown to trust him. Opened up to him. And the more he listened without judging, kept coming back, his expression growing warmer and more inviting with each conversation, the more I'd begun to realise he was on my side, and piece by piece had told him the full, horrible story of what had led me to that day. He was a good man, but I'd never make that final jump, have a man in my space, though I knew he couldn't be more different from Ryan. He was too kind to ever hurt me.

I looked down at the ruined blanket in my lap and silently picked up my knitting needles, wondering how to begin piecing it back together.

'I let you in because the look on your face reminded me of the fear I'd felt every day of my relationship with Ryan. I could see instantly that you were in a panic. That you'd seen an opportunity and grabbed it, for yourself and for Amala. There was a sense of urgency about you... it reminded me of myself,' I admitted.

'You're right,' Jade said softly. 'That's exactly what I did.' Her face was pale, and as I looked at her hands, I realised she was trembling. My story had clearly brought up memories that were still too raw for her to address.

I rose to my feet, letting the scraps of tangled wool fall to the carpet. 'I think I could do with a cup of tea and a big slice of that lemon cake,' I said, though I knew I wouldn't be able to swallow a thing right now. 'Do you fancy it?'

She nodded silently, and I left the room, giving her time to compose herself, wondering if I should have held back... if I'd said too much. I knew she was picturing what could have happened to Amala. Realising just how lucky she had been to get away before it was too late.

THIRTY-TWO

JADE

The soft tap at the door had me jumping up from the chair at the kitchen table, rushing to answer it before Annie came in from the back garden. She'd moved on from digging the pit at the front, it seemed, and now kept disappearing off down the long winding path at the back instead. I was still reeling from her confession earlier, sick to my stomach over what she'd told me, and I'd been glad when she'd subtly excused herself under the guise of letting me rest. It had taken all my willpower not to vomit as she spoke, not to rush out of the house, Amala safe in my arms, and get as far away from this place as I could manage.

I suppressed a shiver and opened the front door to find Aaron waiting there. He held out a small cardboard box, and I broke into a relieved smile at the sight of it. 'You got the phone! Thank you,' I breathed. I had been worried sick about what I would do without it. I *had* to have access to the internet in order to make my plans. Annie was living in the dark ages here, and without a computer, I had no way of figuring out where I was heading next. I gripped the box to my chest, hoping the SIM card hadn't been damaged in her assault with the hammer.

'It wasn't a problem. I hope I got the right one.'

'I'm sure it's fine,' I said.

He was staring at me, I realised, but without the intensity I had grown to expect. Instead, there was a warmth, almost sympathy, that had me confused. He'd been like that this morning too, I remembered. It made me more uneasy somehow.

He stepped back. 'I was going into town anyway. I had to pop into work.' He twisted his mouth. 'I'm sorry,' he said. 'For how I treated you this week. I thought... I don't know what I thought. But I got it wrong. I'm just protective over Annie, you know? It makes me sick to think that piece of shit is still out there, ruining lives. You did the right thing in leaving him. Coming here. I apologise if I made you uncomfortable when you were already going through so much.'

I stared at him wide-eyed as I realised Annie had shared my story with this man. This *police* officer. He'd said he had to go into work... was that because of me? Because of Ryan? I gripped the box against my chest, my knuckles turning white.

Aaron's eyes widened, and he held up a hand in apology. 'Please don't be afraid. I know this is sensitive and we have to act with the utmost caution. I won't do anything until I've spoken to you. He doesn't have any idea we're aware... I shouldn't really have said anything, I just wanted to make sure you knew you can always talk to me. I'm here if you need me, okay?'

I nodded, unable to speak, and I could see that Aaron was regretting his words, wishing he could take them back so as not to unsettle me. I choked out a muttered thanks for the phone, then pushed the door closed, leaning my head against it. Time had run out. Everything was about to fall apart.

I ripped open the box and took out the new phone, then with shaking hands pulled the SIM from my pocket and slid it into the slot, dread swirling in my belly at what I had to do next. I closed my eyes and sucked in a deep breath, knowing I had no choice. I had to call the man I'd hoped to never speak to again.

THIRTY-THREE

ANNIE

The breeze barely ruffled the leaves in the golden hedge, but I was grateful of the shade they provided as I sat, head bowed, on the smooth bench. I felt drained from the conversation I'd had with Jade, though I was glad I'd told her, that we were getting closer at last. I had never expected to talk again about the day I'd left Ryan, especially not with a virtual stranger, but I'd known I had no choice. And deep down, I had been aware of the fact that she deserved to hear every detail, to understand how close she had come to losing her daughter. Perhaps now she would feel able to open up and share her own story with me. It wouldn't be easy for her. There was so much shame and denial involved. He had always been able to twist every situation to put the blame on me. I could so easily picture how he had done the same to her. The fact that she'd been brave enough to leave was a miracle in itself.

The shock on her face had shown me that she hadn't expected my story to be so dark, and I wondered if that was a good thing. Perhaps he hadn't shown her his true colours to their full extent yet. They had barely been married a year, and even if they'd met straight after I left, they could only have been together three years at most. The violence had crept up so slowly in my time with him that I was already trapped before I realised how bad it had become. The control had been his first weapon. And it had been so clever, so sick, I had missed the warning signs. It was possible she'd had more of a sense of self-preservation and had left at the first signs, as I should have done. The thought that it hadn't been so bad for her was a comfort, but I wished she would share what he'd put her through so I could know for sure.

I was almost certain now that Ryan wasn't going to show up. Jade seemed in no rush to leave, and she was such a good mother, I had no doubt that protecting her daughter was her first priority. If she had any fears over him coming here, she'd have left by now. Found somewhere safer to hide.

I'd been so lucky that he had never known of this place while we were together. He'd taken an instant dislike to my parents during the handful of pub lunches we'd shared, though he'd been overtly charming to the point of sleazy, and he'd never joined me when I'd visited them here in the early days of our relationship. It hadn't taken long before he'd guilted me into cancelling my visits in favour of keeping him company. If he'd known where they lived, or bothered to keep in touch with them, he'd have tracked me down the moment he returned from Scotland, seething at having found his mother alive and well, knowing that for once in his life he'd fallen for someone else's game. The image of him arriving home to find the flat empty, tearing it apart in his search for me – to punish me – sent a shiver down my spine, and I rose to my feet, needing to move.

What if he *did* come, though? What if he was just biding his time? My instincts were tingling. Jade still seemed so wary of everything, so jumpy, and though I knew she and I were on the same side, I couldn't help but think of the threats he might have made. She was trapped in a world of fear – a place I knew like the back of my hand – and that frightened me because a scared woman was capable of bending her morals, but a mother would cast her values to the wind if it meant protecting her child... as *I* should have done. I should have slit that bastard's throat in his sleep to save my son.

It wasn't the first time the thought had crossed my mind. I'd imagined ramming a knife into his chest, watching the blood spurt, hearing him beg me to stop, to save him. I'd pictured going back to that first missed period, when I'd tentatively shared the news that I was expecting, only to have him spit in my face. I should have done something then. Poured rat poison in his coffee. Thrown petrol over him and flung a match into his smug face. Anything to save my son.

I was sure Jade had been through the same thoughts during her pregnancy. She'd been strong enough to save her child, and I was glad. And now that she was here with me, we could figure out a way to make sure that man would never hurt us again.

Nervous energy rippled through my veins, and I felt an urgent need to pick up my shovel, move my body, *do* something. I walked briskly back up the path towards the house, stopping short before I reached it. I could hear Jade's voice floating down from her bedroom window. Was she talking to Amala?

I moved closer, making sure to keep to the grass to soften my footsteps, and paused, listening.

Her voice was hurried, harsh; clearly she wasn't speaking to the baby. She sounded like she was on the phone. But how? Hadn't I smashed hers to pieces?

Heart racing, I slipped through the back door and, as quietly as I could, skipping over the floorboards I knew to be creaky, tiptoed up the stairs to listen outside her bedroom door. I held my breath as she spoke.

'I'm not your wife any more!' she said sharply. 'Not for much longer anyway...' There was a pause, and I could hear her pacing across the floor as she spoke again. '*What*? No! Please just answer my question. Tell me what I need to do so we can finish this! I can't live like this any more – I need it to be over!' Another pause. 'I don't *want* to see you. I'm not going to tell you that.'

A burst of white dots exploded across my vision, panic igniting in my chest. I let out a long breath, gripping the wall to steady myself. She was talking to Ryan! Why on earth had she contacted him? What a stupid, stupid girl! What could possibly be worth taking such a risk?

I waited to hear more, but the church bells began to ring, reverberating through the open window, drowning out whatever she was saying. All the bravado, the strong-willed intentions to stand up for myself, leached out of my bones, and I turned, rushing for my own bedroom, stepping into the safe little cocoon and bolting the door from the inside. I would not open it, not for her, not for anybody. I would not let him take me again.

I curled into a ball on the carpet and trained my eyes on the door, knowing it was only a matter of time. He was coming.

THIRTY-FOUR

Only seconds had passed when I heard Jade's footsteps rushing along the hallway. The door handle rattled as she tried it, and then a cacophony of bangs sounded against the thick wood. I held my knees tightly beneath my chin, rocking on the carpet, the muscles in my face twitching involuntarily. I could feel my top lip curving up, the nerve pulsing against my will, and was suddenly reminded of all the tics I'd had when I first arrived here. Every sound would force me into a physical reaction, blinking too much, trembling from head to toe. The way my thumbnail would flick frantically against the inside of my index finger until it wore through the skin. It had been so long that I'd forgotten how his very presence reduced me to this pitiful creature, but now it was like slipping back into an old, worn-in pair of shoes, as if they'd been waiting for me all this time. The Pavlovian response of knowing I was a victim, in danger, was built into my very being.

Jade slammed her fist into the wood again, bashing so hard I jumped. 'Annie, open the door! I know you're in there!'

'No!' I shouted, my voice weak, croaky.

'Annie, you *have* to! He's coming! Oh my God, he's coming now!'

The edges of my vision went dark, and I fought with myself to stay present. The window caught my eye, and I thought desperately that I might climb out of it, escape somehow. Could I slide down the drainpipe? Could I get to Aaron's house? *He* would help me. Protect me.

I saw my reflection in the mirror above the dresser and shook my head in disgust. *Protect* me? Why should he have to? Had I learned nothing in the past three years? Had I grown at all? I would not be reduced to this shell of a human being. I was worth more than this!

I took a deep breath, then stood up on shaky legs as Amala gave a high-pitched cry. I had to help them. I would not be that coward, would not leave Jade and her baby to face whatever vindictive intentions he had in store for them. Squaring my shoulders, I strode over to the door, unlocking it to find Jade gripping Amala, her eyes wide and filled with fear.

'The bells!' she gasped. 'I was on the phone, and he heard them... he heard the bells! He stopped talking – it was as if he recognised them, and then he hung up on me.' She gripped my hand. 'He knows I'm here! He's coming, Annie!'

I nodded calmly, though inside I was screaming. 'Then we have to leave. We'll go next door,' I said, ignoring the way my entire body stiffened at the idea of stepping through the gate. I had no choice. 'Aaron will help us. He'll keep us safe.'

She shook her head, panic lacing her words. 'He won't! We can't trust him, Annie. Why the hell do you think he would protect you? You know that your name is still plastered over the internet? The ads and Facebook page are still running. Why do you think that is, huh?'

I stared at her, stunned. Aaron wouldn't lie to me. He wanted me to be safe, didn't he? He wouldn't lead Ryan here.

I swallowed, unsure how to absorb her words, the shock

paralysing. I didn't believe it was possible, but there was no time to argue the odds now.

'Right,' I said softly, the only choice available to me becoming glaringly obvious. 'Right.'

I walked past her, and she followed. 'What are you doing?'

I didn't answer, but I felt her behind me as I walked as calmly as I could manage downstairs, heading to the back door.

'Annie,' Jade pushed. 'We need to stay inside. Barricade ourselves in and stay quiet! We don't have time for whatever it is you're doing!'

Ignoring her, I headed purposefully down the path to the workshop, unlatching the door. The axe lay on the far side of the bench, and I strode towards it, clasping it in my hands. An odd sensation of certainty settled over me. Ryan was coming. Now. And whatever happened today, I wouldn't let him take me back without a fight. I was willing to do anything to keep my freedom. I looked at the deadly blade, touching my fingertip to the edge, feeling the sting as the metal pierced through my skin as easily as cutting through butter. I gave it a testing swing, glad that I'd spent the past three winters chopping logs for the open fire in the kitchen. I could do this... I *would* do this.

I closed my eyes, my mind racing. I would have to wait till dark to get rid of the body. The pit for the pond was already deeper than I was tall. I'd need Jade to help me move him, but together we could do it. And she *would* help. She'd understand there was no choice. He'd forced us into a corner, and now we had no other option. She wouldn't have to bloody her hands. She just needed to stay back, keep Amala safe. I would deal with the rest. I had to.

I sucked a deep breath into my lungs, the fresh sawdust smell bringing me a sense of solidity, reminding me of everything I was set to lose if I didn't summon my courage. I opened my eyes, half surprised to find Jade staring back at me from just inside the doorway. Her face was set, and I frowned at the sight of something glinting in her hand.

Looking behind her, I saw the door closed, a padlock looped through the thick metal latch. She held the key up. 'We have to stay in here. Hide until he leaves,' she said quietly. 'He'll go if he can't find us.'

I shook my head. 'No, Jade. He'll just come back. Again and again until he wins. Don't you get it? This is his favourite game – cat-and-mouse, hide-and-seek. He expects us to cower away and hope he'll give up, but he won't. Not ever. I have to put a stop to this – for good. I can't live with the threat of him looming over my life any more, knowing he's out there biding his time. We go out there ready and face him head-on. We will *not* be his victims. Never again.'

She stared silently at me, and I watched her jaw flex, a stubborn, decisive expression I hadn't seen from her before settling on her delicate features. She met my gaze, and then, as I stared back, wondering what she was thinking, she turned to the high rectangular window I'd left open to clear the dust and, to my shock, tossed the key out of it.

'What the hell did you do that for!' I cried, shocked.

'You aren't thinking straight, Annie. What, you're going to kill him? Really?' She raised an eyebrow, as if the idea I'd been playing with in my mind for days now was simply ludicrous. 'We stay in here and we keep quiet.'

'No.' I shook my head. 'Absolutely not. I won't do that! Not again.'

The many times I'd hidden from Ryan, huddling in the wardrobe, the coat closet, beneath the bed, flashed through my mind. He had always found me. Had enjoyed the chase, the search, his unhurried footsteps drawing ever closer, as if he were stretching out the inevitable for his own sick amusement. He'd love nothing more than arriving to realise we had set up his favourite game.

'I won't hide in my own fucking garden! Not here. This is my space. *Mine*! He'll be sorely disappointed if he thinks he's going to come here and find the woman who walked out on him. He's in for one hell of a shock!'

'Oh, shut up! Just shut up!' she screamed. She walked past the workbench to the far end of the workshop, Amala in her arms as she lowered herself onto an upturned bucket. 'This isn't about you playing the hero, Annie. It's not a redemption story. This is my *life*. Mine and hers,' she said, looking down at her daughter. 'And I'm not going to let you ruin it, risk her future by doing something stupid. Get over here and shut your fucking mouth before you let the whole world know exactly how to find us! I mean it!'

I stood frozen, looking back and forth between her and the padlocked door. A motorbike engine roared in the lane nearby, and Amala let out a startled cry. I met Jade's eyes and saw pure desperation written on her face. I could break through the door with the axe. Go across the path and be at Aaron's house in a matter of seconds, though Jade's accusation that he'd failed to protect my privacy made me wonder how much trust I could really place in him. I could break out of here. But I couldn't leave her... couldn't walk away from the baby and risk her coming to harm. I wouldn't have another infant's blood on my hands. If Jade wouldn't leave, wouldn't make a run for help with me, I couldn't go either. The realisation made nausea swell in my belly, my palms turning slick.

I gripped the axe, breathing hard as I weighed my options, taking a final desperate look towards the locked door. Then, swallowing my self-disgust, I did the one thing I'd sworn to myself I would never do again. I cowered in the dark and waited for him to find me.

THIRTY-FIVE

The motorbike engine came to a stop, and I gritted my teeth, wondering if it could possibly be Ryan already. There was no way he would have made it from our old flat in such a short time, but perhaps he hadn't come from there. Perhaps they'd even moved. I had neglected to ask, I realised now. I'd taken so much for granted.

Jade was utterly silent, as if she knew exactly what was coming next and was going through a mental checklist of how to prepare. She sat on the upturned bucket, Amala drowsing in her arms, her eyes trained on her feet, shoulders hunched. Her posture reminded me of myself when I'd been at his mercy. The constant, obsessive lists I would make in my head. Had I ironed his shirt with the crease just how he liked it in the sleeve? Had I made the bed to his standard? Would he accuse me of overcooking the steak, even though it had barely touched the pan? All those stupid little rules he'd created in the name of sending me dancing in circles, driving me mad trying to jump through the never-ending hoops he tossed before me. I had been so busy trying to remember everything on the list, I never stopped to ask myself why I was bothering – at least not until it was far too late to get out.

Was Jade making a plan for what she would do to placate him if he discovered us here? She was clearly lost in her thoughts. The only sign that she was on high alert was her hand moving in swift circles against Amala's shoulder, comforting herself more than the baby, I suspected.

I, on the other hand, couldn't keep remotely still. I paced like a caged leopard back and forth beside the workbench, clambering onto my stool to peer out of the narrow rectangular window every few minutes before hopping down to resume my agitated pacing. I was filled with the primal urge to flee before the opportunity was gone. How long would it take before he found us? Would he look out here? Or, I thought, biting my thumbnail and tasting the dirt embedded beneath it, would he for once give up, assume we'd convinced one another to make a run for safety?

Why *weren't* we running for safety? This was ridiculous!

I chewed my nail, my gaze flitting between Jade and the window, trying to see if there was any movement inside the house. I'd locked the front door, I knew I had, but a lock had never stopped him before. I suddenly remembered how Jade had left it unlocked her first night here. What if she'd been out there today and I hadn't checked it? The side gate was wide open anyway, and the back door too, where we'd rushed out in a panic. We didn't stand a chance. He was coming, and it was too fucking late to do anything about it!

Why hadn't I left a week ago? I'd known who this woman was from the day she arrived, known exactly the danger she posed in even setting foot inside my house. From the second she'd walked through the front gate, it had been inevitable that he would come, for her and for me. If I hadn't been so scared of leaving the house, I could have saved myself. But I'd wasted time. I'd tried to talk myself out of the imminent danger. Once again I'd been given an opportunity to stand up for myself, make myself proud, and instead had transformed instantly into a deer in headlights, a victim rather than a fighter.

He would kill me this time.

The realisation was like a bucket of iced water to the face. He would never give me the chance to get one over on him again. He would end my life, heedless of any consequences he might face. He'd once whispered to me, in the dead of night, while he thought I was sleeping, that he almost wished I would try and leave. 'I dream of it sometimes,' he'd said in his gravelly voice – the voice I'd once thought was the sexiest thing on the planet – as he pressed his chest to my curved spine. 'You leaving me... the hunt...' He chuckled in the dark. 'I would destroy you, you know. You wouldn't walk away.'

I tried to keep my breathing even, though I was sure he must know I was listening, aware of every word, the terrifying lullaby he crooned. His huge hand slid up my naked hip, over my breast, coming to rest gently on my throat. He didn't even need to tighten his fingers for the shiver to chase down my spine, my bowels churning as I clenched every muscle in my body, fighting the blind terror he stirred up within me.

'It's not even because I love you so much I want you for myself,' he admitted. 'I don't. I never did. But I *own* you. You're my little slave, Annie. You don't get to leave until I decide I've had enough.' He laughed again, pleased with himself, then grabbed my hand, forcing me to roll towards him. I kept my eyes screwed tightly shut, but he increased the pressure on my wrist until I thought it might snap in two, and with a gasp, I opened them, staring into his malevolent black irises. In the darkness, his ebony skin was barely visible, but the white slash of his teeth showed the wide smile on his face. 'Ah,' he breathed, almost sensually, 'so you're awake. That's good.'

I didn't dare to speak, to say a word in my defence. I could tell he didn't expect me to. Somewhere deep down, a tiny voice screamed at me to fight back. To claw and slap and scream until I either got free or he put an end to this miserable excuse for a life. But I was silent. Just as I always was.

He smirked, the pressure on my wrist easing, and I held my breath, hoping he would roll over and go to sleep. Instead, he eased himself onto his back, propping one muscular arm beneath his head and yanking me on top of him. 'Now,' he said, danger lacing his voice, daring me to refuse, 'ride me like the little whore you and I both know you are.' He let go of my wrist, perfectly relaxed in the smug knowledge that I wouldn't fight, wouldn't refuse. I looked up at the ceiling, cringing at the feel of him as he shoved upwards against me, and as he invaded my body, I tasted bile in the back of my throat and wished I was brave enough to end this. End *him*.

The workshop seemed to be closing in around me as I tried to shake off the memory I'd long since suppressed. My heart was racing, and I found myself gasping for air that wouldn't come, my throat narrowing in panic. I bent double, my hand cramping around the axe I couldn't bring myself to put down, the fingers of my free hand digging into my knees, bruising hard, as I choked against the dust-filled air that did nothing to calm me. There was a ringing in my ears that was growing louder, and I knew that if it didn't stop, I would faint... I would die!

'Shush! Do you have any idea how noisy you're being?' Jade snapped, and I turned to meet her furious eyes.

'I... I can't... help it,' I spluttered. 'I'm having a panic attack!' I gripped my throat, my head spinning. I couldn't wait here. I had to find a way to get free! I spun, rushing for the door, the axe raised high above my head as I prepared to swing it, heedless of the commotion it would cause.

And then Jade was standing in front of me, blocking my escape, her calm eyes meeting mine. She reached out and prised the axe from my aching hand, simultaneously shifting her drowsing daughter into my arms. 'Hold her,' she whispered gently. 'Breathe with her.'

The relief was instantaneous. It was as if this warm, soft baby, her eyes closed, her chest moving steadily up and down, her breath escaping in contented little puffs, had flipped a switch. The frantic thrum of my heartbeat in my ears began to fade, and I clung to her as if she were a lifebuoy in the middle of a thrashing ocean.

I *couldn't* fall apart, not when her safety, her very existence, was at stake. I closed my eyes, letting the panic seep slowly away, my trembling fingers the only remaining clue to how close I'd come to the edge of reason.

Jade gave a short nod, as if she had known it would work, then took up her place on the bucket again, returning to her thoughtful state.

'What will we do?' I said softly. 'When he comes?'

She shook her head, refusing to offer up an answer.

'Do you think he will look here?' I pushed. I longed to hear her own experiences with him, to understand if he was still the monster I'd escaped. Maybe he loved her in a way he'd never managed with me... maybe he would be more forgiving. Maybe he'd see me holding his daughter, and his fatherly instincts would get the better of his vindictive desire for revenge. But then I remembered the sick look of pleasure on his face when he thought he'd risked my pregnancy, and knew it was impossible. A man who'd stooped that low could never come back. He wouldn't be able to survive his own guilt if ever he tried to become a better man. It was easier not to.

'He'll look everywhere,' she murmured. 'Military men never leave a stone unturned.' She spoke so quietly it was as if she'd forgotten she was answering my question.

I frowned. 'Ryan wasn't in the mil—' I broke off as I caught a glint of claret liquid on the floor beneath the bucket. My eyes travelled up the leg of Jade's jeans to where bright red blood pooled at her crotch. 'You're bleeding!' I cried, forgetting for a moment to keep my voice down. Now that I really looked, her face was far paler than it had been earlier, and there was a clammy sheen to her freckled skin. She shook her head as if it was of no consequence. I had wondered if she might be suffering with mastitis earlier in the week, but now I realised it had been something much worse. 'Jade,' I asked urgently, 'how long have you been bleeding?'

She shrugged, shifting the axe onto her lap. 'I haven't stopped yet – since the birth.'

'But it's been six weeks!' I spluttered. 'And that's a lot of blood!'

'It wasn't as bad as this... It got worse today. It's the stress. I'm sure that's all.'

I shook my head, holding her daughter, wondering why she hadn't mentioned it. It explained why she'd been using the washing machine so often. Twice I'd come down to find her bedsheets already hanging on the line, a smell of bleach lingering in the air as if they'd been soaked before she'd thrown them in the machine. I'd assumed Amala had had a leaky nappy, or Jade's milk had let down, but now I realised it had likely been blood. 'You have to go to the hospital. There could be a piece of retained placenta causing it, not to mention an infection.'

'I'm *fine*.'

'Jade,' I whispered urgently, 'I'm serious! You're going to make yourself ill. These things can turn nasty very quickly.'

She closed her eyes as if she could block out my words, and frustration swelled in my belly. 'For goodness' sake—' I broke off as a deep male voice called out.

'Hello?'

I gasped, and Jade's eyes flashed wide open. She pressed her finger to her lips, gesturing frantically with her free hand for me to pass Amala to her. Legs shaking, I moved towards her, but I knocked against a pile of planks balanced against the wall and watched horror-struck as they toppled to one side. In that split second, I had to choose between grabbing them before they collided with the stone floor and keeping my hold on the baby. I squeezed my eyes shut as they clattered to the ground, the sound deafening in the silence.

I held my breath, unmoving, praying that he had somehow missed it, that he was already in the house, creeping through the corridors, hoping to catch us. Slowly, I opened my eyes, staring intently at the door. From across the lawn, I heard the familiar creak of the back door opening wider, and for a second, hope filled my chest. He hadn't heard; he was going into the house! I bit down on the inside of my cheek, silently begging to be spared, just as Amala let out a high-pitched bellow, startled by the noise – or unsettled by my own terror.

There was a bang as the back door was slammed shut, and then heavy footsteps sounded on the paved path, heading in our direction.

THIRTY-SIX

I swayed my hips, holding Amala upright against my chest as I patted her back, trying desperately to get her to stop crying, though it was too late for that. My eyes were still trained on the door, wondering why he didn't try to open it, what the hell he was playing at. I had always hated this part, the waiting, the knowing what was coming next. Jade pressed her hands to her face, her shoulders slumping as if she was too drained to fight any more. It made me angry on Amala's behalf that she wasn't standing by my side, ready to face him head-on. That she'd shrunk back from the danger, not even bothering to grab the axe lying in her lap, a pathetic mirror to my own past. The anger morphed to a realisation, an understanding, that it was myself I was most disgusted with. The person I became whenever he was near.

'Not any more,' I breathed, the words barely a whisper. If Jade wouldn't fight for her daughter, I bloody would! I would *have* to do it. I'd known it from the moment she arrived. 'Jade!' I whispered urgently, fighting to hold on to the baby, who was squirming in my arms, arching furiously. 'Bring the axe here and take Amala, now!'

Jade didn't respond, but the sound of the latch being tried had me spinning back to face the door. The metal creaked, the padlock holding firm, and I edged backward silently. The door rattled, the latch creaking again, and then, after a few beats of silence save for Amala's cries, my captured breath burning to escape my straining lungs, there was a sudden blast, and bright sunlight blinded me as the old door fell from its rusted hinges and crashed to the stone floor. A cloud of sawdust erupted, making me cough, my hand covering Amala's face to protect her. She went utterly silent, her eyes round with surprise.

I blinked hard, focusing slowly, then gasped, shaking my head, utterly bewildered by who was standing in the place of my abusive ex.

'Thomas!' I cried. 'You kicked the door down!'

My brother, dressed in heavy black boots, jeans and a khaki T-shirt, looked no less confused at finding me sequestered away out here, comforting a baby. The last conversation we'd had had been filled with bitter accusations and a complete inability to relate to one another, but the relief at seeing his face instead of Ryan's, the familiarity of his rosy cheeks and freckled nose, his cropped blonde hair, had me rushing forward into his arms. He hugged me tightly, then, gripping my shoulders in a way only he could without sending me into a panic, stepped back, shaking his head in wonder.

'You had a baby?' he asked, his eyes lighting up, reminding me of how boyish he could be, how delighted by life. He touched Amala's hand, and she stared at him, stunned by the sound of his voice. I let out a shaky breath, baffled at what was happening. Was Ryan still coming? It would be a different story now, with Thomas here. I'd explain everything to him, be honest for once about what Ryan was like, and Thomas would stand with us against him. I was safe now. I looked at my brother's face and realised how deeply I had missed him, despite our differences. Despite his inability to look deeper and see the trouble I'd been in back then. How he could have made all the difference...

'No.' I smiled, shaking my head. 'She's not mine.' I stepped back to reveal Jade, who rose in one swift motion to her feet, as if she had suddenly come to life. 'This is Jade. Amala is *her* baby.'

The smile fell from Thomas's face, and he stepped past me, his eyes wide, hurt. 'You had a baby? And you didn't think to tell me you were carrying my child?'

'*What*?' I gasped, looking at Amala in confusion. 'Thomas, you *know* her?'

'Of course I do! She's my *wife*!'

He spun, looking at the baby in my arms again, taking her in properly now. His expression morphed from a kind of wonder, filled with reverence – a man setting eyes on his daughter for the first time – to betrayal. I saw the exact moment his reality shattered, his heart snapping into pieces. He set his jaw, his eyes hardening.

I knew what he was seeing. Amala was a beautiful baby. But her hair was thick and black where his was blonde and fine. Her dark eyes were so very unlike the piercing blue he'd inherited from our father. And her skin, that unmistakable chocolate-brown skin, contrasted powerfully with both his and Jade's. He swallowed. 'She isn't mine,' he whispered.

'No.' Jade's voice was hard as she delivered the single word that wiped out any lasting scrap of hope.

I was too confused to speak. Was she having an affair behind Thomas's back with Ryan? If so, things were about to get very nasty.

'You had a baby with Ryan when you were married to my brother?' I said, the words slow, stupid, not making any sense to me. 'How? *Why*?'

She gave a sigh, as if she didn't have time for my questions, her face glistening with perspiration, reminding me that she was in need of a doctor to see to her bleeding. 'Honestly, Annie,' she muttered, fixing me with a look of absolute disdain. 'It's about time you stopped being such a victim and started questioning the stories presented to you.'

'I don't know what you mean.'

She frowned, clearly irritated. 'I mean I've never even *met* your ex. I had no idea you'd been in an abusive relationship.'

I winced, seeing the shock on Thomas's face at her words.

'But your own fears, your own insecurities... your *guilt*,' she added softly, vindictively, reminding me of how much I'd divulged to her, 'made you so easy to manipulate. You just let me into your home, barely put up a fight. You're lucky it wasn't someone else.'

'But why come here at all?' Thomas asked, folding his muscular arms.

Jade gave a dramatic sigh and lowered herself back down to sit on the bucket, fixing him with a cold stare.

'Oh, Thomas,' she said, her voice soft, impatient, as if she were talking to a small child who couldn't grasp a basic problem, 'I think you know why.'

THIRTY-SEVEN

JADE

It was all going horribly wrong. If I'd had things my way, everything would have come together perfectly. Thomas was supposed to be on tour with the army for another three months yet. I didn't know how or why he'd got early leave, but his impending return had ruined everything. Forced me to flee with only the clothes on my back just weeks after giving birth, still dealing with the heavy bleeding that had gradually worsened this past week. I hadn't had time to figure out all the details of my plan, and it showed. It was a mess!

If it hadn't been for Sarah randomly passing my house as I was putting out the rubbish in my dressing gown – concealing the bulge of my post-partum belly as Amala slept indoors – excitedly sharing the news that our husbands were on their way home, I would never have had time to get out. Trust Thomas to think he was being romantic in surprising me! I hadn't seen Sarah in months, not since before our respective husbands went away, and had managed to hide my pregnant belly from the world so she was none the wiser. Thank heavens! She'd always been an oversharer – of both her own business and everyone else's. It was actually a fact I was immensely grateful for. It wasn't the first time she'd inadvertently given me information that had completely changed my path.

I ran my hand over the still tender bruise on my upper arm, recalling how I'd tripped over the rug, smashing my arm into the wooden bedpost in my hurry to get out. That bruise had probably been the thing that had swayed Annie into letting me stay, though I hadn't realised the significance of it at the time.

Annie was still standing, holding Amala, her leathery, sun-damaged forehead creased in confusion. 'How can you *not* have met Ryan?' She shook her head. 'You're lying. My aunt sent me a photo of you at your wedding to him. I've been searching high and low for it, but I never forgot it. It took me a little while to make the connection, but I know it was you in the photo.'

I pursed my lips, thinking of the envelope that had been jammed down the back of her bedside cabinet drawer and that was now hidden behind the bath panel in my en suite. The accompanying invitation that still had the unanswered RSVP attached.

Thomas scratched at his pale, freckled arms, dragging his pathetic, broken-hearted gaze away from Amala to meet his sister's eyes. 'You're confused, Annie. *I* sent you the photo of Jade last year. It was of her in a white dress at our engagement dinner.' He cleared his throat. 'Along with an invite to the wedding. You never replied.'

Annie shook her head. '*You* sent it?'

He nodded. 'An olive branch. After the way we left things when we last spoke.'

She gasped, clearly remembering, her eyes wide as she rubbed circles into Amala's back, still swaying her hips in the instinctive way mothers always seemed to fall into whenever they held a baby. 'You sent just a scrap of a note with the invite, saying you'd met someone. There was no apology.' She swallowed, and I could see a thousand unresolved emotions crossing her face. 'You didn't take back any of the awful things you called me after Mum and Dad died. Did you honestly expect me to turn up to your wedding?'

He looked down, suddenly sheepish. 'I meant to have a face-to-face conversation with you when I saw you. To get to the bottom of our disagreement. The whole day I kept watching the door, hoping you'd walk in, but you didn't come.'

'I was angry,' she admitted. 'Hurt.'

'I know.'

She shook her head. 'But... there was definitely a letter from Aunt Betty telling me that Ryan had got married. I remember reading it. I was shocked that he'd moved on so quickly. You know, thinking about it now, there must have been two letters around the same time. I guess I blended them into one in my memory.'

'I'm sorry,' he said, his brow creasing as if holding back a wince. I could imagine how uncomfortable he was right now. I'd once been told that he was deep, but that hadn't been my experience of the man. He met his sister's eyes. 'That must have hurt to hear he'd moved on.'

She gave an ugly snort. 'You have no idea,' she replied, her tone filled with disdain, and I played back our past conversations in my mind, watching their interaction, my thoughts racing from one to the next as I tried to work out what to do next. Thomas had never mentioned Annie being in an abusive relationship. Did he even *realise* what she'd lived through? Or had it been easier not to notice. To pretend he didn't see the glaring truth? Men really were pathetic. Always looking for the easiest road.

'I was upset,' she admitted. 'About both of the letters. Yours *and* Betty's. I recall not wanting to face either of them. It was too much to cope with – our fall-out, Ryan's wedding. He *did* get married – there was definitely a photo of a girl with long brown hair, just like Jade,' she said, throwing a glance my way. 'I remember because he had his arm around her and his hand was in her hair. It was made to look romantic, but—' She broke off, shaking her head, her lips paling.

I was hardly about to admit that she was spot-on about there being a photograph of me. I hadn't seen the one of Ryan and his new wife, but if her reaction in the loft having seen the old snap of the two of them in the pub was anything to go by, she would have set it alight the moment she laid eyes on it. She had told me herself that she didn't want a photo of her ex under her roof. The photo of me, though... *that* one she'd kept. I'd found it myself in the back of her bedside table. It was just me in the picture. I had been smiling so much it hurt my cheeks. Not because I was excited for marriage, but because I knew I was close to pulling this off, and Thomas wasn't going to back out. He had been so sure about me, right from the moment we met. The photographer had made me stand under the floral archway, the Italian-style waterfall in the foyer of the hotel artfully behind me, and I had complied, knowing my dress was beautiful, my face youthful and happy, my long brown hair loose and shining.

'Look.' Thomas pulled his phone from his pocket and showed it to Annie. I knew what she was seeing. His lock screen had been that very photo for the past year. 'See?' he said.

'Yes...' she whispered.

My stomach cramped, and I clenched my teeth together, trying to hold in the blood, wishing it would just stop. I let out a long, slow breath, closing my eyes and counting silently to ten, then looked up to find them both staring at me with avid expectation on their faces.

THIRTY-EIGHT

Then

The pub was crowded, and I pushed aside the gravy-streaked dinner plate, picking up my wine glass and leaning back against the red leather bench, taking in the Friday-night activity unfolding around me. At the bar, there were groups of people watching me, not bothering to be subtle, clearly waiting for me to vacate the family-sized table I'd nabbed more than an hour ago. They were out of luck. I had no intention of going anywhere. I poured myself another glass of ice-cold Pinot from the half-bottle I'd chosen, taking a deep sip and sighing with pleasure. I had missed this... missed so much over the past eight months. Oh, but it had been worth it.

The noise of the place was comforting, familiar, easing my transition, and I smiled to myself, thinking of where I'd spent *last* Friday night. The tiny cell in the prison I'd called home for the past eight months in the notorious HMP Bronzefield. The largest women's prison in the whole of Europe.

I'd thrown up when I'd heard I was going there. My lawyer – useless, lying fuck *he* turned out to be – had said I wouldn't go down. He'd been so sure of himself that I'd believed him. It turned out he'd been on the brink of losing his forty-year marriage, having been caught in an affair, and his mind had been elsewhere as he went through the motions, placating me like a child. When the judge had read out the verdict, the sentence, I'd felt like I must be hallucinating.

It was a blessing that I'd been the only prisoner in the van that day; that nobody had seen the sweating, vomiting pile of jelly I'd become when I realised where we were heading. I'd fallen apart completely, crying like a pathetic little child, but by the time the van pulled up at the prison gates, I'd got it out of my system. I'd climbed out of the back, head held high, and from that moment had never once shown a scrap of fear. Even when I'd seen my cellmate have a finger sawn off for disrespecting one of the inmates. Or watched two women on GBH charges hold down one of the new girls and suffocate her with a bin bag. They'd waited for her, known she was being brought in, that she'd messed with someone she shouldn't have, and made up their minds that she wouldn't survive the week. I'd kept my mouth shut, turned my face away and pretended not to see. I'd had to do that a lot. There had been things I had seen whilst trapped in that hellhole that had changed me. Things that had scarred deep inside where I could never reach, but it was the price I had to pay, and I didn't regret the choices that had led me there.

Really, if I reframed it, looked at it from a logical perspective, I was lucky to have stayed in one place for so long. At least I'd been able to learn the ropes, understand who to avoid and who to go to for a favour. So many of the others had been shipped from pillar to post, never able to settle. I had even managed to keep the same cell for the last four months of my stay. It hadn't been all bad.

I took another gulp of my wine, smiling to myself. I'd made some stupid mistakes over the past few years, mistakes that had led to my being locked up – though the money had never been found – but I'd learned some valuable lessons too, and I was excited to put them into practice now I'd regained my freedom.

I clicked my tongue, reminding myself that patience was key. There was no rush – I was hardly on the breadline.

A young, flustered-looking waitress with dark brown pigtails and a heat rash across her chest came over to clear away my plate, and I smiled blandly at her. 'Would you like the bill?' she asked, glancing at the five empty spaces at my table that could no doubt be given to other paying customers.

'No, I'll have another bottle of wine. And the dessert menu.'

'I... I'll have to ask you to move to a smaller table now that it's busy,' she said.

'I'm happy here.'

She swallowed, biting her lip nervously, then, meeting my confident stare, gave a non-committal nod and dashed off. I tried not to let my irritation get the better of me. But not *too* hard. If there was one thing I'd learned in prison, it was that you didn't back down. It never hurt to show your teeth a little, to let people know you might be calm, *quiet* even, but you were no pushover. I glowered at her retreating back, hoping she could feel it.

My attention was dragged away when on the opposite side of the bar, the front door opened and a rowdy group of three men and two women burst inside, letting in a bitingly cold wind that made the flames in the open fire dance, the spaniel sleeping beside it raising its head as if to ask if they'd been born in a barn. My sentiments exactly.

The men were holding on to each other, singing something that sounded like a sea shanty, causing everyone to look their way. All three were clearly drunk. And all three wore the distinctive camo of soldiers' uniform. What was it with army guys thinking they could take over a place like this? And why did the women they were with put up with it? It was crass to make such an obnoxious scene, to have no regard for anyone else trying to enjoy their evening.

I turned my head away, trying not to let their presence ruin my first night of freedom. I'd managed to put up with a lot worse inside. The constant shrieking. The petty arguments and bitchy drama that never seemed to abate – the only source of entertainment for the inmates who didn't have enough brain cells to come up with any better use of their time. I had actually found that worse than the violence. It was the tedium of it, the complaining that made me want to slap them in their stupid little mouths. They didn't realise what a gift they'd been given. *Time,* with no obligation to be anywhere, no pressure to get to work. Personally, I had used every single day of those eight months to plan for the future, so when the time came to leave, I knew I wouldn't find myself back in a cage.

'Can we join you, beautiful?'

I grimaced as I looked up to find one of the camo-dressed buffoons standing over me. His voice was slurred, but there was an unmistakable twang of public school behind his casual request. And I knew from past experience that that came with entitlement.

'Obviously not,' I replied, holding my wine glass close to my chest, not trusting that he wouldn't trip on his laces and knock the contents over my new dress. I'd enjoyed the shopping trip this afternoon. The way clothes seemed to fit better now. I'd been to the prison gym daily, needing the exercise to keep me sane, and the results spoke for themselves. I wished I'd tried it before.

'Oh, go on!' one of the other men jeered.

I looked past him, seeing their female companions heading for the toilets. I wasn't about to let them force me out of here on my first night as a free woman. Besides, I had a reason for coming here. I would hardly find a decent target from the comfort of my sofa, would I? This was the best table in the pub.

It enabled me to see out the window and watch who was coming and going, and to assess the place without having to gawk around like a loser. I wasn't moving. Wasn't leaving. And I'd be damned if they thought they could intimidate me.

Ignoring their bloodshot puppy-dog eyes, hoping they'd fuck off and leave me in peace, I turned away from them and came face to face with the nervous young waitress, holding a bottle of wine and the dessert menu. I already knew what she was going to say before the words left her mouth.

'I'm so sorry,' she stuttered, the heat rash creeping up her neck now, making me narrow my eyes, hating how weak she looked. I couldn't bear it. Wished she had the guts to tell me straight. She might have earned a scrap of my respect then. 'My boss insists that we need this table for larger parties.'

'Are we not a large enough party for you?' asked the blonde man – the one who'd called me beautiful – sliding in beside me, slinging an arm over my shoulder that I instantly shrugged off. The women returned from the toilets and sat down without seeming to notice my resistance to their presence.

The waitress gave a quick, relieved nod. 'Oh, yes, of course... Can I get you a menu?'

'Yeah, please. What are we drinking, ladies? Red?' He glanced at the fresh bottle that the girl had placed in front of me. 'Or *white*?' He winked and reached for the bottle, topping up my glass, and I snatched it back, jamming it into the ice bucket.

I could feel his eyes on my face as he spoke. 'Three bottles of that stuff,' he said, 'and five more glasses.'

One of the women giggled. 'You don't even *like* wine, Thomas.'

He grinned, flashing a glimpse of straight white teeth. 'I do tonight.'

He rested his arm on the bench behind me, as if we were old friends, and I scowled, trying to focus on the dessert menu in my hands. 'Fucking tenacious, aren't you?' I muttered under my breath, seeing him break into a grin in my periphery. If I wasn't enjoying my freedom so damn much, wasn't so good at keeping my cool, he'd be lucky to make it out of the pub with both his balls.

Almost an hour later, one of the women slid into the obnoxious man's place on the bench as he and the other men got up to go outside for a smoke. As if he could make himself more repugnant. He would come back stinking of cigarettes and lech all over me again. I'd had enough. I'd managed to eat the double chocolate brownie with whipped vanilla-bean cream, savouring every decadent mouthful, whilst the group who had infiltrated my evening chatted noisily amongst themselves. I'd had another glass of wine, and a coffee, and now I was ready to call it a night. On *my* terms. I was glad I hadn't scurried off with my tail between my legs and let them ruin my evening completely.

'He likes you,' said the woman, her leg inching ever closer towards mine, her breath pure alcohol fumes as she leaned into my personal space. Her name was Sarah. I'd heard it across the table enough times that it felt like fingernails scraping down a blackboard now.

'What?'

'Thomas.' She laughed, shaking her head as if I was stupid.

'I'm sure he doesn't. You have nothing to worry about,' I replied, my tone so icy it would have served as a warning to a more sober woman. Sadly, in her current state, she was incapable of picking up on that. How ridiculous it was that women allowed themselves to drink until they became a walking target. She'd surrendered every ounce of control and had nothing but blind hope that the men she was with would keep her safe. I couldn't do it. Leave my fate up to the good judgement – good nature – of others. I liked a glass of wine as much as the next person, but I forced down a pint of water or a black coffee after every two drinks, knowing it was the sensible choice. This woman needed a few harsh truths, some near misses to give her a damn good wake-up call.

She let out a high-pitched burst of laughter. 'Oh, I'm not worried. I'm with Graham, the one with dark eyes. We've been married almost two years.' She grinned, wiggling her fingers close to my face to show me her wedding ring, a simple band dotted with tiny diamonds. I wondered where her engagement ring was. Why some women decided to wear only the wedding ring once they'd signed the papers. I'd want both. I wanted it all.

'Congratulations.' My tone was dry, and I gestured to the waitress to bring my bill, but she didn't see me. Irritated at the thought of having to go up to the bar to pay, I rifled through my bag for my new purse, stuffed with cash.

'Poor Thomas has been single for years,' Sarah continued conversationally, as if we were the best of friends. She reminded me of those awful drunk girls in the toilets on a Friday night – the ones who tried to make you their best friend and tell you their life story whilst badly reapplying their lipstick in a smeared mirror. Why did they always try and hold your hand as you were walking back out to the bar? It made me want to slap them away.

She gave a dramatic sigh, as if begging me to ask for more information, and when I didn't, she went on as if I had. 'He finds a girl he likes, and then a few weeks in, he realises there's nothing below the surface. Vapid.' She laughed again, then slung an arm round my shoulder. '*I'm* not vapid,' she whispered, too close to my ear, the fumes making my eyes water. 'I'm actually a teacher. Primary school. They say kids drive you to drink, don't they?' She answered her own question with another gulp of wine, then, mercifully, leaned back, trying to focus on my face.

'Thomas might not seem like it tonight, but he's deep. He

doesn't go out like this often. He's more likely to be off hiking or wild swimming than at a bar. But the boys just got leave and' – she gave a sudden wide yawn that showed her surprisingly perfect back teeth – 'we missed them. Rose is with James. Four years.' She touched my hand. 'He *likes* you,' she repeated. 'Give him a chance. He's been so unlucky. Girls find out he comes from money and they change, you know? Start sizing him up for a Birkin.'

I paused, already halfway out of my seat, lowering myself down and turning to face her. 'He attracts gold-diggers?' I asked, meeting her bloodshot eyes.

'Oh, like you wouldn't believe. His parents—' She broke off, burping long and loud, then giggled, wafting the smell away with her hand. 'Sorry. Too much wine.'

'His parents?' I pushed, interested now.

Her eyes widened. '*Rich...*' She pressed her hand to her mouth as if she was spilling state secrets. I hoped she wasn't about to evacuate her stomach over my nice dress, but I wasn't worried enough to walk away from what was turning out to be a very enlightening conversation. She dropped her hand. 'So very, very rich,' she finished. 'Thomas doesn't give a shit about money, though.'

'But he'll be getting an inheritance someday, though, I should think?' I mused.

'Oh, they died a year or two back. Boating accident or something. He never talks about it, but from what I can tell, he walked away with a small fortune... or a big one!' She laughed again, pleased with herself. 'Their house was like something out of a movie. Picture-perfect, and the biggest in the best spot of a very la-di-da village. I could do country living,' she added, more to herself than to me now. 'I'd love my own sheep...'

She glanced up at the sound of male laughter as the men returned to the warmth of the pub. 'Shh,' she whispered, far too theatrically. 'They're coming back.' She squeezed my arm, and I didn't shrug her off. 'Just give him a chance, okay?' She moved out of his space without waiting for an answer, going to join the other woman and the barmaid, who were cackling loudly about some idiotic joke.

Thomas slumped down on the bench, and I waited a few seconds, then adjusted my position, my leg pressing firmly against his. Slowly, I turned my head, meeting his eyes, and smiled, a slow, sexy smile, letting my hand brush against his as I reached for one of the half-empty wine bottles and topped up his glass. 'I had this one at a little pub in the South Downs a few weeks ago,' I said, making my voice husky, a skill I'd practised to perfection. 'It's good. Hits the spot. Especially after a long day of hiking. Nothing like a country pub roast after a day out in nature. But I suppose in your line of work you don't get much time for walking for pleasure?'

I pressed the glass into his hand, our fingers grazing briefly, smiling softly at the unmistakable light that now shone in his eyes. He opened his mouth to correct me, instantly reminded of his favourite spots in the South Downs, and I leaned in, giving him my full attention. I hadn't expected it to fall into my lap. I hadn't thought it would be so easy.

THIRTY-NINE

ANNIE

Now

'You never told me your parents were rich. Lord and lady of the manor, it would seem. Must have been a nice childhood...' Jade met my brother's eyes with a look of pure spite I hadn't imagined she had in her. I felt like I'd been dropped from a tall building, freefalling, trying to grasp hold of something that might make sense. I'd spent a week jumping at every noise, waiting for Ryan to slam his fist into my front door, alternating between wanting to protect Jade and thinking this was all some elaborate game. But now it was sinking in that Ryan had nothing to do with any of this. He wasn't coming. Hadn't found me. The relief I should have felt at that realisation was notably absent. Instead, I was just confused, and watching the way Jade regarded my brother, the disdain in her eyes, I suddenly experienced a feeling of familial protectiveness that had lain dormant so long I hadn't known it was in me.

Thomas blinked. 'Jade, the last time I saw you was six months ago. You were kissing me goodbye at the train station.' He lowered his voice, his pale cheeks turning pink. 'You said you didn't know how you would sleep without me cuddling you.'

'I managed just fine.'

'You were pregnant. That day at the station. You had to have been.'

'Yes. I met someone. The timing wasn't ideal, and I didn't intend for it to happen.'

'You didn't intend to cheat? Or to get pregnant?' He was trying to speak without emotion, but it broke my heart to hear how destroyed he was, how hard he was working to keep control of the torrent of hurt simmering beneath the surface. Jade gave no indication that she was sorry, that she even cared.

She pressed a hand to her belly and sighed. 'To get pregnant,' she said, the words coming slowly, as if she were talking to a small child. 'I took the morning-after pill, but clearly it didn't work.'

It was chilling to hear her speak so clinically about her daughter. Instinctively, I held Amala a little tighter. She had fallen asleep in my arms as I swayed back and forth in the hot, dusty workshop, and I undid her babygrow down to her belly button, worried she might overheat. I should take her back in the house; we should all get out of here. I opened my mouth to say as much, but Thomas spoke first.

'So... it's over then. You've left me no choice.' His words were firm, but his eyes begged her to disagree, to fight for their short-lived marriage. It reminded me of how hard I'd tried to make Ryan be the man I needed rather than the monster he was. No amount of talking, begging, had made him change. 'I'll sign the divorce papers, and we can leave this marriage exactly where it belongs. In the past. I don't want to ever see you again.'

'You won't have to,' she spat. 'I can get my lawyer to deal with yours. I'm very interested to find out how much I'm entitled to. Very interested indeed.'

He snorted. '*Entitled* to? Babe, you cheated. You won't get a penny from me. The prenup couldn't have been clearer regarding that.'

'Oh, and why don't you remind me what it said regarding hidden assets?'

'What?'

'You know, that was the most interesting thing I learned doing my law degree. How a prenup can be watertight, but if you hide little bits and pieces – a house here, an inheritance there – it isn't worth the paper it's written on.'

'I didn't hide anything.'

She broke into a slow, cruel smile. 'Darling Thomas, we both know you did. Now, I don't want things to get nasty between us. Not when we started out with so much love for each other. I'm sure we don't need to get lawyers involved if you're honest... *reasonable*. We can come to an agreement of a fair sum, don't you think?'

He shook his head, genuine confusion crossing his features, and I felt a cold wave of realisation as to why she'd come here. She wanted the house. *My* house! A combination of indignant rage that the whole time I'd been hosting her she'd been after my sanctuary and righteous satisfaction that she'd had a wasted journey fizzed through my veins.

Thomas shrugged. 'I have a small army pension, which I declared. I don't own anything. No property. No stocks and shares. And you read the clause that said you'd get nothing if you cheated. I only did the prenup in the first place because I didn't want us fighting over any pets. Remember? The clause that said if I bought a dog, in the event that we separate, I get full ownership?'

Jade made a choking sound, her eyebrows shooting up, and Thomas laughed. 'There's nothing else. You can whistle, love. I hope you enjoy claiming benefits. I'm sure you can get plenty now you're a single mother. Or are you planning to go back to the other guy?' he asked bitterly. 'Maybe you'll have more luck fleecing him.'

The look on Jade's face told me that conning Amala's father was indeed part of her plan.

'Why did you come here?' I asked, needing answers.

'Because I wanted to find the paperwork. The deeds to the house. Your parents' will. They aren't in our flat – I've searched through all his stuff. Sarah told me they left a fortune, and I want my share!'

I met Thomas's eyes. A vindictive pleasure in ruining this poisonous woman's plans passed between us. For once, we were both on the same page.

Thomas took a deep breath. 'I suppose that's why you married me? For the money?'

'Why else? Look at you!' she exclaimed. 'Do you think a woman like me wants to spend my weekends eating warm cheese sandwiches in the middle of some bloody tick-ridden field in the arse-end of nowhere? Have you even once taken me to a nice restaurant? A weekend away somewhere worth going, rather than the bloody YMCA hostel in Snowdonia? Have you bought me a piece of decent jewellery?'

She yanked a silver chain from inside her shirt, engagement and wedding rings hanging from it. 'I had these valued. They're a piece of shit. Not even worth a grand between them. Is that how much I mean to you, Thomas?' She laughed bitterly. 'I want more. More than you're willing to give. So yeah, I mean to take it, and then we can say our goodbyes. It's only because of the pregnancy that I've let it drag on this long. I was too sick to have the energy to do anything before Amala was born, and,' she added, gesturing with disgust to the blood on her jeans, 'I haven't exactly been at my best since she arrived. You coming back early was a nightmare, to be honest with you.'

He shook his head. 'Sorry to inconvenience you.'

She sneered. 'You can't understand it, can you? How it feels to have nothing? To realise you have the power to change that? Do you really expect me to feel guilty over using what options I have to make my life better? While you were swanning around in your blazer and tie at the local prep school, eating home-cooked dinners and playing tennis at the weekends, I was picking fleas off my little sister in sheltered accommodation. Do you know what it's like for two young girls to grow up in one room, with a single mother who brought men in to buy sex from her while we pretended to sleep? Do you know what it feels like to go to bed hungry night after night? To watch as your sibling wastes away. They took her... put her in foster care, and I don't know what those bastards did to her, but she was dead within the year. *You* wouldn't understand any of that, would you? How could you? You had a silver spoon from birth. Only the best.'

I pressed my lips together. 'I'm sorry you went through that. It sounds like a difficult childhood.'

She glared at me. 'I'm not interested in your pity, Annie.'

'No,' I replied, moving to stand beside my brother, holding Amala with one arm and reaching out with my free hand to squeeze his shoulder as I looked coldly at the woman who'd dared to hurt him. 'So it would seem. You've come for money.'

'Obviously,' she spat.

'And you've been searching for paperwork? Proof that Thomas owns half this house and our parents' fortune?'

'That's right.'

I nodded, then smiled.

'I don't see what's funny. Like I said, we don't need to involve lawyers. You have two choices. Sign over the house to me, or – even easier – you can do a bank transfer. I have an offshore account. It'll be done and dusted in a matter of minutes.' She held out her hands, palms facing up, as if she were presenting lunch options at a conference, asking something so simple it didn't require more than a few seconds of contemplation. 'Give me what I came for and I'll give you a divorce.'

I met her eyes. 'Thomas signed over the house to me three years ago. That was the last time we spoke.'

'*What?*'

'You heard me. He called me after the funeral, and when he found out I had moved back in here, he called me a money-grabber. Said that if I cared so much about the house, I could have it. You must have noticed he doesn't have any interest in money. He didn't want anything from our parents.'

Thomas cleared his throat. 'I didn't want anything that might change me as a person, make me become like them. I wanted to make my own life, be free of them for good. I'm sorry, Annie. For how I spoke to you back then.'

Jade stepped forward, shaking her head in disbelief. 'No!'

I ignored her as I met his eyes. 'It was never about the money for me, Thomas. It was freedom. From Ryan. I should have told you earlier what I was going through. Made you understand the kind of man he was. Asked for your help.'

Understanding dawned on his face, and he stepped back, joining the puzzle pieces. 'Oh fuck... I'm sorry,' he said, his voice gruff, full of emotion.

I shrugged. 'It's in the past.'

'So he *was* abusive?'

I dipped my head in confirmation. 'It's a story for another time. But yes. Badly, and for a long time. This place was my chance at freedom. He never once came here, didn't have a clue about where I'd grown up. He never cared enough to ask, and that turned out to be a blessing. A chance for a fresh start.'

Jade held up a hand, cutting off our conversation. 'Hold on. So you're saying...'

Thomas looked at her as if she were a piece of dirt on his shoe. 'You've wasted your time.' He folded his arms, regarding her. 'I have no claim to this house, and I didn't take a penny from my parents. I didn't want to inherit privilege. I wanted to make something of myself, show them I didn't need them. That despite all the ways they thought I was a failure, I had made it on my own. I wouldn't have been able to live with myself if I'd used their money – the money they made being cold-hearted, narcissistic, smug—' He broke off, taking a breath, then said simply, 'I signed it all over to Annie.'

Jade was silent for a moment. 'Right,' she said softly. She dipped her head, and for a moment, she appeared utterly broken. Then she looked back up, her eyes meeting mine. 'In that case, *you're* going to pay me.'

I laughed. 'Why would I do that?'

She broke into a smile. 'Because if you don't, I'm going to track down that delightful ex of yours and let him know exactly where he can find you. Along with all the not-so-pleasant things you've been saying about him. So,' she went on softly, 'why don't you hand my daughter back to me and we'll go inside and talk numbers?'

FORTY

I laughed at the sheer outlandishness of her demand, even as butterflies swarmed in my belly at the horrific threat, the idea that anyone could be so intentionally cruel.

'I think it's time you got your stuff and left,' Thomas said coldly, standing strong beside me.

Jade folded her arms, even as more blood dripped from the leg of her jeans. She no longer seemed aware of it, her entire focus now on me.

'Jade,' I said, a disbelieving high-pitched tone bursting from my lips. 'Even if I wanted to – which having heard what you've put Thomas through, I *don't* – I don't have it to give you. A few months after Thomas signed everything over to me, the debt collectors came. It turned out Mum and Dad had made some pretty poor financial choices. By the time I cleared what they owed, there was only a small sum left, and I gave that to a handful of conservation charities more than two years ago.'

At the time, it had felt important to make my own money, start selling the things I'd kept to myself for so long, put my woodworking skills to good use. It had brought me a sense of pride, something I'd forgotten I was capable of. Now, with things growing increasingly strained with Ron, I half wished I'd kept a little cushion to fall back on, but it was too late for regrets. 'It might have escaped your attention,' I went on, 'but I live a pretty simple life here. I don't need millions for fancy holidays and caviar.'

Thomas looked at me in surprise, and I could see he was re-evaluating every assumption he'd made when our parents died. 'You really gave it all away?'

I nodded.

Jade pointed a long finger at me. It was crusted in dried blood. 'You still have the house. You can sell it.'

'I *live* here. It's my home. Do you seriously expect me to move onto the street so you can benefit from the profits?' I laughed. 'Go home, Jade. Do better, *be* better, for your daughter.'

She shook her head vehemently. 'Don't you get it? I'm doing all of this for *her*! For her future. A decent life. There are two kinds of people in the world today. The rich, and everyone else. I won't be left behind to bow and scrape my way. I deserve more.'

'*Do* you?' Thomas asked.

'Look at me!' she shrieked. 'Look at how easy it was to make you fall in love with me. You were begging me to marry you less than six months into our relationship! Of course I deserve the best. I was born to *have*, to acquire, to be *given* things. We're not the same, not alike in the slightest. Surely you realise that?'

'Oh, I do. You're nothing like me. Or my sister.'

His words brought a surge of comforting pleasure at the acknowledgement that he finally saw things as they really were, not how he assumed they had been. Outside, the church bells started up again, and he shook his head in wonder.

'What?' I asked.

'Those damn bells. I hated them growing up here. You, Mum, Dad – you all slept through the night, but I could never manage to tune them out. I'd just be drifting off to sleep and they'd start up again. I used to wonder why – who on earth needed to know it was quarter past four in the morning? Not me. The sound of them is imprinted on my brain. I can't delete them.' He snorted. 'Sometimes, if I wake suddenly at night, I still hear them. My imagination playing tricks on me. When Jade called me today, refusing to tell me what the hell was going on, why she'd disappeared without so much as an explanation, *they* were what gave away where she was.' He looked at her. 'I couldn't understand why you'd come here, or why you'd bothered to call if you weren't going to tell me anything of use, but now I get it. I suppose you were recording the call? Planning to ask me about the house and get me to admit I owned half of it?'

Jade's silence was all the answer we needed, the livid expression on her face giving away her intentions.

He shrugged. 'Well, sorry to disappoint you. And if you think you're going to threaten my sister, scare her out of her home, I've got news for you. It won't fucking work. If that worthless ex of hers turns up here, he's going to find a whole battalion waiting for him,' he added vehemently. 'You don't mind if we stay a while, do you, sis?'

I shook my head, shocked that he would do that for me. That he would step up. The thought of letting him and his fellow soldiers into the house wasn't in any way frightening now. Despite everything, the arguments, the estrangement, I knew that he would keep me safe.

Jade bowed her head, defeated, and I let out a long breath, relieved that she'd finally seen reason. I would be the bigger person. Let her leave without making a scene. I hitched the sleeping baby higher on my shoulder and began to turn for the doorway, the broken door lying on the ground, leaving nothing but a splintered frame, the light fading beyond. I was desperate to get back out in the fresh air. It stank of blood in here. She needed to go to the hospital. Find out what was causing it.

Suddenly, her head snapped up, and she let out a shrill screech that had me spinning back to face her. 'You bastard!' she spat. 'You've wasted a whole year of my life! I won't let you walk away without giving me what I'm owed!'

'Perhaps you should have thought about that before you went behind my back with another man,' Thomas said sadly. 'You might have been entitled to a chunk of my pension, but now you won't even get that. You voided the contract the moment you got into his bed.'

Jade launched herself forward, shoving him hard in the chest, slamming her fist into his belly with more strength than she should have had whilst bleeding so heavily. She swung the axe, and I screamed as the blunt edge smacked into the side of his head. As he stumbled back, clearly not expecting the attack, Amala woke in my arms and began to cry, startled by the altercation.

'Watch out!' I cried as his foot caught in a coil of chain I'd left on the floor. He fell backward, grasping at thin air, and I saw the silver flash of the axe in Jade's hand as she raised it, her eyes wild as she prepared to swing it again.

'No!' I shrieked, clutching Amala. I looked around for somewhere to put the baby down safely, but I was too late. Thomas gave an agonised bellow, and I spun back just in time to see him tumble out of the open doorway. He rolled to his knees, crawling away, the chain still wrapped around his ankle, and as he disappeared from sight, the most horrific moan filled the air. Then there was silence.

'*Thomas*!' I rushed forward, but Jade got to the door first, holding the axe up in front of her, barring my way.

'Give me my daughter *now*,' she demanded, her eyes gleaming dangerously.

'I have to go to him! I have to help—'

She swung at my face with the axe, and I was so shocked that Amala nearly slipped from my arms. Her cries were frantic, deafening, and I felt disorientated, terror seeping through my bones. 'Are you out of your fucking mind?' I yelled. 'I'm holding your daughter!'

'Oh, don't play Mother Teresa with me, Annie, it doesn't suit you. You *killed* your own baby. Stop trying to play the saviour with mine! I don't want your filthy hands anywhere near her. You're a murderer! You failed your son, chose yourself over him because you were too damned weak to find a way out of the life you'd let yourself end up in.' She gave a cruel laugh. 'Do you think you've changed? That you're such a good person now? Is that it? I know you think you're finally ready to stand up to your ex and fight, but it's too late! You're a joke! Nothing you do is going to bring your son back. It's pointless. You *failed*, Annie. You failed your baby, and you failed yourself. And you can tell yourself your little fairy stories about how the next time you see him it will all be so different, you'll be strong, but we both know you don't have it in you. You're pathetic. You could never take the necessary steps to end him, no matter what you might let yourself believe.'

I shook my head, her words cutting right to my core. 'I don't know what you're talking about,' I said coolly.

'Right.' She nodded, narrowing her eyes spitefully. 'So it's just a coincidence that the moment you thought Ryan was headed this way, you started work on that pit in the front garden? Do you think I didn't realise exactly what you were dreaming of doing? I knew you were mad – I mean, it's obvious, isn't it? For a while there, I even wondered if you were planning to toss me and Amala into it. But then you told me about Ryan and it all clicked. It was for him, right?'

'It's a pond! It's going to be a pond. For the wildlife!'

She smirked. 'Oh, yeah, sure it is.'

'I need to see Thomas!' I cried, listening for any sound of movement and hearing nothing. Was he lying out there on the lawn, bleeding to death? 'We need to call an ambulance! Did you cut him?'

Jade acted as if I hadn't spoken, as if my brother was of no interest to her now. I met her eyes and saw red.

'You're right, okay?' I hissed. 'You're right. I didn't know it myself to begin with, but yes, the deeper the pit became, the more I realised what I was making. What I had to do. If you'd lived even a year in my shoes, you would understand, but you haven't, have you? You've no idea what I've been through. So yes, I would have killed Ryan with my bare hands if it meant not going back to that life. I would have done whatever it took and concreted over his rotting corpse without the slightest ounce of regret.'

I was pulsing with rage now. 'Thomas was kind to stand up for me just then, but it wasn't necessary. If Ryan sets one toe back into my life, he's going to find me a very different woman from the person I was when he knew me. I don't need your permission, your fucking assessment of my character. You don't know me. You don't have the slightest clue what I'm capable of. If Ryan comes here, he *will* pay for what he did to me... And you're wrong about my son. I have blamed myself for far too long. Taken on the guilt for crimes I didn't commit.' I shook my head. 'I *didn't* kill him. I *wasn't* responsible. I did everything I could to get out. I risked my safety time and again. It wasn't my fault that Ryan was too clever, too quick, too fucking disturbed to let me leave. It wasn't my fault he broke me down until I was too afraid to try. It wasn't my fault,' I breathed, letting the words fill me, heal me.

Jade shrugged. 'If that's what you need to believe to help you sleep at night...'

The axe glinted again, and I wondered if this madness had always been there, waiting to be unleashed.

She nodded towards her daughter. 'Hand her over.'

'No.' I couldn't give Amala to her in this state. I would never forgive myself if anything were to happen. I would protect her at all costs.

Nearby, the sound of sirens echoed through the still, windless air, and I wished there was a way to alert them, to get them to divert their path and come here instead of wherever they were heading.

Panic gripped Jade. 'Now!' she screamed. 'Give me my baby. I have to go!'

I backed further into the workshop, holding Amala firmly in my arms, my eyes not leaving the axe. The baby wailed and jerked her head, and I knew she was getting hungry, but I couldn't hand her over. Jade was unhinged.

As if in confirmation of my doubts, she lunged forward, swinging at my legs with the axe, and I jumped back, the walls closing in on me, the splintered, cobwebbed wood pressing into my bare shoulders.

'Give her to me!' she screamed.

The sirens grew louder, then came to an abrupt stop close by. I heard heavy footsteps running up the path, urgent voices, someone yelling for an ambulance, and then, to my shock, Aaron appeared in the doorway, dressed in his police uniform. 'What are you—' I began, but Jade spun to face him with the axe clenched between her shaking fists.

'Danielle Lake, drop the weapon and put your hands where I can see them!'

I blinked, confused. *Danielle?*

'I really got it wrong with you, didn't I?' he went on, shaking his head. 'I thought you were an investigative journalist, come to dig up the past. It was always a miracle to me that the story never got leaked. Annie's abusive ex, the investigation into the death of her child. It would have been tabloid heaven for some halfwit hack, and I made it my mission that she wouldn't suffer that after everything she'd already endured.

'One of the PCs who'd been on duty back then was recently

sacked for misconduct, and since then, details of a few cases have been leaked to the press. I had a hunch he'd been putting out feelers, trying to get one over on us and make a bit of cash into the bargain, so I'd been half expecting it. And then here you were. The moment I saw you, I knew there was something off about you. That you were here for nefarious purposes. Annie always glosses over the worst parts of a person's character. She searches for the best. And you did such a good job of making her feel sorry for you – *responsible* for you – that she almost managed to convince me you might actually be telling the truth. You should go into acting, Danielle, because you really do play the part of pitiful lost soul to perfection.'

He snorted. 'To think I was worried about you coming to dig up Annie's secrets, to cast her as a killer in the papers and ruin the life she's made for herself here. The truth was way beyond what I imagined. I have to say, you're pretty good at coming up with new identities for yourself, aren't you? Laura Jarvis, Michelle Oliver, Joanna Prince, Lacey Rogers… I *think* we uncovered all of them. I already suspected there was no such person as Jade Ashton, so we did some digging, and with a picture I took of you from my window a few days ago, I was able to discover your true identity. Quite the record you have, Danielle. Married under your real name four times, divorcing each of the husbands less than a year into the marriage and taking half their fortune. All legal, very clever. But your fourth husband didn't slink away with his tail between his legs, did he? He made it his mission to destroy your reputation.'

He glanced at me, though I could tell he was still hyper aware of the axe clutched in Jade's hand. 'If you type her real name, Danielle Lake, into Google, there are too many results to read through. Articles her fourth husband wrote describing how she conned him, the tricks she used to make him think she loved him.' He looked back at Jade. 'The way you pretended to be clueless about the prenup, all the while finding ways to work it to your advantage. You wrote the wrong date of birth on the forms, and then flirted with his lawyer, a young, inept puppy, who didn't notice. Voided the whole thing, didn't it?'

'Oh my God,' I whispered.

'I know.' He nodded. 'Like I said, clever. We spoke to him,' he went on. 'He isn't the kind of person I'd mess with. You made an enemy for yourself there.'

'As if I care!' she bit back. 'Let him cry into his empty bank balance. I got what I wanted and that's all that matters.'

He shook his head as if shocked that anyone could be so calculating. I liked that about him. That even after years in the police force, dealing with some terrible situations, he still had the capacity to be surprised by how cruel people could be. He was so good he couldn't bring himself to see the worst in people. Even me.

'So,' he continued, 'you couldn't use that name any more, so you started creating new identities. You'd seduce some unsuspecting rich guy, then go through the farce of marrying him, though it wasn't legally binding. You'd even sign the prenuptial agreements; that part was especially clever because it was your leverage, wasn't it?'

'What do you mean?' I asked.

'She scares the life out of them – reminds them of the prenup and tells them she'll take them for half of everything they've got. Then when they panic, believing that they're legally bound to pay her, she plays the kind-hearted hero, getting them to transfer the money to some offshore account without getting lawyers involved. Always a hefty chunk, but far less than half, so the husbands think they've escaped lightly. But here's the most interesting part,' he added, and I could tell he was enjoying this just a little bit. I supposed it made quite a change from arresting petty shoplifters and graffiti artists. 'Just over two years ago, Danielle Lake was convicted for fraud and sentenced to nine years in HMP Bronzefield.'

'*What*?' I gasped.

He met her eyes coolly, and I could see the rage pulsing through her. I wanted to warn him to stop goading her, to back down. He was pushing her too far. I knew that look, that simmering energy that grew steadily more volatile in the moments before an explosion. I'd experienced the consequences first-hand from Ryan. He and Jade had a lot in common, it would seem.

'Most prisoners who escape don't make it a week,' he went on. 'I'm not sure how you managed it, but you did well to get this far. That law degree taught you all you needed to know, didn't it? Just a shame you didn't put your knowledge to better use.' He glanced at me. 'Did she ask you for money?'

'Yes. She married my brother… that's why she came. For money. The house.' I frowned. Aaron had said that her previous marriages weren't legally binding. My eyes widened as I took in what that meant. 'So Thomas isn't even married to you!' I broke into a smile, then quickly schooled my features as I caught the seething rage burning across Jade's pretty face. She had nothing over him. My brother was free to walk away from her with no legal repercussions.

Aaron nodded, seeing that I understood.

'Thomas!' I cried suddenly. 'Is he—'

'The paramedics are out there with him now. I think his leg is injured and he's concussed, but he's conscious.'

I let out a long sigh of relief. 'Thank God.' I patted Amala, swaying gently. She'd stopped crying and was losing the battle against sleep, her eyes heavy, her breathing slowing, giving just the occasional hiccupping sob.

Aaron took a pair of handcuffs from his belt and nodded over his shoulder. Three officers appeared behind him, as if they'd been waiting there the whole time. 'You've had quite the adventure, Danielle. But it's time to go home now. I'm sure the staff at Bronzefield will be ready to welcome you back with open arms. Put the weapon on the floor and your hands in the air where I can see them.'

'I won't go back there,' she cried. 'I have a daughter now! I have responsibilities. You can't take her from me. I won't go back to that place!' She let out a scream that made the hairs rise on my arms, then rushed forward brandishing the axe.

I wanted to close my eyes, to make sure I didn't carry the memory of what was sure to happen next with me for the rest of my life, but I couldn't bring myself to look away. Aaron deserved more. Without thinking, stopping to reason, I grabbed the first thing to hand, a tin of paint, and, clenching my fist around the handle, swung it with all my might, then released it. It flew through the air, smashing into the back of Jade's head just as the other three officers pushed through the doorway, their bulk filling the dusty space. She went down like a sack of potatoes. Trembling, I looked up into Aaron's eyes and found him smiling at me. 'I knew you had it in you, Annie,' he said softly.

I gave a tiny nod. 'So did I, I think,' I breathed. 'So did I.'

EPILOGUE

Aaron and I watched the ambulance drive away, my brother in the back. The paramedic had said that the axe had only gone an inch or so into his thigh, thankfully missing any major arteries, though the blow to the head had caused him to pass out. He was concussed and needed stitches in the leg wound, but he would be up and about in no time.

Before he'd left, having already been given a dose of morphine, he'd smiled and said, 'When I'm discharged, I'll come over and see you, Annie. We have a lot to catch up on.'

I'd smiled and hugged him, watching them wheel his stretcher into the back of the ambulance, grateful to have him back in my life and determined to hold on to my relationship with the sibling I'd never truly understood. Perhaps this time it would be different between us. I hoped so.

Aaron turned to me now, looking at Amala, his brow creasing. 'I suppose I'd better call social services to come and pick this little one up. We're going to need to track down her real father.'

'Let *me* take her to the station,' I said, meeting his eyes. 'She knows me. She'll feel safe. I don't want to hand her over to some stranger.'

'You want...' He looked towards the gate as if he didn't quite believe I could leave this place, even if I wanted to. '*You're* going to bring her to the station?'

I gave a firm nod. 'If you'll take us?'

His face broke into a wide smile. 'Of course I'll take you, Annie. Anywhere, any time.'

'Let me just get my bag.'

Carrying the sleeping baby, I walked carefully back up the path, opening the back door and heading through the kitchen. My bag was on a hook in the hall, containing only tissues, my purse and some gum. It was dusty, I realised. It had been hanging there unused for so long. I grabbed it, not allowing myself to linger inside, to have any opportunity to back out of my offer. I didn't know what had even made me say it – only that I couldn't bear for Amala to be frightened. She was going to have a difficult time ahead of her, and if I could soften that transition in any way, I would.

When I walked back out, Aaron was standing alone, waiting for me. The rest of the police had left, taking a screaming Jade with them, and I wondered how long it would take for her to be moved back to the prison. Aaron had promised she would be seen by a doctor to assess her bleeding, but the paramedic had declared her fit to be taken to the station for the time being. I imagined her sentence would be extended significantly, and her freedoms – if she'd had any – would be greatly diminished this time around. It would be a very long time before she got out again.

I was devastated for Amala. She would have to grow up without a mother. It was a harsh start to life, and I felt livid with Jade at having been so reckless. She must have known that sooner or later she'd be caught and taken back to prison. She'd said she was doing this, fleecing Thomas, for her daughter, *her* future, but she hadn't seemed to have considered the stakes, the price Amala would pay when it all went to shit.

Aaron pushed open the low wooden gate without a word. I was glad he wasn't making a fuss about what a big step I was about to take, expanding the already massive bubble of fear in my belly. As I followed him to the waiting squad car, I couldn't help but smile at the sight of him in his uniform, noticing how well it fit him. He caught me looking, and I glanced away.

'Here,' he said, opening the back door. 'There isn't a car seat, I'm afraid, but I'll put the blue lights on, and we'll take it nice and steady. Face her towards your body and put your hand on her head to support it.'

I dipped low, stepping into the car, noticing that Aaron had put his hand between my head and the door frame to cushion it. He seemed unaware of his innate habit of protecting me, little gestures that to him were just being kind, a gentleman, but that made me feel safe, comparing him to Ryan and remembering how he had loved nothing more than when I got hurt. My heart thrummed faster as I met Aaron's eyes.

'Do you want help with the belt?' he asked.

I nodded, and he leaned in, gently clipping it in place, his hair brushing my cheek, the smell of his skin, warm and clean, filling my nose. He carefully shut the door, then headed round the car, climbing in the driver's side and speaking into his radio. He placed it back in its holder, then turned to me. 'Ready?'

'We're ready.'

The engine roared to life, and then we were moving. I couldn't help but stare as the house grew steadily further away. My heart began to race, my mouth dry though my hands were drenched in sweat, but I soothed myself, patting the baby, breathing in her sweet, calming smell, absorbing her warmth as I reminded myself it was her I was doing this for. She deserved someone to be strong for her.

The house disappeared from view as Aaron turned the

corner, and ahead I saw huge arches of roses on the village green. 'What are those?' I asked, curiosity overcoming my anxiety for a moment.

'Oh, there was a village fete at the weekend. Stalls, Punch and Judy, coconut shy, cider tent. A quintessentially English affair.' He grinned. 'Didn't I mention it?'

'No,' I said softly. Now that I thought about it, I had a vague memory of hearing music on the breeze, but I'd passed it off as someone having a summer barbecue. I felt a pang of regret at how much I'd missed. The community I had refused to embrace because I was too afraid.

The sun was sinking lower now, though there were still a few hours until night would fall, and the burnt orange light made the fields of rapeseed glow, the cloudless sky streaked with colour, the endless expanse of it making the world feel bigger than I'd remembered. It was like seeing a painting I'd forgotten about, the beauty – the possibility of it – overwhelming. I couldn't look away. We drove in silence for a while as I soaked up every scene, every stunning picture. As we reached the town, I felt myself gape in awe at the people sitting outside cafés and bars, laughing and drinking and making the most of the balmy summer evening.

'I've missed such a lot,' I said softly. 'I forgot what it was like to be amongst people. To go where I wanted, when I wanted.' I shook my head at the realisation of what I'd lost. 'I'm so completely institutionalised, I didn't even consider I might *want* to leave the safety of my home. I let myself think it was all I would ever need. He made me a prisoner for ten years, but I continued my own sentence for a further three. I left him, but I was never free.'

Aaron shrugged, but in the rear-view mirror, I could see his eyes sparkling as if rejoicing at my unfolding revelation.

He slowed the car to a crawl and pointed to a particularly lively café. 'That place does the most amazing tapas and sangria. I'll take you if you like?' he offered casually. 'This week?'

I met his hopeful stare and broke into a smile. 'Do you know what, Aaron? I think I'd like that.'

I sat on a squashy blue sofa in the police station staff room, Amala full from the bottle of milk one of the PCs had produced and wearing a fresh nappy, sleeping soundly on my lap as I ate a fairly reasonable chicken sandwich, trying not to drop crumbs on her. I was listening to, and occasionally joining in with, a lively conversation between two female officers on their break, and was surprised to discover how at ease I felt. I'd expected a cold welcome, for people to remember the last time I was here, during the investigation surrounding my son's death, but whether Aaron had warned them to be kind or for some other reason, there had been no indication that they even remembered me from back then. Everyone had been warm and friendly.

I had forgotten how good it felt to talk to other women, to smile and laugh. It was as if the person I had been before I'd met Ryan had stuck her hand up, waving at me to notice her, and squinting, unsure, I watched as she walked towards me, growing steadily clearer with every step. I had forgotten her. Become someone else, a caricature of what I thought I needed to be to survive. What *I* had wanted, any desires or interests or personality traits that didn't align with keeping me safe, had been squashed and erased. But now I remembered. I had been happy once. Not just safe and content, as I had been over the past three years. But raucously, unashamedly happy. I'd been loud and fun and excited by life, by adventure, by challenge. Ryan had seen that in me and taken great pleasure in dousing the flames, but now the embers were smouldering once again, and I would never let another person dampen my spirit. I wanted that woman back.

The two policewomen broke into laughter, trading disastrous dating stories back and forth, and I leaned back against the sofa cushions, struggling to swallow the bite of sandwich through my own laughter.

The door to the staff room opened, and I looked up to see Aaron standing there, dishevelled but gorgeous as ever. 'You're still awake!' He smiled. 'You really didn't have to wait all this time, Annie. It's been hours. Someone would have driven you home, and there's no shortage of willing volunteers to cuddle the baby.'

I shook my head, looking over at the clock on the wall, surprised to realise it was past midnight. The time had flown by. 'I wanted to stay with her. To make sure she felt safe.'

He nodded, and I could tell that he understood. I hadn't been able to protect my own baby, but I wouldn't repeat that mistake.

He swallowed, then met my eyes. 'He's here. They're waiting,' he said, and though I'd been preparing myself for those very words, I felt my whole body tense.

Tears blurred my vision, and I blinked them away, looking down at Amala. Once we left this room, I would likely never see her again. The thought made me want to cling to her. To fight against the inevitability of what I was about to do. My throat constricted, and I remembered how just a few days ago, the idea of holding her had made me recoil. I hadn't wanted to revisit the memories of the last baby I'd held in my arms. Hadn't thought I was strong enough. I knew exactly why Aaron had been afraid of me being around her. It was because he knew I had never really come to terms with my son's death. He was worried that all that suppressed pain, that awful grief and guilt, would come flooding out.

I could see now that he'd been terrified of what I might do.

He'd had to watch the blood trickling from my slashed wrists; he knew what I was capable of if the darkness became too great. Losing my son had made me cold, emotionless, shutting that side of me down to protect myself, and I couldn't blame Aaron for being concerned when he saw me with Amala. But things had changed now. Holding her, allowing myself to care about her, had opened up something inside me that I'd long since forgotten about. I didn't want to lose that now, didn't want to let her go.

I gave a shaky sigh and reminded myself that this wasn't about me. It was about what was right for *her*. She wasn't my baby to keep, but perhaps, in time, I would get another chance to be a mother. And I wouldn't let fear stop me if that opportunity came around.

I lifted her gently from my lap, pressing a kiss to her soft, round cheek. A tear slid down my face, and I tasted salt, but I met Aaron's eyes, determined to do the right thing, as hard as it might be. 'Okay.' I smiled. 'Let's go.'

He led me down a wide corridor and paused outside a glossy walnut-coloured door, raising his eyebrow towards me in a silent question. I nodded, and he pushed open the door. Two people were sitting inside, and I could see the tension coiled in their bodies at having been kept waiting. Aaron had told me that finding Amala's father hadn't been too hard. He and his mother had been actively searching for her and had filed a missing person report days after her birth. He knew Jade as Lacey Rogers. She had sent him photographs of his daughter and told him that if he wanted to see her, he would need to transfer an outrageous sum of money into an offshore account. The idea that she would use the baby as leverage – that she would use a father's love to bribe him – was hard to stomach. It was the kind of thing Ryan would have done.

The man stood, and I took him in, silently assessing him, though I knew I had no say in anything that happened next.

Amala was his, and I had no right to prevent him from taking her. He was around five eight, black, with strong, broad shoulders and kind, nervous eyes. He reached behind him, gripping the hand of a much older woman. She had the same warm, hopeful smile as him, and a head of wiry salt-and-pepper hair. Both of them looked kind, and as I took a moment to silently check in with my instincts, I felt no fear in my gut. They would love Amala. They already did.

Aaron cleared his throat. 'Sorry to keep you waiting. This is Annie, and *this*' – he gestured – 'is your daughter, Amala.'

The man stepped forward, the woman, Amala's grandmother, flanking him. 'She's exactly as I dreamed she would be,' he breathed. And then he was holding out his arms, tears streaming down his face, and I was letting her go, knowing she was in safe hands.

The woman touched a finger to Amala's cheek and spoke in a strong Jamaican accent. 'Hi, baby. I'm your granni. I've been waiting to meet you for so long.'

The man passed the baby to his mother, then held out a hand to shake mine. 'Josiah,' he said, his voice trembling. 'Thank you so much for taking care of her.'

'It was my pleasure,' I admitted.

'I had no idea Lacey— sorry, *Danielle*,' he corrected, 'had it in her. She seemed so sweet. She was never interested in money. Our first date was hotdogs cooked on a disposable barbecue on the beach. I thought I'd finally found someone who wanted me, not my money. She seemed perfect.'

'Too good to be true,' his mother said darkly, cocooning Amala against her breast. 'And not nearly good enough for you. I never liked the girl. There was something off about her.'

Amala opened her eyes and stared up at the woman as she spoke, her face blank as she took her in. The two of them shared a long look, and I watched, holding my breath. Then Amala broke into a gummy smile, snuggled into her and clutched hold of her finger.

'You weren't to know,' Aaron said. 'Danielle Lake was a professional con woman – she had years of practice learning her craft. I'm just glad she's back behind bars, where she belongs.'

'So I'm not actually married?' Josiah asked, gently taking hold of Amala's foot, as if he needed to touch her to keep reminding himself that she was real. 'I don't have to go through divorce proceedings?'

'Nope. The marriage wasn't legally binding. And of course Annie's brother was also under the impression *he* was her husband. We're going to do some digging and make sure there aren't any more of her victims waiting to hear from her. She's been a very busy woman.'

'So it would seem,' he replied quietly.

They left, thanking me profusely as they tucked Amala into a car seat in the back of a very expensive-looking SUV. I could see exactly why Jade had targeted this man. Aaron had already told me that Josiah was a hugely successful entrepreneur and on track to becoming one of the richest men in England. For Jade to have found him, got close enough to seduce him and conned him, all whilst keeping up her lies to Thomas, was a mark of her experience and skill. I couldn't help but be sad at the thought that though she hadn't got away with either man's money this time, she'd taken something far more valuable. Their trust in women, their ability to have another relationship in the future without second-guessing their partner's motives. I hoped they would both be able to move past the hurt she'd caused and find happiness one day.

As I watched the car disappear into the darkness, I felt Aaron step closer. 'You all right?' he asked.

I nodded. 'Surprisingly, yes. She's going to be loved. Safe. That's all I care about,' I said, but my voice cracked, and he nodded as if he could read my mind, see how painful it had been for me to let another baby go. He pulled me into his arms, and I clung to him, burying my tear-streaked face in his shoulder. It had been a very long time since anyone had held me like this, but it didn't feel scary. I felt safe. I breathed slowly, letting my tears fall, knowing in my heart that if I wanted to stay here all night, he would stand with me. Hold me until I was ready to let go.

Finally, I looked up at him. 'Did someone go out to check on Ryan's wife?' I asked. I'd insisted on it. Even though he'd turned out to have no connection to Jade, it was the right thing to do. If he hadn't hurt her yet, it was only a matter of time. A man like Ryan would never change.

'Yes.' He screwed up his face. 'And it was serendipitous timing. She was sporting a black eye and a broken wrist, and she said it wasn't the first time. She'd been trying to leave for a few months, but he had locked her in. Apparently, he started working from home just before their wedding, and it meant she never had an opportunity to escape.'

'That's my fault. He wouldn't want to make the same mistake twice.'

'It most certainly isn't your fault. It's his.'

I nodded. 'You're right.'

'Ryan's been arrested. He isn't here,' he added quickly as I glanced back at the police station in horror. 'He's been taken to the next town for questioning, and his wife is being treated in hospital. But you should know she's keen to press charges. She wants him behind bars.'

I met his eyes. 'And you think that will be more likely to happen if I give a statement too?'

He pressed his lips together, his brown eyes warm as they met mine. 'There are hospital records. You never mentioned his involvement in the loss of your child, but it's not too late. There's a lot you have to say that will at the very least diminish his character in front of a jury. You don't have to—'

'I'll do it. Anything. I'll make a statement tonight. I'll stand up in court. Anything she wants, anything to get him convicted. I should have done it the moment I heard he was married. I could have helped her, *warned* her.' I had known it back then, but the fear had been too great, the idea that he might drag me back into his web and the certainty that if he did, I'd never get free. But it was different now. *I* was different.

'We'll get you in for an interview tomorrow, and you can tell us everything on record.' He smiled. 'I'm proud of you, Annie.'

I opened my mouth to tell him he shouldn't be, but then remembered to be kind to myself. I had been a victim of abuse. I had been afraid. That wasn't my fault, and I was going to do something to make amends now. 'Me too,' I whispered.

He rested his forearms on my shoulders and fixed me with a quizzical look.

'What?'

'It's too late for tapas tonight. But would you like to come back to mine for a glass of wine?'

I met his eyes, my hands wrapping around his waist, and smiled. 'I would love that.'

He stared at me, and I gave a nod, knowing exactly what he was asking. His lips met mine, and I realised I had found my way back to the woman I thought I had lost. And I would never let her go again.

A LETTER FROM SAM

I want to say a huge thank you for choosing to read *The Girl with the Baby*. If you want to keep up to date with all my latest releases, just sign up at the following link. Your email address will never be shared, and you can unsubscribe at any time.

www.bookouture.com/sam-vickery

If you enjoyed reading *The Girl with the Baby*, I would be very grateful if you could leave a review. I'd love to hear how you felt about the story.

Find out about my upcoming titles at www.samvickery.com, or on my Facebook page.

Until the next time,

Sam

www.samvickery.com

facebook.com/SamVickeryWrites

ACKNOWLEDGEMENTS

I'm so lucky to get to do this work, and it's something I'm reminded of every time I hold a new paperback in my hands and see all the effort that has gone into it brought to life. Even now, after more than twenty books, I still find it incredible to see the final package come together.

Google informs me that there have been no known inmate escapes from HMP Bronzefield, the largest female prison in Europe, so I hope you won't mind that I've taken advantage of my artistic license when it comes to Jade's great escape!

Creating a book takes so many highly skilled people. From the cover designer, Aaron Munday, who grabs your attention and compels you to pick up the book, to my wonderful copy-editor, Jane Selley, and proofreader, Laura Kincaid, who ensure every detail is correct so the story flows without confusion. Charlotte Hegley, who readied the manuscript for editing, and my hard-working publicist, Sarah Hardy, who organises blog tours and gets the story into the hands of the readers; not to mention the wonderful book bloggers who read it in advance and share their reviews with their followers. This is my ninth novel with Bookouture, and throughout my time with this incredible, innovative and proactive publishing house, I have had the good fortune to have Jennifer Hunt, my talented editor, by my side. Her insight, understanding of the market and openness have led to many inspiring conversations and helped feed my creativity, making the writing process so smooth and enjoyable.

I want to thank all of you for your hard work in bringing this book to reality!

PUBLISHING TEAM

Turning a manuscript into a book requires the efforts of many people. The publishing team at Bookouture would like to acknowledge everyone who contributed to this publication.

Commercial
Lauren Morrissette
Hannah Richmond
Imogen Allport

Cover design
Aaron Munday

Data and analysis
Mark Alder
Mohamed Bussuri

Editorial
Jennifer Hunt
Charlotte Hegley

Copyeditor
Jane Selley

Proofreader
Laura Kincaid

Marketing
Alex Crow
Melanie Price
Occy Carr
Cíara Rosney
Martyna Młynarska

Operations and distribution
Marina Valles
Joe Morris

Production
Hannah Snetsinger
Mandy Kullar
Nadia Michael

Publicity
Kim Nash
Noelle Holten
Jess Readett
Sarah Hardy

Rights and contracts
Peta Nightingale
Richard King
Saidah Graham

RAISING READERS
Books Build Bright Futures

Dear Reader,

We'd love your attention for one more page to tell you about the crisis in children's reading, and what we can all do.

Studies have shown that reading for fun is the **single biggest predictor of a child's future life chances** – more than family circumstance, parents' educational background or income. It improves academic results, mental health, wealth, communication skills, ambition and happiness.

The number of children reading for fun is in rapid decline. Young people have a lot of competition for their time, and a worryingly high number do not have a single book at home.

Hachette works extensively with schools, libraries and literacy charities, but here are some ways we can all raise more readers:

- Reading to children for just 10 minutes a day makes a difference
- Don't give up if children aren't regular readers – there will be books for them!

- Visit bookshops and libraries to get recommendations
- Encourage them to listen to audiobooks
- Support school libraries
- Give books as gifts

There's a lot more information about how to encourage children to read on our websites: **www.RaisingReaders.co.uk** and **www.JoinRaisingReaders.com**.

Thank you for reading.

hachette UK

Printed in Dunstable, United Kingdom

78217873R00143